THE SLAUGHTERHOUSE

Janie Bolitho

Constable • London

First published in Great Britain 2002
by Constable, an imprint of Constable & Robinson Ltd
3 The Lanchesters, 162 Fulham Palace Road,
London W6 9ER
www.constablerobinson.com

ISBN 1–84119–506–5

Printed and bound in Great Britain

A CIP catalogue record for this book
is available from the British Library

For Paddy and Helen Foley
(after all these years)

Prologue

Flight-bag in hand, Marty Rowland stepped down on to the hot tarmac and was almost blinded by the sun. Chatting to another member of the cabin crew she did not notice June Hoffman, her immediate boss, waiting just inside the terminal building behind the thick glass doors.

'Marty, can we have a word?'

June was tall, slender and usually jolly. Marty looked up into her solemn face and started to shake. 'What is it? What's wrong?'

'Let's go to my office.'

They walked along the corridor in silence, oblivious to the passengers, the ground crews and the flight being called. There was a jug of filter coffee on top of a row of cupboards in the office. June poured two cups and placed them on her desk, pushing one towards Marty whose face was pale. 'You've probably guessed it's bad news. I'm sorry, Marty, but your mother's had an accident.' She paused to allow time for the information to sink in and for Marty to prepare herself for what she must know was to come. 'She's dead. She died instantly,' she added quickly.

'How?' Marty's head was bent, her whole body shook. The sunlight picked out the gold in her wavy red hair.

'She fell. Apparently she was doing something in the loft of the barn and she slipped.'

'The slaughterhouse.'

'I'm sorry?'

Marty shook her head. The slaughterhouse, not the barn, but it didn't matter, not to June, anyway.

'The police have been trying to contact you. It seems your mother only had your previous address – anyway, they found out where you work and spoke to us. Obviously you're on compassionate leave as from now. Is there anyone you'd like to telephone, someone you'd like with you?'

'No, I'll be all right, June. Thanks.' She stood, the coffee untouched. The tiny freckles across her nose stood out against the whiteness of her skin. 'When do you want me back?'

'Whenever you feel up to it.' June watched her replace her uniform hat and leave the room. She very much doubted that Marty Rowland would be all right, she was a little strange at the best of times.

Marty worked out of Exeter airport but she lived in Plymouth. The journey of just over forty miles did not take long. She drove without thinking, with nothing more on her mind than the traffic around her. Reaching home she parked in her allocated space behind the small block of flats and carried her flight-bag up the stairs to the second floor. The first thing she did was to ring John Lavant, her mother's solicitor. He promised to let the police know she had been informed of the death so Gloria Rowland's name could be released to the press. 'It's a terrible shock, Marty,' he said. 'Your mother was so fit and strong. If there's anything I can do just let me know. There won't be any problems over the estate, there's a will, everything's in order and she tied everything up neatly. Why don't you come and see me tomorrow and we can talk about things. Would eleven suit you?'

'Yes, that's fine.' Marty thanked him and hung up. She was still shaking. Looking around her modern flat she thought how similar it was to the anonymous hotel rooms she stayed in when abroad. Now she could move, she could leave all this behind her. Her lips curved in a smile.

'No more. No more travelling, no more waiting,' she said as she stripped off her uniform and flung it on the bed.

She filled the bath and sank beneath a thick layer of foam. Steam rose, misting the mirror, as she lay and relived the last three years. Now he will come to me, she thought as she got out and towelled herself dry, now there is nothing to stop him. I can provide everything he wants. Dressed in a silky robe she walked from room to room, opening the windows. It was six fifteen and still warm. Champagne, she decided, remembering there was a bottle in the fridge. She bit her lip and frowned. It had been bought for another occasion, the third anniversary of their meeting, but he hadn't turned up. It didn't matter now, things would be very different.

With her hair hanging damply around her shoulders, Marty stood looking out of the window enjoying the sharp tang of the bubbles as she drank. 'To the future,' she said, raising her glass to the trees on the opposite side of the road.

In the morning she put on a simple dress which failed to disguise her sexuality. John Lavant shook her hand and tried not to stare at her legs when she sat down. Having expressed his sympathy he explained her position. 'As you know, your mother sold off parcels of land to neighbouring farmers over the years. However, what's left will become yours: the farmhouse, the outbuildings and a few acres of land.' He paused, aware that Marty might not be fully aware of the situation. Gloria had told him they had had no contact for over seven years. 'And, of course, the money your mother invested.'

Marty held her breath. Sitting there, the sun fierce on the back of her neck, she felt the room begin to spin. The sickly scent of lilies in a jug on a shelf filled the room. Just over three-quarters of a million pounds, she thought John Lavant had said. The floor rose and Marty thought she might faint.

She sipped iced water as he explained that there was no one to challenge the will, that Marty was the sole survivor.

'You can have the keys immediately,' he continued. 'There'll be things you need to attend to, and it won't take long to finalize matters.' John Lavant smiled gently. Gloria's daughter probably felt awful. She had lost contact with her mother but had still inherited everything. Remorse and guilt were harder to bear when the person who had induced those feelings was dead. 'I think that's settled, then. Make another appointment on your way out. One of my partners will advise you on investments.'

'Thank you.' Marty did so then stepped out into the busy street. There'll be a funeral to arrange, she realized as she walked to where she had left the car.

She drove straight to the farmhouse. The roads narrowed once she left the city and she was surrounded by the Devon countryside. The hedges were overgrown; behind them crops were ready for harvesting or already stood in bales. The air was still and dry, the only sound was that of a tractor in the distance. She turned into the lane, bumped over the hard-packed ruts of mud, and swung into the yard.

Weeds pushed up through the cobbles and the windows of the house stared back at her blankly. The whole place had an aura of dilapidation. Marty got out of the car and walked towards the front door. To her right was the slaughterhouse, the place where her mother had died. She ignored it. The key slid into the lock. Marty opened the door and stepped inside. She gasped. Nothing had changed, she might not have been away for seven years. I can't stay here, she decided, not yet, not until I've changed things. Even when the money came through she would carry on working until the builders had finished.

A month later Marty handed in her notice and put her flat on the market. The funeral was behind her. Several other people had attended, a few women from the nearby village and the postman who had found the body. None of them had acknowledged Marty's existence.

At the end of October she moved into the farmhouse. Now that the main reconstruction work was complete she

found she could live with the mess and the plaster dust.
Her mother's furniture had been disposed of and a new
kitchen had been fitted.

'She's not all there,' Marty overheard a workman say as
she burned the old bedding and curtains in an oil drum,
the fabric splashed with methylated spirits. She had been
talking to herself.

She shopped for furniture, crockery and linen. The bal-
ance of the money had been reinvested, she could live off
the interest.

The place was redolent with the smell of new wood and
wool carpets and it was a pleasure to use her kitchen
equipment. But there was still work to be done outside.
The yard needed weeding, the fields fertilizing and the
shed would revert to a hen-house. 'Hens for eggs, good
soil for vegetables,' Marty told herself, realizing she was
far more like her mother than she cared to admit.

Christmas passed into the New Year but still he didn't
come. He had lied, he had not moved in with her. 'I will
not be abandoned again,' she screamed, her voice bounc-
ing off the walls of the slaughterhouse where she was
checking the tools. By being murdered her father had
abandoned her; she would not allow it to happen a second
time.

She sat on the cold concrete floor where she had sat
many times before and began to plan.

I'll get in touch with Jenny Greene and then I'll go and
see Hannah, she decided.

Later, in the comfort of the lounge, she wrote a letter
explaining the situation and asking for Jenny's help. She
knew it would be forthcoming, Jenny had always been in
awe of her.

'It isn't illegal and it won't cost you anything,' she had
added. 'Please don't let me down, this is very important to
me. You have no idea how much I love him.'

She posted the letter the following morning.

11

Chapter One

The automatic glass doors slid back as Hannah approached them. Moving stiffly she crossed the modern, brightly lit concourse of Plymouth station. Her body seemed to belong to someone else, still functioning when it ought not to have done. She had no idea what she hoped to achieve; she only knew that to remain inactive had become impossible. Three days had passed, the weekend was behind her but she couldn't imagine how she had survived it.

The police had provided her with a bleeper in order to be able to contact her at any time. It was switched on, as was her father's mobile phone in the side of her handbag.

'Where to, love?' the ticket seller inquired when she asked for a return.

'London. London Paddington.' How could he not know? Her painful longing was so intense everyone ought to feel it. And had he not seen her picture on the front of the evening paper? Her reflection was little more than a shadow in the glass dividing her from the man behind it but Hannah cared little that her face was puffy and blotchy from crying, that lines and shadows had appeared overnight. Inside her was a knot of rage, a held-back scream of despair.

She signed her name on the credit card slip: it no longer mattered that the surname was Laurence's, her ex-husband's, that she could choose to stop using it now if she wished.

'Platform 7,' the Great Western employee told her kindly as he handed back her card, aware of some inner turmoil in the woman who stumbled away blindly.

The train had not yet arrived. Hannah pulled a packet of cigarettes from her coat pocket, although she could not recall purchasing them. Having thrown all her lighters away when she had given up smoking five years previously, she lit one with a match. Someone had told her you could no longer smoke on the train, whose pointed nose now appeared, followed by the curve of carriages as it rounded the bend and slowed at the platform. Hannah opened the door and boarded it.

A man entered the same carriage and paused by the table at which she was sitting. He carried a briefcase. There were plenty of empty seats. His eyes dropped to her legs. 'Is this seat taken?'

Hannah looked up. His smile was confident, half leer, half inquiry, that of a man whom women did not refuse but who would cast them aside once they had served their purpose. 'Why don't you fuck off?' This was the new Hannah; she would never have said those words a few days ago. Her suffering had diminished the world, all that existed was a deep void.

The train pulled out of the station. Hannah leant back against the seat and closed her eyes, sensing that the stranger had moved away.

Sonia was not expecting her, but that was intentional. One way or another she would discover if her suspicions were correct. Suspicion of everyone she knew had made her irrational, a fact she had so far managed to conceal.

When had it all started? Fifteen months ago, she thought, on that miserable March evening. The scene still remained vivid.

Laurence was in Cannes when her GP confirmed she was eight weeks pregnant. Filled with joy she had driven home to their secluded house in the Tamar Valley with its view of the river. She loved the place and it was large enough to accommodate several children.

For three days she kept the news to herself; Laurence must be the first to know and she wanted to tell him face to face, not over the telephone.

He rang from the airport. 'I should make it by six,' he told her. 'Did you miss me?'

'I always do,' she had replied, although she also enjoyed having some time to herself.

The meal was ready to cook and the table was laid when she heard his car. She poured some wine, two glasses. The doctor had said the occasional drink wouldn't hurt and this was a celebration.

'It's good to be back,' Laurence said, kissing her cheek as he dropped his hold-all on the kitchen floor.

'Here, you look as if you need this.' Smiling, she handed him the wine.

Laurence followed her to the lounge, beyond which the dining-table could be seen through the connecting archway. Unable to wait she had turned to him and blurted it out. 'I'm pregnant, Laurence,' she said, still smiling.

'What? You can't be.' Colour drained from his sun-tanned face. With his next brutal words he had destroyed her. 'Then you'll have to have an abortion,' he said, pointing a finger in accusation.

Hannah, gripping the back of a chair, unmoving, stared at the man she loved, unsure if it was the words or the body language that accompanied them, emphasized them, which had stunned her more.

The beautifully laid dining-table over which she had intended telling him had become a cliché. The light from the table-lamps was reflected off the cut glass. The glint of silver and the erect yellow tulips in their vase seemed to mock her. 'Did you mean that?' Hannah's hand trembled as she raised it to brush back her long, fair hair.

Laurence was pacing the room, his head forward, glowering the way he did when he was angry. 'Yes, Hannah, I did mean it. A child would ruin what we have.'

Hannah had felt too sick to cry. No explanation, no excuses. As always, Laurence's whims must not be denied.

Why had she never noticed this before? She had wanted to touch him, to tell him not to worry, that she would cope, but she had not done so. Behind the pain had begun the stirring of a realization. 'I won't do it. I would never do it,' she told him quietly, her throat aching with held-back tears. 'I'm having this baby, Laurence. Our baby.'

His stubborn green eyes met hers. Soft brown hair lay across his forehead, making him boyish. Casual trousers and an open-neck shirt beneath the cashmere sweater accentuated his leanness. He looked so vulnerable. Hannah stood her ground. A baby was meant to enhance, not ruin what they had.

'I'm going out, I need some air. Think about what I said and we'll discuss it later.'

The front door closed and the car started. Hannah walked towards the dining-table and sat down. There was nothing to think about, nothing to discuss, she was not having an abortion.

But the scene had clarified something Hannah had refused to admit because she loved him. Laurence was selfish. During the four years of their marriage she had made excuses for him, failing to listen to her friends and her mother who had dropped enough pointed hints regarding his character. Now she realized that the nature of their marriage had precluded her from seeing his faults. He was away as often as he was at home. Each return was a homecoming, not to be marred by petty arguments. But there had been times when she had glimpsed the frightened child in him although she saw no reason for it. Maybe he had not been able to bear the idea of sharing her. Maybe it was that simple. What a fool I have been, Hannah thought.

He returned within the hour. Hannah put down the soup spoon in which she had been studying her upside-down reflection and studied Laurence's face instead. It was set, his eyes cold. The optimism she had felt in his absence dissolved. He was not going to change his mind.

They did not hold a conversation for three days. No

words were exchanged other than a tight-lipped 'Excuse me' or 'Have you finished in the bathroom?' In bed at night Hannah lay next to the hard, masculine body of her husband whose sperm had helped create their child but she had no desire to touch him. She felt no need to make amends, to ease the way for Laurence. Those days were over.

On the fourth day as he set off for his next trip he stopped at the door. The hold-all Hannah had packed wordlessly with clean clothes sat at his feet. 'Eight weeks, you said. Well, nine now, I suppose. Then there's no immediate panic. You've still got time to change your mind.'

Wordless and otherwise unresponsive, Hannah shocked him by laughing. And you'll have a lifetime in which to change yours, she thought. I am having this baby.

With a puzzled frown he turned away and closed the door behind him.

No one else, apart from the doctor, knew of her condition. The more who did, the more support she could summon. She rang her mother first. 'I'm having a baby,' she began, but got no further because her throat had tightened. Tears fell and ran over her white knuckles which were clenched around the receiver.

Within the hour Joyce Gregson was with her daughter, making her coffee and calming her down. 'You know how I feel about Laurence,' she said as she placed cups on a tray. 'He's intelligent and he works hard. He's also witty and charming, but only when he gets his own way. There's something lacking, Hannah, I've always thought so. He simply can't face responsibility and commitment.'

'But he married me.'

'Yes, he married you, but he walked into a house you'd already bought and renovated. And he still has his freedom. His job takes him all over the world and when he returns you're waiting for him. Any man would be happy with that arrangement, Hannah. I really can't see what he's got against a baby. It'll affect you far more than it will him.'

Hannah poured the coffee. 'Who else knows you're pregnant?' Joyce asked. She was filled with excitement at the idea of a grandchild, knowing instinctively how much she would love it.

'No one.'

'Then I suggest you tell Pauline and Andrew before Laurence gets back. They might be able to talk him round.'

'Poorly Pauline?'

Mother and daughter laughed at the shared joke. 'Oh, dear, she can't help it.' Joyce shook her head in amusement. 'Poor old Pauline. Poorly Pauline. If she knew what people said about her she'd wish she'd been given any other name but that. Still, for a hypochondriac she looks pretty robust to me. Anyway, this might be just what she needs, somebody else to think about for a change.' Joyce sighed. 'I could stay here for ever but I really must go. Will you keep on teaching now?'

'Yes.' Hannah had realized that she might have to go back to work after the baby was born. But her art and design students weren't difficult, they were keen, with her because they wanted to study. She did not envy her mother who was the headmistress of a primary school.

'If you're free next weekend give me a ring. Come into Plymouth and I'll treat you to lunch somewhere in the Barbican.' She paused. 'You'll be all right, Hannah. You know Dad and I will do anything we can to help.'

'I know.' Hannah had hugged her then walked with her to her car, waving as she drove down the lane which divided the house from the river. Then she went back inside and dialled her mother-in-law's number. The congratulations she received were genuine.

She then rang everyone else she could think of, leaving Sonia, her best friend, until last. Sonia was a fashion photographer, at the stage in her career where she could pick her assignments. Hannah did not want to leave a

17

message, it seemed too impersonal, she would ask her to ring in the evening. But surprisingly Sonia was at home, between shoots, and entertaining. A lunch party, she guessed because glasses had chinked in the background.

'A baby?' Sonia shrieked. 'How will you manage?'

'Like every other mother, I imagine,' Hannah replied drily.

'If it's what you want, then I'm delighted.' Sonia, who never disclosed her age, was roughly a decade older than Hannah and found the idea of children disgusting.

'It is what I want.'

'Ah, but Laurence doesn't.'

Sonia had seen through Laurence too. Everyone seemed to know her husband better than Hannah did. 'No, he doesn't.'

'Is he there?'

'No. He's on a job.'

'Look, can I ring you later for a proper chat? I've got a bit of a houseful.'

'Of course.'

Her long telephone conversations with Sonia were normally a source of pleasure, but the one later that evening had not been because she had admitted to the cracks in her marriage. 'I'm not even sure that he loves me,' Hannah had added.

When she wasn't at work she filled the time until she had to face Laurence again by meeting her mother for lunch and inviting her friend Lorna for supper. In between she tried to picture her baby and longed for its arrival.

Laurence came back. He was browner than ever. More handsome than ever, too, Hannah noticed. As she was diminished, so he was enhanced. At one point she almost capitulated, not to a termination, never that, but to her old ways. But there was no reaching out, no pleading with him, no taking him upstairs to their king-size bed where their child had been conceived. Whatever happened next would be up to him.

'I've been thinking, Hannah,' he began as he plugged in

18

the kettle. 'Why don't we compromise?' He smiled; a mixture of pleading and embarrassment. That little boy look that had once charmed her. 'I thought we had an understanding about children. You know I've never shown any interest in having them, but if you go along with me this time I'd be prepared to try again in five years.' He reached for her, so sure of his reception.

Hannah took two steps backwards. 'No. You'll do the same then. I am not killing my baby.'

He blustered, talked about them having more time alone together. Hannah did not listen.

'Don't waste your breath. Even your mother sounded pleased.'

'My mother? You told her behind my back?'

'Oh, really –' she began before her head snapped back and her fingers came up to meet her reddening cheek. Laurence had struck her.

He had never done so before.

'Hannah. Oh, shit, I'm sorry. God, I'm so sorry.'

She ran from the kitchen and locked herself in the upstairs bathroom ignoring Laurence's entreaties to come out. The truth hurt far more than the flat of Laurence's hand had done. Sitting on the lid of the toilet she saw what had happened to her, what she had allowed to happen to her. Marriage to Laurence had turned her into a victim. A mental victim only until that day. But she was aware of the downward spiral to hell that could follow one slap. She had loved him too much to see his shortcomings. At that time she still loved him.

Time passed and Hannah realized that the house was silent. She went downstairs when she heard the telephone. Pauline at least had had the decency to let her know where Laurence was. 'He's staying here tonight,' she had said. Hannah thanked her and replaced the receiver without offering any explanation. It would differ from whatever Laurence had told his mother.

It was not yet spring. In the late afternoon Hannah felt cold in jeans and a sweatshirt. Shivering, she picked up a

19

jacket and went outside hoping the silent smooth river would soothe her. She was alone, and, at that moment, glad to be.

Orange streaks of a dying sun were reflected in the water as the tide ebbed. There were no boats, few ventured that far up the estuary, but the waders who had not yet migrated for the summer settled on the mudbanks to feed, to eat the molluscs the water had uncovered. Oyster-catchers called, their cries melancholy in the thin evening air. The branches of the trees on the opposite bank took on the hues of darkness and the orange sky turned purple, the colour of the bruise on her cheek.

Hannah was ten weeks pregnant. In a little over six months she was to become a mother but she did not know if she would still be a wife.

Standing in front of the house, shadows lengthening, dusk descending, Hannah knew that it was more than the end of another day, it was the end of her marriage as well. She loved Laurence, she could not help that, but she knew he wasn't coming back, that it would never have taken much to make him decide to leave her.

The last of the light had left the sky. Night sounds drifted up the valley. Hannah did not notice the darkness through the tears which burned then cooled on her face . . .

Nor did she notice the darkness now as the train entered the first of the five tunnels hewn out of the red Devon rock which ran alongside the sea. She only opened her eyes when an announcement, distorted because of the bad public address system, told her that they were approaching Exeter. She had missed the best part of the journey, the beauty of the estuaries of the Teign and the Exe. Not that it mattered, nothing mattered now. She touched her face. It was wet with tears. Hannah wiped her eyes, uncaring if other passengers saw she was crying. How could she ever have thought that losing Laurence was the worst thing that could happen to her?

Time passed. The train reached Taunton. It slid to a halt

with a hiss of brakes. Weeds grew through the tarmac beneath the advertising hoardings in the centre of the station. Waiting passengers on the opposite platform peered anxiously down the line as if they could will their train to appear more quickly.

Hannah's carriage filled up; there were several minutes of chaos as people tried to find their seats, reserved or otherwise. Behind her, a teenager switched on a Walkman. Hannah ignored the relentless throb of the bass and merely nodded when a man asked if the seat next to her was free. He unrolled a newspaper making it clear that he had no intention of talking, which was a relief. Hannah settled comfortably in her seat and thought back to the day her son was born.

Gazing out of the grime-streaked window of the train she found it hard to believe he had once been so tiny. Now his sturdy little legs were dimpled and she had a struggle to catch him when he took off in a fast crawl. He was able to haul himself up on the furniture and soon he would take his first steps.

In those first fleeting seconds when Josh was placed in her arms she had seen only a miniature replica of Laurence. 'He's like you,' the midwife told Hannah kindly, aware of her situation, aware of what she was thinking and of the tears which were held in check.

Reality had been suspended during the days of her hospitalization after the birth. She had stayed in for a week because, without her mother taking time off work, there was no one at home to look after her. Food was brought to her by the staff, flowers and visitors arrived, sometimes together, sometimes separately, and there was always someone on hand to alleviate her doubts about Josh. But there had been no word from Laurence, not then. How would she cope? How could she possibly be responsible for someone so tiny and fragile? she had asked herself on numerous occasions.

Her parents came each evening after work and Lorna and Sonia sat on the side of the bed exchanging gossip

21

with her. They were both waiting at the house on the day she was discharged.

Her father drove her home, glancing in the rear-view mirror every other second to check that Josh was safe in his little seat with the handle which was strapped in place by the seat-belt. 'He's a beauty, Hannah,' he said, more than once, a smug grin on his face, as if he had had a hand in the miracle.

The house felt different somehow, as though Hannah had been away for a long time. Then she realized why. It was the first time she had spent a night away from it since Laurence had left and therefore the first time she had returned to it as a single woman. Her friends exchanged a look and took over before she felt too keenly the absence of the baby's father.

Sonia's perfume had already impregnated the air. She always wore too much. Overriding it was the smell of roasting meat. Hannah raised her eyebrows in a question.

'It's all Lorna's doing,' Sonia had admitted, hands raised, palms at right angles as if she was denying her part in a serious crime. 'You know I can't cook.' She did not add that she had paid for the food, it was her way of contributing to the occasion.

Josh was settled in his carry-cot in the lounge where a fire burned in the grate. Sonia had lit it as a sign of welcome in place of the husband who should have been there to welcome Hannah home. Apple wood scented the air. It was a raw October day. The sky and the estuary were steel grey, the leafless trees on the opposite bank stark, almost black as they bent to the wind which had brought the rain. But the kitchen was warm. Enveloped by cooking smells, condensation running down the windows, the three women sat at the large table in the alcove eating lamb which was crisp on the outside, pink in the middle, and sipping the champagne which Sonia had provided. With a wave of a thin, braceleted wrist she declared, 'It's nonsense, all that business about red wine being obligatory with red meat. Give me champagne any time.'

22

Hannah wondered if she ought to be drinking at all but she was not breast-feeding. After thirty-six hours of discomfort and tears and frustration Josh had been put on a bottle and they had both settled down. The champagne relaxed her and she smiled in gratitude at the efforts made on her behalf. She listened to rather than joined in the conversation which flowed across the table, unable to understand how three very different people could have become such good friends. Sonia belonged in cities. All bones, but sleek and perfectly groomed; rose-painted nails matching her lips, her strawberry silk suit costing as much as an average monthly mortgage repayment, a name in the world of fashion photography about which she was now talking. Lorna, more rounded and bouncy, wore her fine ginger hair in a pony tail. In jeans and trainers and a childish sweatshirt she was countryside fresh and might have been a farmer's wife, But Lorna was a barrister, married to a teacher with whom Hannah worked.

And me, Hannah had thought, what or who am I? A mother. Her stomach had churned. So much responsibility, now and for ever. But she was happy, overflowing with maternal love. But no longer a wife, soon to be not even legally married. Laurence had wasted no time in consulting a solicitor. Pregnant, alone, deeply depressed, missing him yet hating him, Hannah had not had the energy to fight. She had agreed to a divorce on the grounds of mutual consent. Pointless to hang on to a husband who no longer wanted you. However, she had acquired a certain dignity through her abandonment. She might not possess the glamour of Sonia or the deceptively youthful ebullience of Lorna but – although Hannah was unaware of the fact – hers was the most interesting face, because her beauty was harder to define.

At that time there had been no word from Laurence other than through his lawyer. No card had arrived upon Josh's birth, no flowers were sent and he had not been to see his son. Laurence had meant what he said. Each day had been endured, beginning with hope, ending in despair. Once her pregnancy had advanced Hannah had believed that he would come back, that he would see he had no option other than to face the inevitable. He had not done so. And now he never would.

'Has Pauline mentioned Laurence at all?' Sonia asked, realizing that they could not refrain from bringing him into the conversation indefinitely. Whatever stance he took, he was still the baby's father.

'She says she told him when he last telephoned, and she gave him the hospital number.' Hannah shrugged and tried to smile, to show she was not devastated. She did not fool her friends.

Poorly Pauline and Andrew had come to the ward bearing sleeping suits with teddy bear motifs and a hand-crocheted blanket from Pauline's mother who was too infirm to come herself. Andrew had been embarrassed, either by Hannah's predicament, by his own son's behaviour or by the fecundity which had surrounded him. Pauline had cooed and smiled and fussed around the plastic crib but seemed fearful of picking Josh up. 'He's so small,' she said, as if she had not had a child of her own. 'I'd be terrified of dropping him.' By the following day she could not hold him enough. They were his grandparents, Hannah would not deny them access whatever their son might have done.

After lunch on the day she returned from the hospital they carried their coffee into the lounge with its long windows overlooking the river. Josh, in his carry-cot, woke and was fed. Hannah's coffee went cold. She knew that was how it would be from then on but she felt no resentment. Josh was everything.

It had rained all afternoon and the sky darkened into a premature dusk. But Hannah was cocooned in the warmth of the four-bedroomed house which had once contained her husband and three mature students to whom she had rented rooms to cover the expense of the repairs She had thought at the time that she might have to consider doing so again as she had no idea where she stood with Laurence

24

financially or how she would cope if she went back to teaching.

'You must talk to someone, sweetheart,' her father had advised. 'Get it sorted out before the divorce is finalized.'

'I don't want his money, Dad.' Laurence did not have a monopoly in stubbornness.

'You mightn't, but what about Josh? He's his son. And the law –'

'Please. Don't.' Near to tears, Hannah had cut him off. She had wanted to wait, to test Laurence's reaction. If he did not volunteer to help support his child then she would know for certain how he felt. Even then she was still giving him last chances. Even as she gave Josh his bottle that day, watched by her friends, she was listening for his car on the drive, his key in the lock.

Josh went back to sleep, a milky dribble in the corner of his mouth. His translucent blue-veined eyelids twitched. Hannah wondered if babies could dream, if Josh knew he was fatherless.

'Motherhood suits you,' Sonia commented when the taxi she had ordered finally arrived. It would drop Lorna off on its way to the station. She embraced Hannah. 'But I don't envy you one bit.'

'He's gorgeous,' Lorna had added nostalgically because by then her children were both at school. 'He really is.'

'I know.' Hannah had smiled with maternal pride. 'Thank you both for today. It made things so much easier.' She watched them leave with tears in her eyes. Although her parents were coming to stay she had never felt more alone.

The taxi turned out of the gate. Above the rear lights Sonia's head was a pale blob; Lorna's was almost invisible. The rain fell harder from an oyster sky. Concentric circles dotted the surface of the river as large spots hit it like hail. Hannah hated herself for wanting to cry, hated Laurence for not being there. Knowing that hormones partly accounted for her mood swings did not help.

When her parents arrived she let them take over. Her

father made supper, her mother heated Josh's bottle and asked if she could feed him. Hannah said yes. Exhausted, she went to bed early and sobbed quietly into her pillow . . .

It's strange how far Laurence has receded from my thoughts now, Hannah realized as she asked the man beside her to excuse her. She lurched through the rocking train to the buffet for coffee. Occasionally she would see something, a reminder of happier days, or someone would say something and a clear picture of their life together would form in her mind, only to blur again almost immediately.

Hannah returned to her seat. The coffee was black and scalding, too hot to sip yet. She removed the plastic lid and watched the steam rise.

The time had passed so quickly, those happy days as she watched Josh grow and her love for Laurence faded. But he had come at Christmas, bearing gifts. Far too many for a two-month-old child. Guilt, Hannah had guessed. But she had been polite, hating it when he held his son, hating seeing the resemblance between them. She wished she had not answered the door, but while she could have denied Laurence his son she could not deny Josh his father. 'I just wanted to make sure you were all right,' he said.

'We're fine, Laurence.'

'And the money's sorted out?'

'Yes.' She did not thank him. It was for Josh, not herself. Laurence had stayed no more than fifteen minutes. He had telephoned several more times since then, asking if he might call in. Each visit was similar to the previous one. They made small talk, Laurence held Josh briefly, unsure what to do with him, then he said he must leave. Hannah felt nothing when he had gone: the birth of her son had helped ease the pain.

It was just after Laurence's first visit that she had met Jenny; Jenny who drove out to see them whenever her job allowed. On a crisp January morning she had been pushing the pram up the lane. Josh had been fretful, unable to

26

settle. Hannah knew from experience that movement, especially outdoors, sent him to sleep. Few people used the public footpath so it was a surprise to see the young woman walking towards her. They spoke and Jenny admired the baby. Hannah found herself inviting her in for coffee, realizing that there were times when she felt isolated, in need of adult conversation. Their friendship had grown from there. But now Jenny had gone, changing career in mid-stream by going off to Bristol to train as a nurse. I miss her, Hannah thought, I miss her lovely grin and her eternal cheerfulness. She'll make a terrific nurse.

The man beside her coughed. Hannah turned to look out of the window in case he had decided to instigate a conversation. What was it that prompted my suspicion of Sonia? When, exactly, on her last visit did I realize she was somehow different, cagey almost? And it was odd, her coming for a whole week. Had she planned it then? Did she stay under my roof knowing that she was going to destroy me?

By the end of January Hannah had developed a routine which suited both her and Josh. With the promise of an early spring came an upswing in her mood. Teaching colleagues came to visit, her parents doted on Josh and called in whenever they could, and each Monday Hannah met Lorna in Plymouth for lunch. Dear Lorna who had offered to be there at the birth, an offer Hannah had refused. There were visits to Laurence's parents and evenings when she would cook a meal for Jenny. Hannah began to feel fulfilled.

Sonia rang regularly, then, during that last week of January, invited herself down. 'My next commission isn't for another ten days, and, to be honest, George is being a bit demanding,' she had said.

Hannah had nuzzled the warm creases in Josh's neck as she replaced the receiver, adept by then at performing tasks one-handed. 'Mummy's friend's coming to stay,' she said. She had not met George Allison but she knew he was the mainstay of Sonia's London entourage. 'Moths to a candle. One of the by-products of being beautiful,' Hannah said. She talked to Josh constantly but she rarely mentioned Laurence.

Two days later she had driven into Plymouth to meet the train. Unstrapping Josh from the back of the car, she placed him in his sling and watched his wide eyes blinking in confusion at the loud station announcements. His lips puckered as they stood on the windswept platform but he decided not to cry.

Sonia was not alone. She hurried down the platform and hugged Hannah without squashing Josh. The man carrying her luggage stood several yards away waiting to be introduced. 'Hannah, you look marvellous. You've got your figure back and, well . . .' she held her away from her body, her hands on her elbows as she scrutinized her, 'you look happy and healthy.'

'I feel it.'

'Oh, this is James Fulford.' He had stepped forward. 'He's a friend of George's. They're both in electronics and go way back. We've met a few times and as James lives in Plymouth we decided to travel down together. James, this is Hannah Peters and her son, Josh.' Sonia rarely used her car for pleasure. It was mostly garaged in London. When assignments took her overseas her taxi and air fares were paid by whoever happened to be employing her.

James shook her hand. Hannah was surprised when he touched Josh's little hand very gently. But she smiled weakly, wondering if this was Sonia's latest conquest and if she was expected to put him up too. When they walked across the concourse and over the road to the car-park James was still carrying Sonia's luggage. 'Can I give you a lift?' Hannah asked to clarify the situation.

'No, I'm fine, thanks. There're plenty of taxis.' He indicated the rank of black cabs outside the station.

Once she knew he was not going to be staying, Hannah felt more generous. 'Look, it's no trouble. Go on, get in,' she told him.

On the journey from the station he had to sit in the back

28

next to Josh in his car-seat because Sonia was already in the front but he seemed not to mind.

Hannah drove through the wide streets of the city centre. In the rear-view mirror she saw James tickle Josh. A man used to babies, she thought. Married then. Not handsome, but – what? Comfortable, pleasant to look at. It was the first time since Laurence had gone that she had assessed a man in that way. She took another quick look. Short dark hair, firm features, drop-sleeved shirt open at the neck. That was all she was able to see.

They stopped at a set of lights at the large junction at the bottom of Western Approach. Toys-'Я'-Us on one corner, a store Hannah guessed she was destined to visit, the Plymouth Pavilions on another, forthcoming events flashing digitally across the top of the building. It would be a long time before she would be attending any of them. The lights changed to green. Hannah turned left and crossed the roundabout into Royal Parade. The glass edifice of the theatre glided past. She had last been there with Laurence. How long would it be before places did not remind her of him?

'Left here, please, Hannah,' James said several minutes later. 'You don't know how glad I am to be back. I always look forward to the occasional conference in London but after a couple of days I find I've had enough. Slow down. Sorry, I should've said. Stop here, anywhere you like now, this is where I live.'

Hannah did not know the area but it was pleasant with enough greenery to soften the outlines of suburbia. The houses were pre-war, part of the ten per cent of the buildings which had survived the bombing. There were steep steps up to the house and sloping lawns either side. Hannah thought that it would be a struggle with a pram, then smiled because she now related everything to her new status as a mother.

'Thank you. Bye, Sonia.' James picked up his bag and got out of the car. He waved to Josh who ignored him and continued to suck his thumb, then leaned across to thank

Hannah again for the lift. He seemed reluctant to go. She could smell his aftershave – and she had come to know it well since that afternoon.

Josh fell asleep as they reached the Devon countryside. All around were bare fields, the rich red Devon soil neatly ploughed. Here and there the green shoots of early crops showed through the ridges. The river came into view. A man in a dinghy was fishing. The trees on the opposite bank would soon lose their wintry sharpness and become misted with budding leaves. Hannah turned into her gateway full of optimism for herself and Josh and looking forward to having Sonia with her.

'How do you stand it?' Sonia asked as they unpacked the car: bags and luggage, Josh and baby paraphernalia. So many things for such a short trip 'I know it's beautiful and very peaceful here, but now you're stuck with a baby don't you long to socialize again?'

'No. I'm perfectly happy. Grab this, will you?' She held out her handbag. 'I get visitors and I go into Plymouth, I'm not exactly a recluse. I'm quite content, you know.' And she was. Speaking the words aloud had affirmed something she had not realized. Even then Laurence came into her thoughts less and less.

They woke to a mild winter's day. Hannah put Josh on a blanket on the lounge floor where he thrashed his limbs without co-ordination. His eyes followed the sound of Hannah's voice as she moved around. He was already three and a half months old. Sonia sat on the floor beside him, unaware that she was being observed from the open kitchen door where Hannah was preparing lunchtime sandwiches and reaching for the corkscrew in order to open a bottle of wine. Sonia's shiny blonde bob fell forward as she leant on one narrow hip to stroke the baby's cheek.

Hannah was puzzled. For a woman who had an aversion to children and motherhood the gesture was out of character. But Sonia had mellowed in some way. Even upon her arrival she had seemed different. Hannah had put it down to being in the company of a man.

When she returned to the lounge, a tray in her hands, Sonia was on the sofa, her arms clasped firmly around her bent knees. She knew instinctively just how to sit or stand to create the greatest impression. Her figure was that of a model and she was often mistaken for one.

'And I thought London was civilized,' she said casually as she accepted the glass of cold wine.

'This is purely for your benefit. We don't live like this every day.' Hannah gulped at her own wine. She hated having to use the money Laurence had agreed to pay but her father had been right. Pride was no substitute for disposable nappies and powdered milk. She would soon be going back to work. She had talked it over with her parents, she did not want to stagnate and the extra money would be useful. At the time the idea had been unbearable but she had soon become used to leaving Josh in someone else's hands and it was only for a couple of hours each day.

During the time Sonia was with her Hannah tried to decipher what had caused the subtle change in her friend. She had softened, that much was obvious. Her edges were less defined both mentally and physically. Hannah said nothing, aware of the state of near anorexia to which Sonia would revert if she thought she had gained any weight. No matter how beautiful and successful she had become, the insecurity of the fat, unloved child was never far from the surface.

'He's cute,' Sonia said, poking Josh experimentally. 'But it would drive me crazy spending all day running around the way you do. I know I've told you it's the reason Brian left me. He wanted children desperately. It took me six years to convince him there was no way I was having any. Still, once he married the bimbette he didn't waste much time, three in four years.' It was said without bitterness, they still got on well. Sonia laughed. 'But I never imagined he'd fall for a stereotype.'

Hannah turned away to hide a smile, not wishing to point out that, yes, she had heard the story many times and that Sonia had been young and beautiful and blonde when Brian had married her, and that the bimbette, as they both called her, was only a substitute. Sonia admitted that she had driven Brian away. 'It gets easier, Sonia – looking after a baby, that is,' Hannah had told her.

Later, when Josh woke, crying before he had opened his eyes, Sonia remarked, 'You can tell he's a male. He's demanding food and attention before he's properly awake.' It was more like her old self, her London persona.

They idled away the next two days, talking and reading. Sometimes, wrapped up against the cold, the plastic hood of Josh's pushchair snapping in the wind, they wandered along the bank of the river bumping him over the rough grass. The strain had left Sonia's face. She was ready to get back to her life in the city.

Hannah mentioned Jenny and her plans for the future. 'You'd have liked her,' she told Sonia.

'A nurse?' Sonia was horrified. 'All those bodily excretions? Yuk. I don't even like cutting my own toenails.'

'You don't,' Hannah said with a grin. 'You pay a pedicurist to do it for you. Anyway, she'll make a wonderful nurse.'

'James liked you, you know,' Sonia said on her last night as she handed Hannah a disposable nappy.

'Pardon?' She turned around, her fingers still clasping Josh's ankles as she manoeuvred the nappy into place.

'James Fulford. He likes you.'

'How on earth do you know?' Hannah was startled.

'I could tell.'

'Isn't he . . .'

'One of mine? No. Not my type. And he's not married either. Can I use the phone?'

'Of course.'

Hannah put Josh to bed but as she came back downstairs she could not help overhearing part of the conversation, something about a baby. 'Were you talking about my son?' she asked with the conceit of a new mother for whom, temporarily, no other topic was worthy of discussion.

'No. My baby. Timmy.' Sonia seemed a little embarrassed. 'A bundle of black fluff. That was my neighbour, Marion, she's catsitting for me.'

'You've got another cat?'

Sonia's shrug was nonchalant. 'As they say about children, two are as easy as one.'

Hannah wondered if Sonia had bought the cat because she had had a baby, if it was a touch of subconscious competition. Maybe beneath the London gloss lurked some maternal instincts.

Life reverted to normal until, a week later, James Fulford telephoned.

That was it, Hannah thought, as the train slowed and pulled into Paddington station, that's why I didn't make the connection. I was too preoccupied with Josh and then James. Five months. She suddenly realized that it was five months since she had last seen Sonia. Time went so quickly when you had a baby. She knew, Sonia knew back then what she was going to do. And when I find her, what then? What will I do? If I find her.

Hannah swallowed hard. No more tears, she had done enough crying.

'. . . Please make sure you take all your belongings with you,' a disembodied voice was saying. The train had come to a halt. Hannah stood up and reached for her coat.

On the platform people knocked into her, moving on without apology. She was shaking, her hands were cold. It might be June but it was damp and chilly. Amongst the crowds and the noise she felt alien. People pushed and shoved, hurrying importantly down the steps to the Underground as if no one else mattered. They appeared so certain it left Hannah feeling weak and disorientated. There was no certainty in her life. She took several deep breaths and walked towards the rank of black cabs where each departing one was rapidly replaced by another.

Within minutes the people ahead of her in the queue had been driven away. Hannah stepped into the next taxi and gave the driver Sonia's address. It was in West London, not far from the station.

The journey took fifteen minutes but only because the traffic was heavy. It seemed like a bad omen.

The driver pulled up in a wide, tree-lined street. The three-storey terrace of red brick was uniform; at intervals came the entrances to the groups of luxury apartments housed within, three inside each solid wooden door. Above, tall windows gleamed beyond the wrought-iron railings guarding balconies with enough space for only a few plant pots. And above all this was an arc of milky-white sky with a hint of sunshine in the distance.

Hannah paid the driver and added a tip which he didn't acknowledge. She stood on the pavement staring up at the third floor wondering what might be going on behind those blank, unopened windows. The sound of her heart-beat thumped in her ears just as she recognized the roar which would have preceded her fainting had she not sat down on the low wall at the base of the steps and bent over, her head between her knees. Am I that close? she thought. Have I really discovered the truth? She refused to accept the reality of what she had seen. It was a mirage caused by hunger and exhaustion; her brain wasn't functioning properly.

One or two cars passed down the street but there were no pedestrians. It wasn't that sort of area. Hannah approached the front door, reached by three narrow steps. To either side were glossy shrubs. Earlier rain had left its mark, dimpling the leaves, spreading the dust of the city to expose greener spots. There was also an estate agent's board hammered into the soil which provided the shrubs with their mean nourishment. 'Third Floor Apartment to Let', it said beneath the name of the firm. She swallowed, uncomprehending. It was not a mirage. There was only one flat to each floor behind the sequence of entrance doors. Sonia's flat was on the third floor.

It was a mistake. The taxi had deposited her outside the wrong number. She stepped back to check.

It wasn't a mistake. Hannah's mouth was dry as she pressed the intercom buzzer, already aware that the slip of cardboard bearing Sonia's name was no longer behind the protective plastic. The space was empty. Hannah waited. On the last occasion she had spoken to Sonia she had said that she was taking some time off work. Perhaps she had gone on holiday. But that would not explain the garish board at her side or the lack of a name by the buzzer. She pressed the entryphone button again, keeping her finger there for a long time. There was no reply. She had not expected one, it was an act of panic. With a shaking hand she took her father's mobile phone from her handbag and dialled the estate agent's number. 'I just happened to be passing,' she began, hoping that she did not sound as hysterical as she felt as she gave Sonia's address. 'I wonder if it would be convenient for me to view the property sometime this afternoon? I know it's short notice, but I'm only in London for the day.' Barely listening as the man who had answered reeled off figures for rental and service charges, she glanced at her watch. It was almost one o'clock. She realized he would not want to waste his time if she could not afford the expensive apartment. 'Yes, that was about the amount I was expecting to pay,' she told him.

Andy, who had given no surname, agreed to meet her outside at two.

Knowing the area from previous visits Hannah was aware that there was a small parade of shops and a decent wine bar not far away. She would go there and try to eat something, enough to ward off the dizziness, although it was doubtful she would succeed.

Having ordered a glass of red wine she made it last almost the whole hour. The plain jacket potato went cold on her plate. She had eaten two mouthfuls.

Andy was five minutes late. He pulled up in a brand new car, jumped out and locked it with a beep of an electronic device and, with a wide smile, held out his hand. 'Hi, I'm Andy. It is Mrs Peters, isn't it?'

'Yes.' He was about twenty-five, a few years younger than Hannah. She had forgotten how much more pushy Londoners were in comparison with the more gentle way of doing business in the West Country. Plymouth may be a city but it had a small town feel, it was a place where you were likely to bump into someone you knew in the street.

'I'm sure you'll love the apartment. And it's a great area to live in.' As he unlocked the front door and led her up the stairs he continued to point out all the advantages, apart from the fact that there was no lift. Hannah had known this already.

Andy undid Sonia's front door and opened it, standing back to let the full impact of the light, high-ceilinged interior hit her. All the doors to the rooms had been left open deliberately. Hannah stepped inside. The place was empty. There was no furniture, no pictures on the walls of the wide hall and no sign that Sonia had lived there, not even a cat hair. She walked from room to room, ignoring whatever Andy was telling her.

She turned suddenly. Something was wrong. At some point in Andy's monologue she thought he had mentioned that the owner had never occupied the place, that it was one of the few apartments in the road that were let, nearly all of the others were leasehold purchases. 'I'm sorry, did you say the owner didn't actually live here?'

'That's right. She had an accident just before she was due to move in. It was the lack of a lift, you see, she was left disabled.'

Hannah had believed that Sonia owned the place. But Sonia hadn't actually said so. How many other things had she taken for granted? 'When did the last occupant leave?'

'Oh, about a month ago.'

'A month?' Hannah stared at him. She must not let him see how desperate she was, she needed information. How could the police have spoken to Sonia if she no longer lived here? How could Sonia have avoided mentioning her move in their last long telephone conversation a fortnight ago? The answer was obvious now, as was Sonia's hesitation when she had rung to see if there was anything she could do after she heard the news. With a smile Hannah stood straighter and pushed her hair back from her face. She noticed Andy's glance drop to her body as her coat fell open. Was it possible that a man could still find her attractive despite what she was going through? Perhaps she was hiding it better than she knew. She no longer thought of herself as a woman, only as an automaton with one objective in mind.

'Does it matter?'

She laughed quietly. 'No, of course not. I was just curious.' Despising herself for doing it she used her femininity. With one hand on her hip she half turned to look out of the window, allowing Andy a view of her profile, of her hollowed-out cheeks and her breasts which had filled out since Josh's birth, pleased that she had chosen a clinging wool dress. 'Why did she leave such a lovely place?'

Andy shrugged. 'I've no idea. Probably decided it was time to buy. She'd been here for eight years.'

Since a year before I met her then, Hannah thought. She shook her head. 'I don't know why, but when I saw this place I had the peculiar feeling that I might have known who lived here. Silly, isn't it?' She grinned. 'Her name wasn't Grant by any chance?'

Andy's fixed smile faded. There were always cranks, people who made a hobby of viewing properties they had no intention of renting or buying, but Mrs Peters had not struck him as one of them until then. If she had known who had lived there she would also have known the apartment had been available for renting weeks before. 'I'm not sure that I should . . .' But something in Hannah's face made him decide to answer the question. She looked close to breaking point and he could almost feel her tension. Maybe Mrs Grant had done something dreadful to her, stolen her husband or maybe owed her lots of money. 'Yes. Yes, it was,' he said.

Hannah nodded. 'Thank you.' She had rung Sonia herself two weeks ago. How stupid she had been. Sonia's telephone system was always up to date. Calls were transferred from her home number to her mobile if she was out. With all her business contacts she would obviously have taken her old number with her. It was ex-directory, Hannah would not be able to get an address via an operator or a phone book, but she could at least telephone. How would Sonia explain herself? She had already provided the police with a statement. They would have dialled the number Hannah had provided but to cover her tracks, to ensure no one knew she had moved, Hannah guessed that Sonia would have volunteered to go to a police station to answer their questions, possibly the one nearest to this apartment. Hannah was now certain that she had been totally deceived. 'I'll just have another look around, if I may.'

The curtains and carpets had been left *in situ*. The windows were large, floor to ceiling, and the shape of the apartment meant that the fitted carpet would not be suitable anywhere else.

Hannah moved from room to room trying to plan her next move, to think why the certainty now existed. Did Gareth Chambers know that Sonia had moved and was he, as she stood there, trying to find her? Had he known and not told Hannah?

How different the place seemed now that it was bare. The lounge at the front overlooked the street, as did the study next to it where Sonia had kept her computer and camera equipment. The hall wound left-handed around the curve of the stairwell on the other side of the wall. On the right was the bathroom followed by the master bedroom, as Andy had called it pretentiously. Beyond that, around the curve was the second bedroom and, to its left, the wide kitchen which spread over the landing below. What was she hoping to find? There was nothing to see other than the indentations in the carpets where furniture had once stood and a few lighter patches on the walls where pictures had hung.

Standing in the doorway of the second bedroom Hannah tried to recall what it had held. She had slept there on several occasions. There had been a double bed, a dressing-table and stool, and a chest. The wardrobe was built-in, a small walk-in affair with hanging rails and shelves. Surely the oatmeal carpet had extended throughout the whole of the flat apart from the kitchen? This carpet was new. It was pale blue. She steadied herself against the door-frame. It was pale blue and new and springy beneath her feet as she crossed the room trying not to cry. In the corner nearest the window were four marks left by the feet of something. They were the only indentations. They were too closely spaced to have been made by a single bed. A dressing-table, maybe? The room tilted. Or had it been a cot?

Yes, a cot. Sonia had Josh. Sonia had taken her eight-month-old baby. Hannah felt sick with fury. A primeval scream rose in her throat. She held it in. She thought she could smell his baby smell. To hold him, to touch his soft hair, to feel his little arms around her neck, she would kill for that. The pain was too much to bear.

'Mrs Peters? Mrs Peters, did you hear me? Are you all right?'

No. No, I'm not all right, she shouted silently. Had Sonia planned this for months then realized she could not keep Josh where he would be so easily found?

Inhaling deeply, she turned to face Andy whose look of concern was genuine. 'I'm fine. I've seen enough, thank you,' Hannah said with a tight smile. 'You've been very generous with your time.'

He made the place secure and walked to his car with Hannah at his side. 'You wouldn't happen to know where Mrs Grant went?' she asked.

'No, I'm afraid not. She rented on a six-monthly basis and gave us six months' rent in lieu of notice.'

'I see.'

'Look, take your time, think about it. If you decide to take the place or you'd like to look at something similar, call me. Here's my card.' He reached into his suit jacket pocket and produced one.

'Thank you.' Hannah put the card in her handbag and began to walk down the road, aware of Andy's boyish face beneath his short cropped hair watching her. She did not know what she felt, relief that at least she knew who Josh was with or rage and disgust that Sonia could have done such a thing. At least now they would be able to find her. No one could live in isolation. But Sonia earned enough that she might have taken him anywhere, out of the country, even. At that moment she hated Sonia so much that had she appeared then she would have killed her without hesitation. All that talk about not wanting a baby had been to deceive her. She thought she had been a friend but she had used her. Hannah leant against the rough bark of one of the trees, waiting for the shaking to stop. There was nothing she would not have sacrificed to feel Josh's warm little body against hers, to nuzzle his neck, to feel his lips on her cheek. She felt dizzy with longing, she was sinking into a black hole.

Andy watched her. The woman's sadness was tangible, her aura of tragedy touched him. She needed help which he knew he could not give. He drove the short distance to where she stood. 'Can I give you a lift somewhere?'

'Yes, please.' But where did she want to go? Where could she go? Home, she decided, once she'd rung Inspector Chambers to tell him what she had found out. 'I've got to catch a train. Is Paddington out of your way?'

'Not at all.' He reached across to open the passenger door, feeling protective towards the lovely but vulnerable woman who sat beside him. Her naturally fair hair framed her face. Thickened by the damp atmosphere it emphasized her fragility. He smiled. Some of it was tucked into her collar. He wanted to reach across and free it.

'Don't forget to ring if I can be of help in any way.' They had arrived at Paddington in no time at all.

'I will. Thank you. And thanks for the lift. It was kind of you.'

In the bustle of the station the world seemed a little more real. Hannah queued to use one of the telephones which stood in a row. It seemed more anonymous than if she used the mobile in the midst of so many people. Lifting the receiver she slid in some coins and dialled Sonia's number. It was unobtainable. How could that be? Gareth Chambers had rung her recently. Had she known Hannah would come? Tears of frustration were stinging her eyes when, from nowhere, a memory flashed across her mind. She disconnected the line, wondering if it meant anything.

'He's a real darling and he never lectures me on my lifestyle,' Sonia had said.

'Probably because he realizes he'd be wasting his breath,' Hannah had told her with a smile.

'I felt so ill before that trip to Florida I thought I'd have to cancel. Whatever he gave me did the trick. Marcus Gould is the sort of doctor everyone should have. He makes you feel better just for seeing him.'

If he was that understanding he might be able to lead Hannah to Sonia. No doubt he kept his patients happy in ratio to the fees he charged them. It was unlikely that he would break the code of professional conduct but if he knew how desperate her case was he might let something slip. She rang Directory Enquiries and obtained the number of his practice, asking to speak to Dr Gould when she got through.

'*Mr* Gould. He's with a patient at the moment. Can I get him to ring you back?'

'I'm in a call box. It's rather an urgent matter.'

'Ah, I see. Are you one of Mr Gould's patients?'

'No, my name's Hannah Peters but my friend recommended me. Mrs Grant. Sonia Grant.'

'Oh, well, in that case I'll see what I can do.' There was a click. Strains from a Viennese waltz floated down the line. Hannah waited. 'Are you near by? I can fit you in at five thirty if that's convenient?'

'Thank you. I'd be most grateful.' Hannah replaced the receiver. She had over two hours to kill.

Chapter Two

Inspector Gareth Chambers had not been surprised when WPC Yvonne Francis reported that her services were no longer required. Yvonne was a Family Liaison Officer, trained to deal with situations such as the one Mrs Peters was currently in. But Hannah Peters had advantages over many of the people with whom Yvonne came into contact: strong support from parents and in-laws, a group of worried, caring friends and an inner strength which would see her through this however things turned out. Hannah, housebound since Friday evening, had told Yvonne that she was going mad, that she had to try to look for her son. 'My mother's agreed to stay here,' she'd added. 'There'll be someone here at all times to answer the phone.' Yvonne was too experienced to point out that Hannah could do nothing the police were not already doing. The disappearance of a child affected women in different ways. Hannah needed action, she was not the sort to stay at home and weep.

Gareth understood her feelings far more than most people would have given him credit for. Some time ago he had thought his life had turned into one of those hackneyed tales, that he had become another overworked policeman who didn't give enough time to his wife. Many of his colleagues' marriages had broken up. Judy was taking more of an interest in clothes and had started visiting the hairdresser more frequently. She seemed different, glowing with health. Gareth believed she was having an affair. He had finally confronted her. When she laughed he had been shocked by her reaction.

'No, oh, no, Gareth,' she'd said, shaking her head. 'God, men are so thick at times. It's just that I feel so feminine again. I want to look good for you, especially now.'

The especially now had been an even bigger shock. At the time he had been forty-one, Judy thirty-nine. They were going to have their first child, the child they had given up hope of ever conceiving, and Gabrielle was now approaching her second birthday. Inspector Chambers knew exactly how he would feel if she was missing for even one night. He would walk the streets until he found her and, unless someone stopped him, would kill whoever had taken her. He guessed how Hannah must have felt on the night Laurence told her to have an abortion. What a kick in the guts that must've been. Then to have this happen.

'You might as well push off, unless you think Mrs Gregson needs you there,' he told Yvonne when she telephoned on Monday morning to say where Hannah had gone. 'It might do her good to be out. She's got the pager.'

The case puzzled him. No ransom had been demanded, although kidnappers often waited until nerves were stretched to breaking point before making contact. But it was more likely that whoever had taken Josh was within Hannah's circle of friends and acquaintances.

On Friday afternoon two officers had responded to an emergency call made from Hannah's house in the Tamar Valley. Minutes later, the information having been relayed to him, Gareth had driven out there too. It had been a sunny but not unduly hot day; typical June weather. He had rounded the bend, almost blinded by the reflection of the sun in the window panes. It promised warmth but once inside the house there was only the chill of dread.

Two officers, one male, one female, had been waiting for him, along with James Fulford, whom he now knew to be Hannah's boyfriend.

Hannah, he discovered, had already left the college

44

where she taught and was on her way home. 'I rang there first but they told me she'd left. She's got a mobile phone,' Fulford told him, 'but I . . .' He had almost broken down at that point.

'No,' Gareth agreed. 'It's best to wait until she arrives.'

Had Hannah not stopped for petrol and a few grocery items she would have reached home ahead of Gareth.

They heard her car. Fulford went to open the door. Hannah would have seen the police car and another strange one beside it. 'Where's Josh?'

Gareth heard the soft voice ask before she entered the lounge and went to intercede. 'You'd better come and sit down, Mrs Peters.' He had actually used those dreadful words which always precede bad news. 'Your son is missing,' he told her, his throat dry. Her cry of anguish made his hair stand on end. It was Fulford who had handed the PC a recent photograph and who explained what had happened. But Fulford was still a suspect.

Throughout the next couple of hours Hannah had sat motionless on the cord settee which was a colour somewhere between mushroom and pink, staring at the carpet. Gareth guessed she was recalling how each of the small stains had appeared: a soggy biscuit crushed beneath crawling knees, a spot of Ribena or orange juice, the telltale marks with which a child decorated its home, as little Gabrielle had done his own house. In a chair in the corner sat a knitted rabbit, Josh's favourite toy. It was the sight of this which unleashed Hannah's tears and later enabled her to speak.

'His bunny,' she had said, looking at it with desperation. 'Oh, God, he hasn't got his bunny.' Sobs tore from her throat as she rocked back and forth, her arms clasped tightly across her chest protectively, as if she might hold them in.

'We've got everyone available looking for him,' Gareth told her, trying to reassure her while all the while wondering if Fulford had done away with the boy.

'I don't understand how it could have happened,' Hannah said when she was calmer.

'Let's concentrate on finding Josh first. I need a list of everyone you know, family, friends, tradespeople, colleagues at work. Anyone and everyone who might know where you live.' Even then he appreciated the unlikelihood of a complete stranger coming across the sleeping child and taking him. It really did point to the boyfriend or the child-minder.

'You might as well take this.' Hannah reached into her handbag and handed him an address book.

One of the two original officers had already left with the photograph, to have it copied and distributed. Soon afterwards Yvonne Francis had arrived and Gareth got down to business.

'You returned to part-time teaching two months ago, and you work from one thirty until three forty-five on weekdays. Is that right, Hannah?' So far, any information had come from Fulford.

'Yes.'

'Who would know that?'

Hannah had shrugged. 'Everyone who knows me.'

'Including your ex-husband?'

'Yes. No. I'm sorry, I don't know. If he bothers to visit it's at the weekend. I may have mentioned it but I really can't remember. He never stays more than fifteen minutes.'

'How often does he see Josh?'

'Maybe ten or a dozen times since he was born. He wanted me to have an abortion, that's why our marriage broke up.'

'I see.' Apart from Fulford and Valerie Mayhew, the father had seemed the next most likely candidate. But it appeared he wasn't particularly interested in his son. 'And your in-laws, do you get on with them?'

'Yes. We're not close, but we've got Josh in common. We see them about every ten days or so.'

'Hannah, will you tell me what you know about Valerie Mayhew?'

46

Gareth remembered her looking away, guilt written in her face. If I hadn't gone back to work this wouldn't have happened, she must have been thinking.

'She's a trained nursery nurse. She was recommended to me by a friend, Lorna Freeman – I work with her husband. I interviewed her and asked her to come for a few days while I was here so I could see how she and Josh got on. She certainly knew what she was doing and Josh took to her at once. She wouldn't . . .' Hannah had bitten her lip. But someone had. 'Oh, God. My parents, they don't know. Can I ring them?'

'Mr Fulford has already done so. They should be here soon.'

When they arrived Joyce and Phillip Gregson had been white with anxiety. Without speaking, Joyce had gone across to Hannah and held her tightly. 'It has to be Laurence,' she finally said as she stroked Hannah's hair. 'It's his way of punishing you. Don't worry, darling, we'll get Josh back.' But the tears in her eyes proved that she was aware there was no guarantee she would ever see her grandson again.

Yvonne made tea. When everyone was seated Gareth began questioning James Fulford again. 'I know we've been through this before but I want you to tell me again exactly what happened this afternoon, starting from the time before you left the factory.' Fulford owned an electronics factory and could please himself when he went in. He looks ill, Gareth had thought, and it's no wonder he can't meet Hannah's eyes.

James ran a hand through his hair. He stood in the window recess, his cup rattling against his saucer as he placed it on the sill. 'I'd planned to take Hannah and Josh out. I'd discovered a pub with a family room and high chairs where Josh could have had his tea. It would have given Hannah a chance to have a couple of drinks and relax because I'd have been driving. I left work early, hoping to surprise her. God, it's so awful. I wanted to have

Josh ready, I wanted to show her that he means as much to me as Hannah does, unlike . . .'

'Unlike Laurence, you mean,' Hannah had finished for him coldly.

Gareth had read her mind. At least Hannah had known Laurence was irresponsible.

'I arrived about two forty-five. Val was here, of course. She'd put Josh outside in his pram for his nap. It was warm and sunny and he always sleeps better outdoors. She told me to wake him no later than three thirty. I could see his pram through the french windows. The hood was up as there was a bit of a breeze.

'Val knows me. I said she could go home, that I'd be fine. She wasn't keen on the idea but I insisted. Anyway, she left about ten past three knowing that Hannah would be home within the hour.

'Soon after Val left I went to check on him, to wake him gently if he hadn't stirred.' He paused. 'Josh wasn't there. The pram was empty.'

Gareth had realized the child might have disappeared before Fulford arrived. He asked a few more background questions, such as how he and Hannah had met. Mr and Mrs Gregson had little to add, but anxiety and fear aged them as the evening progressed. They could think of no one who could be responsible except Laurence.

By the time Gareth Chambers left that miserable household, he too was beginning to suspect that Laurence Peters had taken his own child. From what he had learned about the man he was capable of such an act, especially if he knew his ex-wife was seeing another man.

Now, on Monday morning, having spoken to everyone listed in Hannah's address book, they were no further forward in finding Josh. But there was still Laurence Peters to interview. At the moment he was somewhere in the Atlantic Ocean. The questions they wanted to put to him were best asked face to face, not over a ship-to-shore radio, thus giving him a chance to offload the child if he had him, or putting into some foreign port and disappearing.

On Monday afternoon, aware that Hannah had gone to London, Gareth paid a second visit to Valerie Mayhew. She had now had a couple of days to get over the shock and to recall anything which may have slipped her mind. There were too many incidents of nannies abusing their charges. And fathers abducting their children. And mothers, like Hannah, abandoned, having to return to work and, finding it all too much, removing the obstacle to their freedom. The same could apply to Fulford, of course. Professing that he loved the child did not make it true. Maybe he had decided he wanted Hannah without encumbrance.

The Mayhews lived in the Milehouse area of Plymouth. The house was thirties-style. Painted white, it had a red-brick archway around the porch and green paintwork. It had been well cared for. There was a small path leading to the front door and pots of geraniums on shelves inside the porch. The house and the family who inhabited it came within the range he would describe as average. But had Miss Average tired of being so and decided to go for notoriety instead? The thought of having to dig up Hannah's garden or dredge the river sickened him, but it might have to be done. Not yet, though, not until Peters had been questioned.

Mrs Mayhew answered the door. She had taken some time off work because she could not face the questions of the other staff who shared her office. 'She's in here,' she said, opening the door to the tidy living-room; its natural state, Gareth realized, for he had not been expected.

Valerie was not looking her best, which was under-standable. She sat in a chair, her slippered feet tucked beneath her, her eyes red from crying. At the sight of the inspector more tears welled up. Mrs Mayhew clicked her tongue, impatient with her daughter, and left the room.

'I need you to go over it one more time, Valerie.' Both a sergeant and Gareth himself had already spoken to her. She looked rattled enough to confess if she was guilty.

'It's Hannah's husband you should be speaking to, not me.'

'Oh?' This was a new development. Valerie had not mentioned him before. 'Her ex-husband, you mean? What makes you say that?'

'Josh is his son, too. Hannah told me he doesn't see him very often, but that doesn't mean he doesn't want him. And he knows the layout of the house and garden, he'd have known how to get in from the back.'

The same thought had crossed Gareth's mind. 'May I sit down?'

He took the lack of response as assent and did so. The chair was uncomfortable, stiffly upholstered and hard-backed, although Mrs Mayhew had used it on his previous visit. But that lady's leanness and hardness of manner seemed appropriate to that particular piece of furniture. Conversely, her daughter had chosen a plump green Draylon-covered armchair. Hunched up, a roll of fat bulging over the top of her jeans, she seemed to sink into it. It was a strange observation to be making, but Gareth felt that the preferred seating arrangements of the Mayhews were a reflection of their personalities. 'Any other reason why you think this?'

'Mr Peters was married to Hannah for four years, he'd know she'd be a good mother, he'd know she'd like Josh to get plenty of fresh air.'

It was a shrewd observation, but why would Peters wait until the boy was eight months old? He had not wanted him in the first place and how would he cope with him when his job entailed so much travelling? 'Did you ever meet Laurence Peters?'

'No. He never came while I was there.' More tears ran down her face. Gareth wondered if her grief was a little excessive.

'Just tell me again about Friday afternoon, Valerie?'

She did so, reaffirming all that James Fulford had said. They had already reconstructed the scene with the girl and Fulford, using an officer to represent the kidnapper and Josh's own pram. They had hoped to catch one or the other of them out, for one of them to say, no, it wasn't like that,

I did this or I did that. All that had been proved was that it would not have been a problem for someone to come into the garden over the fields, pass unseen along the hedge at the side of the house then reach in and take the child. But they would have had to know he was there in the first place. Which led them back to Valerie, Fulford, Peters or Hannah.

Unbeknown to Hannah, they had checked her movements on Friday. She had been at the art college during the afternoon, the local garage had produced a timed copy of a Switch card slip which she had used to pay for petrol, and the lady in the village shop had confirmed that Hannah had called in on her way home. But none of this precluded her from somehow being involved in his disappearance.

She didn't do it, she had no part in it, Gareth told himself. Her grief was genuine, of that he was certain. And why go rushing off to London if she knew what had happened? The problem was that neither Fulford nor Valerie Mayhew knew whether Josh was still in his pram during the time the two of them had been together.

He was aware of Mrs Mayhew's disgust with her daughter for allowing such a thing to happen. This might account for the tears and the added guilt. The guilt would have been there anyway, anyone would blame themselves. If the girl was innocent she needed support not antipathy.

There was nothing to be gained by staying. He said goodbye and saw himself out.

Back at Charles Cross police station in Plymouth city centre, he dialled Hannah's number and spoke to her mother.

'We haven't heard from her yet,' Joyce Gregson said. 'There haven't been any other calls either.'

'Okay. Let me know if she does call you.'

'I don't suppose there's any news?'

'Not at this stage. We'll keep you up to date.'

'Thank you.'

Gareth hung up. Not at this stage. For one awful minute he thought that there might never be any news. It happened. Be positive, he thought. Just get on with the job.

And then, at six fifty, Hannah telephoned. What she had to tell him amazed him.

When he finally got home that night he hugged Judy tightly then took the stairs two at a time. Gazing down at the sleeping Gabrielle, he sighed with relief. Very gently, so as not to wake her, he stroked her curly hair, then he went back downstairs to try to eat some dinner.

Chapter Three

Marty smiled to herself as she made tea. It was a warm Monday evening in June. There was no more work to be done inside or outside the farmhouse. The waiting was almost over, merely a matter of days now, no time at all when she had already been patient for so long. Everything was in place. By the end of the week he would be with her and her life could begin.

She carried the tea through to the lounge; the front room her mother had called it. It was lighter now that she had knocked two rooms into one and had replaced the sash windows with tall paned glass doors. Through them she could see the neat yard at the front and the rolling country-side at the back. The slaughterhouse was not visible from where she sat. In a few minutes she would make her rounds and shut in the hens. So far no foxes had troubled her. If they did Marty would shoot them, using her mother's shotgun for which she had no licence. Going through Gloria's things she had destroyed any papers relating to it and, if asked, would deny any knowledge of the gun.

On Friday she had driven to Exeter, a rare excursion since she had moved back. There she had stocked up on things which the local delivery service could not supply. She had felt nervous amongst the crowds. In less than a year she had adopted some of her mother's reclusiveness. Nobody had come to visit, no one from the village had called to welcome her home. They would know she was there, news travelled fast in a small community. 'The postman will've told them anyway,' Marty said. Quite often she spoke aloud just to break the silence.

Dusk was falling when she went outside. She scattered a few grains to draw the hens to her then locked them in for the night. One pecked at her shoe. She kicked it away.

The slaughterhouse was padlocked. Taking a key from her pocket she undid the door. It was a fitting place for her mother to have died. Perhaps she had landed on the exact bit of concrete beneath which Marty was sure that her father was buried.

They didn't believe me, she thought as she stared at the straw in the corner where some wisps rustled. The breeze was a little stronger than earlier in the day. For a second she found it hard to remember why she had put it there. Then she grinned. Of course, it had to be there, in the same spot she had sat with her father. The police are fools. She killed him then she buried him. She couldn't wait to concrete the floor. I hated her. She deserved to die.

Painful memories disturbed her. She did not want to recall those nights with Edward Rowland when they had come to the slaughterhouse and he had shown her how much he loved her. 'He loved me more than he did my mother,' she whispered. She could still feel his hands on her body. She had only ever allowed one other person to touch her in that way and soon he would do so again.

Frowning, she relocked the doors of the building where her great-grandfather had killed his own pigs before the law made it compulsory for them to be taken to an abattoir. Around her the fields were full of ripening crops, not hers, but those belonging to neighbouring farms. The breeze picked up. The ears of the grain undulated in a gentle, soothing semicircular movement. Marty stood and watched the sky change colour. Clouds were tipped with pink and the purplish hues of night-time showed over the hilltops. Soon it would be dark. Then she would pour a drink and cook her meal.

What was left of the land, Marty had given over to

vegetables. The skills her father had taught her had come back effortlessly. There would be too much for her to eat, the surplus might be a problem. She would not demean herself by trying to sell it via the village shop or having a stall at the end of the lane. No one passes here anyway, she realized. She did not question why she had had the tractor overhauled and planted the things in the first place. It was just something she knew she had to do. Edward Rowland had always done so.

I was so happy until she killed him, she thought as she made her way back to the house. She had been fifteen at the time and what made it worse was that she had no one to confide in, she had been friendless. As hard as she tried, the girls at school did not get on with her. She knew there was gossip but not what it was. But she had shown them all, she had got out, become an air stewardess and travelled the world.

'You're such a fool, Marty,' her mother had said when the police had been and gone. 'God knows what people will think of you.'

'I don't care,' she had screamed, frustrated because of the way in which she had been treated by the police, as if she was someone to be humoured. The locals might think her father had gone off with another woman, but Marty knew different. He would never have abandoned her.

'She was a cold bitch, she was jealous of me,' she muttered as she approached the house. 'But I'm back now, I've usurped her. There are no reminders of her, I have made the place my own. Ours,' she added, smiling, amazed at how quickly her moods could change.

She always ate late. The nights were when she came fully alive, maybe because that was when he usually came to her, maybe because of the times she had spent with her father. Often she would wander through the unlit house, going from room to room, talking to herself, reliving the past and visualizing the future. Those days of flights and airports and foreign hotel rooms seemed a lifetime ago. They might never have existed. I'll never travel again, she vowed as she washed salad under the tap, a gin and tonic at her elbow. I'm home, and I'm home to stay. No one can take this away from me.

The telephone rang. Marty jumped, her arm jerked sideways knocking over the drink. It ran down the draining-board into the sink. Ignoring it, she ran to the hall to answer the phone. Seconds later she slammed down the receiver. 'Stupid fucking idiot,' she shouted. It had been a wrong number.

But it was too soon for his call, deep down she knew that. With shaking hands she refilled her glass and took several deep breaths. At least Jenny Greene hadn't let her down, at least she had kept to her side of the bargain. How anyone could leave the airline to take up nursing was a mystery but in this case it had proved to be so useful. Having Jenny in Bristol was ideal, having her for a friend was even better.

The correspondence had been taking place for the past couple of months and it would continue to do so for as long as was necessary.

Chapter Four

Hannah moved away from the row of telephone boxes. She had reached the taxi rank before it struck her: not Dr but *Mr*. Marcus Gould was a surgeon, not a GP as Hannah had imagined. And how was it she had been given an appointment so easily?

She glanced at her watch. It was a little after three thirty. There was plenty of time to find somewhere to stay. She couldn't face the journey home however the meeting with Marcus Gould turned out. 'Could you take me to a small-ish hotel in the Harley Street area?' Hannah asked the cab driver as she climbed into the back of the taxi.

'This should do you, love,' he said when he dropped her outside a white-painted building with smart black woodwork. She paid him and walked up the shallow steps to the front door which was flanked by two bay trees in pots. The metal railings either side of her shone. The driver had done her well. The inside was clean and comfortable and the rates reasonable by London standards.

There were tea-making facilities in her room. She used these and sat on the bed to drink the tea. Later, she would ring her parents. They would be frantic if they hadn't heard by that evening. But not until I've spoken to Sonia's doctor, she thought.

She lay on the bed and closed her eyes. Never before had she felt so exhausted, not even during the nights when Josh was teething, but sleep wouldn't come. Instead, she pictured her mother, desperately trying not to show how worried she was, trying to keep their morale up. Like

Hannah she had fair hair, the thick, wavy kind with a mind of its own. Joyce wore hers shorter now, mindless of the streaks of grey which had appeared. She was still pretty, despite the fine lines in her face and a slight thickening of the hips. Her father was tall and angular with thinning sandy hair. His eyes changed colour with the light or emotions which he had never been able to disguise. Hannah knew how much he was suffering. And I'll have to ring Gareth, she thought. Now that she knew Josh was with Sonia she felt encouraged. Sonia would never harm him. And if she couldn't cope she had the money to pay for someone who could. But what if Josh had already forgotten her?

She got off the bed and splashed her face with cold water in the en suite bathroom. Having combed her hair she picked up her bag and left the hotel.

For the next hour she walked. Retracing her steps she arrived ten minutes early for her appointment. Mr Gould's rooms were shabbier than she had anticipated. A sharp-featured female in a white coat admitted her and showed her to a comfortable waiting area where the magazines were recent editions. Hannah ignored them. Impossible to read, but worse still if she came across some of Sonia's work.

It seemed an age before she was shown into a room where one wall was lined with books. A man in his early forties sat behind a leather-topped desk. He rose and stretched out his hand in greeting. In Hannah's imagination all Harley Street doctors were in their sixties and wore understated suits and glasses. The handsome, suntanned man in shirt-sleeves came as a shock. Suddenly she saw the pointlessness of her visit. There was no reason on earth why this man should help her.

'Please have a seat, Mrs Peters.'

Hannah took the chair at the side of his desk and clutched her handbag tightly on her knees.

'I understand you're a friend of Sonia Grant. We've known each other a long time.' He smiled. 'I'm more than willing to treat someone she knows. How can I help you?'

'I'm not sure.' She was aware that his eyes had dropped to her wedding ring which she still wore.

'Do you have any children?'

'I . . . yes. One. A little boy. Oh, God, I'm sorry.' She tried to swallow the tears.

'Please, it's quite all right. Take your time, I understand.' He had pushed a box of tissues towards her.

'I can't help it, I keep crying.' She looked up. What did he mean, he understood? How could he unless Sonia had told him?

'Mrs Peters?' Marcus Gould looked concerned.

'What do you understand?' Hannah said, leaning forward.

'Sonia recommended my practice, therefore you have come for one of three reasons. You are either trying to become pregnant again, but can't, you are pregnant but you do not wish to have another child or you are experiencing problems with your reproductive system. Which is it, Mrs Peters?' The coldness of his tone did not have its usually sobering effect. His new client looked even more dazed.

'You do abortions?' She was aghast. How cruel fate was to have brought her here. An abortion was what Laurence had wanted. All she wanted was Josh back.

'Please understand I do not perform them on demand. The same rules apply to me as to any doctor. I do hope you haven't been misled.'

'No. No, you don't understand. There's nothing wrong with me.' She paused, knowing her voice had been raised. 'It's Josh. My baby.'

Marcus Gould picked up one of the telephones on his desk and spoke quietly into it. 'I have arranged for some tea, unless you'd prefer something stronger.' He indicated a cabinet at the side of the room. Hannah shook her head. 'Tea, then. Now I think you'd better explain exactly why you're here.'

59

Hannah did so, pausing only when the white-overalled woman brought in the tray. Marcus Gould stared into his empty cup as he listened. His mouth was dry. He believed every word Hannah Peters uttered and, with his knowledge of Sonia's medical history, began to believe her theory was correct. His conscience dictated that he should say nothing to Hannah but, instead, contact the police immediately. Common sense argued that they would repeat to her what he told them anyway and he could not bear to keep her in further suspense.

'I just hoped you'd somehow be able to help me to find her,' Hannah finished.

Marcus sat back in his chair. 'Look, I'll be quite frank with you. I might be able to help, but only in one way. I am prepared to give you certain information which, in ordinary circumstances, would be confidential. However, I shall also be giving the police the same information.'

Hannah nodded. Even her new address or telephone number would suffice. 'Thank you.'

'Sonia has been coming to see me since the second year of her marriage. She was desperate to have children but all that resulted was a series of miscarriages. Between us we tried everything but she never managed to carry full term.'

Hannah felt sick. Lies. All of it lies; their friendship was based on deception. Sonia couldn't have her own child, when time had run out for her she had taken Hannah's.

'Did you ever meet her husband, Brian?'

'No.'

'He wasn't as bothered as Sonia, although she refused to believe this. He loved her deeply. Whatever she wanted, he wanted. From things she said I gather she eventually drove him away. She believed everyone thought the same way as herself and that she was depriving Brian of a chance to have a family. Sonia went through some very bad times. She –'

'But I didn't know any of this.' Hannah's voice was shrill. She did not want to hear about Sonia's bad times.

Whatever she had suffered was nothing compared to what she was causing Hannah to suffer now. 'She convinced me she hated the idea of children.'

'She was probably trying to convince herself. Look, I'm a gynaecologist, not a psychologist, but from experience I know how out of proportion these things can become to women who cannot have babies. Sometimes they take matters into their own hands. If you are right then I think I'm safe in saying that she won't harm Josh.' He paused to see how Hannah was taking this. 'I really thought she'd finally accepted the fact that she would remain childless. I thought that was why she stopped coming to me. She was having a long-term relationship with someone, he even came with her on several occasions. I rather hoped he had talked her round.'

George Allison, Hannah thought. Sonia had said he was becoming a bit of a nuisance. But if she had planned to take Josh naturally she wouldn't want him on the scene.

'It's almost a year since her last visit. No request has been made for her notes which I hold here so she hasn't gone elsewhere for private treatment. That's what finally convinced me. However, she may have been treated by her GP.'

'I see.' If Sonia had not seen Mr Gould for that length of time he would not know where she now lived. 'Until this afternoon I thought you were her GP. She's never mentioned any other doctor. What's his or her name?'

'Mrs Peters, I have to draw the line there.' He had probably already said too much. 'But you have my word I will telephone the police the minute you leave. I'll explain the situation and answer any questions they need to ask. I really hope I can be of some use.'

'So even after Brian left she was still coming here regularly?'

'Yes. I think by that time she no longer cared who the father was as long as she had a baby. Lately, of course, her age was against her. Then, as I said, I thought she'd accepted the situation.'

Marcus Gould now looked tired, and probably was. Hannah realized that while he might be able to afford long holidays in the sun, he had to deal with trauma and misery all day long. She wondered how he coped, switching from one patient who would give anything to conceive to another who wanted to kill an unborn baby. 'She's moved. I don't suppose you'd know her new address?'

'Not if she's moved within the last ten months.'

The surreptitious glance at his watch did not go unnoticed by Hannah. She stood, still clutching her handbag. Her palms were wet. 'I can't thank you enough. Oh, I'd better give you my address.' She fumbled in her bag for a pen.

'Your address?'

'You need to know where to send your account.'

Marcus Gould was on his feet. He came around the desk and took her arm. 'Mrs Peters, I wouldn't dream of billing you and, rest assured, I'll make that call immediately.' He led her towards the door. 'I hope you get your little boy back soon,' he said quietly.

Hannah could not speak. There was a lump in her throat. She was overwhelmed with frustration; to have come so far was amazing but she knew she could go no farther. Matters must now be left in the hands of Inspector Gareth Chambers.

Traffic was still heavy in the streets. A wave of exhaustion swept over her as she threaded between people on the pavement. She needed sleep and she needed to eat but doubted if she could manage either. Entering the first snack bar she came to she ordered a sandwich and a mug of coffee and forced the food down even though each mouthful made her want to gag.

Half an hour later she returned to her hotel and rang Charles Cross police station, relating all that had happened to an astonished Gareth Chambers. Her second call was to her parents who had been staying at her house since Friday evening. 'I'll be back tomorrow,' she told her mother. 'I just couldn't face the journey tonight.'

'Did you see Sonia?'

'No. Look, it's a long story, can it wait until I get back?' There was too much to think about, too much to absorb before she could make any sense of it. And by the morning Gareth might have found Sonia and Josh.

'Of course, darling. Try and get some sleep. We'll be thinking of you.'

Hannah hung up and took off her dress. It was hot in the room and the window didn't seem to open. She lay on the bed in her underwear and fell asleep within minutes. When she opened her eyes it was morning and the events of the previous day gradually filled her consciousness.

Swinging her legs over the edge of the bed she caught sight of her apricot wool dress on its hanger. Her raincoat was over the back of the chair. She could not remember removing either article of clothing. Her feet made contact with the carpet and she stood unsteadily. Light-headed through lack of food she gripped the edge of the dressing unit. Josh, she thought, oh, Josh, as misery washed over her. If Gareth had found him her bleeper would've gone off. She grabbed it from the bedside table in case she had slept through its persistent tone. Nothing. No one had called. Had Marcus Gould kept his word? Yes. She had trusted him. Please let Josh be with Sonia, she prayed because the alternatives were unthinkable.

She made coffee and ate the complimentary biscuits in the cellophane packet, her stomach rumbling as she did so.

If anyone knew where Sonia was it would be George Allison. He had been her main escort throughout the seven years Hannah had known her. But there was no number listed in the directory she found in a drawer. Unless, of course, Sonia had lied about him, too. No, she couldn't have, because he was also a friend of James's. Hannah barely hesitated before picking up the receiver and dialling James's number. It would be the first time she had spoken to him since Josh had disappeared. He had tried to contact her, every day he had called at least once and asked to speak to her but Hannah had refused to go to the phone. Only now did she realize what he, too, must be going through.

'Hello?' James's voice was thick with sleep.

'It's me. Hannah. I know it's early but I need George Allison's telephone number. Do you have it?'

'Oh, Hannah, for a moment I thought you were ringing with good news. God, I'm sorry, that was tactless. Yes, I've got his number. Do you have a pen?' James recited it and listened while Hannah repeated it back. 'It's unlisted, he's very fussy about who has it. Tell him I gave it to you.'

'Thank you.'

'Hannah, how are you?'

'I don't know, James. I really can't answer that. Nothing matters any more, you see. Nothing at all.'

'Shall I come up? I could drive you back.'

'There's no need. I'll be on a train around lunchtime. I didn't intend staying in the first place.' He would confuse the issue. In his presence Hannah would have to think about what he had started to mean to her and why she had turned against him so cruelly when Valerie was probably more to blame than him, and she had no spare energy for that.

'May I ring you later?'

'Yes. Sometime this evening.'

'Thank you.'

He sounded so grateful. How easy it was to give someone pleasure. If only someone could do the same for her. The smell of breakfast reached her and Hannah knew she would finally be able to eat something.

In the bathroom she stepped out of the clothes she had worn all night and fiddled with the gleaming shower controls until rapid jets of hot water sprayed over her. Dressed and feeling marginally better she picked up the telephone receiver. It was seven o'clock. 'May I speak to George Allison, please?' she said when her call was answered.

'Who's calling?'

64

'My name's Hannah Peters.' She frowned. A woman had answered. Surely no housekeeper or cleaner would arrive that early in the morning. Maybe George was married, maybe that was another of Sonia's little secrets.

'Just a moment, please.'

'Hannah Peters! Good morning to you. I've heard so much about you from both James and Sonia and now, at last, we speak. But I gather this must be important for you to be ringing so early. Not that it matters, I'm virtually an insomniac.'

'Mr Allison, I do need to speak to you urgently. Is it possible I could meet you sometime today?'

'Certainly. I have a meeting at three but I'm free until then. In fact, I'd be delighted to see you. Would tennish suit? Oh, I take it you're already in London?'

'Yes. And ten would be fine.'

'Then why don't you come to my place? I'll give you directions.' He did so then said goodbye.

He sounded extremely eager to see me, Hannah thought as she made her way downstairs to the dining-room. Had Sonia put him up to something?

She ordered a full breakfast and a pot of coffee then took her time eating it because she had a couple of hours to spare before setting off to George's address. The other guests were mainly businessmen and one or two couples. Whatever their reasons for staying there, none could be as bitterly sad as her own. One or two of them looked in her direction but only with the cursory glance reserved for females on their own in hotels.

She ordered a second pot of coffee and lit a cigarette, trying to keep calm as the minutes passed slowly.

She paid her bill on the way back to her room then collected her raincoat and left the building. The sky was bright blue and it was already warm, so different from yesterday. It had to be a good omen. Tennish, George had said, maybe she could arrive early. Waiting for a cruising taxi Hannah staggered backwards. Across the road a woman pushed a pram exactly like Josh's. I can't bear much more, she thought as she flagged down a black cab. She was flung into the corner of the seat as the driver executed a U-turn and set off in the opposite direction.

George Allison had been watching for her even though he was not expecting her for another half an hour. A male figure moved away from the tall Georgian window and before she had paid the fare the front door stood open.

Hannah's first impression was that he was ex-military. The small clipped moustache, the straight back and the perfectly knotted tie were deceptive. George had been in electronics all his working life and was, besides, too young to have served in the armed forces during the war.

'Hannah, hello. How nice that we should finally meet. Do come in.'

She followed him down the wide hallway which was lined with closed doors. The room into which she was shown was at the back of the house and was a cross between a study and a sitting-room. The windows looked out over the garden and sunlight filled the room.

'Have a seat, I'll get Mrs George to make us some coffee.'

'Thank you.' They were the first words Hannah had spoken because she had no idea where to begin. Mrs George? His nickname for his wife? I like him, she decided as she looked around the room. There was a small computer on the desk, the screen displaying lists of numbers. Piles of untidy paperwork surrounded it. George Allison appeared to have been working prior to Hannah's arrival.

When he returned he carried the tray himself. Placing it on a side table he fumbled with the cups and spilled milk as he poured it. He seemed nervous. With the light from the windows shining directly on to his face it was obvious he had not slept well, that perhaps he had not done so for some time.

'There. I hope that's to your liking. I try not to put Mrs George to too much trouble, she has arthritic knees.'

'Oh.'

George smiled. 'Ah, of course. I know what you're thinking, but she isn't my wife. She was my father's house-keeper and I took her on. She's retiring next year and I don't have the heart to let her go sooner. Mrs George is her actual name. We always joke that it's as well her first name isn't Alison.' He ran a hand through his springy brown hair and sat down. He wore casual trousers and a checked jacket over his shirt and tie but his clothes looked tailor-made. He looks ill, Hannah thought, and he's waiting for me to explain myself. He has no more idea than I have what to say next. About to begin, she placed her cup and saucer on the table but George forestalled her.

'I'm surprised Sonia didn't tell you I wasn't married. At least, not any more, not for the past twelve years. But that's beside the point. Why are you here, Hannah? May I call you that? What is it you want to tell me?'

Disappointment showed in her face. The man was decent and honest. He would not be able to help her. 'You obviously don't know, there's no reason why you should unless Sonia's mentioned it.' She swallowed. 'My little boy's missing. Someone took him from his pram in our garden.'

'My God.' George's shock was genuine. 'I'm so sorry, Hannah. But how do you think I can help you?'

'I hoped you'd be able to tell me where Sonia is.' To suggest Sonia's guilt might alienate him. She must gauge his reaction carefully.

'Ah, yes. Sonia.' He leaned back and rested his elbows on the arms of the leather chair. His face was sad.

'I've only just discovered she's moved, you see. I had no idea, she didn't tell me she was leaving the flat.'

George Allison was not stupid. 'And you think she's got your son,' he said.

Hearing the words in his mouth made Hannah doubt the truth of them. 'I don't know. I just need to make sure one way or another.'

'I see.'

There were several seconds of silence as he digested this.

67

They were filled with the ticking of a clock and the creak of leather as George changed his position. 'When you telephoned I built up my hopes again. Foolishly I thought you'd come as Sonia's envoy. She's a stubborn and independent woman and I knew she wouldn't make the first move herself. Some months ago she ended our relationship without explanation. I put my cards on the table, I told her I wanted to marry her. After ten years she refused to even give me an explanation of why she wanted to end it. I'd have gone along with her on any terms, that's how much I care. I'd hoped you'd come to tell me where she is.

'Forgive me, how selfish I am. Your child is missing, that's far more important.

'Anyway, earlier in the year she made it clear she no longer wanted to see me. We've spoken on the phone since then but lately she stopped returning my calls and then two days ago I discovered her number is now unobtainable. I've written but received no replies. I had no idea she'd moved – like yourself I had to find it out the hard way by going to the flat.

'That, I'm afraid, Hannah, is all I can tell you.'

'Did she ever mention children, wanting to have them?'

He nodded. His face was flushed with emotion. 'Yes, I went to a clinic with her once or twice. I apologize for being personal but she told me there was no need for contraception because she was unable to conceive. But surely if the police know all this they'll be able to trace her.'

'I know. I just wanted to find Josh first. It's the not knowing.'

'Oh, Hannah. Don't.' George stood and searched around for tissues which he found in a box on the windowsill.

'I'm sorry.' She sniffed. 'I have to be strong, but it's so very hard.'

Me, too, George thought but did not say. His loss was painful but nothing to what Hannah was going through. But Sonia? It hardly seemed credible, although the circumstances fitted. 'Have you tried to contact her through work? She's got loads of connections in London.'

'No, I haven't. But the police told me she kept a recent appointment in Scotland. I can't understand it, they spoke to her on Friday night and then she rang me. She still had the same number then. George, are there any other friends who might know where she is?'

'You mean men. I've tried everyone I can think of. Hannah, you know Sonia, it might be that she's simply taken off on a long holiday or shut herself up in a health farm for a month. The last time I saw her she'd put on a bit of weight and you know how obsessional she is.'

'That doesn't explain the flat.'

'No, you're right, it doesn't.'

'And . . .' She stopped. About to describe her visit to Marcus Gould she knew that she could never break that confidence, not to someone who felt as much for Sonia as George obviously did. 'Well, anyway, I think I'd better go now. Thank you for talking to me.'

'Let me have your telephone number. I'll ring you immediately if I do hear anything.'

She gave it to him and left. George saw her to the door. She was aware of his eyes on her back as she walked down the road in the direction of Paddington. As she crossed over she turned and waved.

He lifted his hand in response but his shoulders had sagged.

There were forty minutes to wait for the Penzance train which would take her to Plymouth. The wait seemed interminable.

At last the journey began. Hannah sat back and closed her eyes. She had scribbled a note to Jenny explaining the situation, maybe there would be a reply upon her return, maybe Jenny would come down and see her. Her parents had been wonderful but at that moment Hannah felt she needed a friend. How vital Jenny was, so full of life and so easy to talk to. She had even talked to her about Laurence and their life together. Jenny had understood and although the two had never met she had been able to offer some insights into his behaviour. Meeting the pretty girl on the footpath had led to a catharsis. 'I realize I don't love him any more and I wonder if he ever loved me,' Hannah had told her. 'But now there's Josh, and, despite everything Laurence said, he does come and see him. He just won't admit that he cares. That's our only link now.'

'You still seem sad when you talk about him,' Jenny had pointed out. 'Perhaps you won't admit it either.'

'I am sad. If Laurence hadn't acted so rashly things might have been different. Josh might've had a real father.'

'You're better off as you are, you know. It was better you found out what he was like sooner than later.'

She was right, Hannah thought as the countryside flashed past. Another hour and she would be home and maybe Gareth would have some news.

Chapter Five

Laurence Peters was sweating. It had been a rough trip, each of them taking a turn at the helm and keeping a careful eye on the computerized instruments. Because of unexpected heavy weather and one of the five-man crew developing an incapacitating migraine they had been hot-bunking. The two-watch system had fallen apart and each of the four able-bodied men had been eating and sleeping as they could. Fortunately the forty-foot ketch handled well and the inflatable dinghy on the foredeck was brand new should the worst have befallen them.

They had kept to the schedule but it had become increasingly difficult the more tired they had become. To cover the thousand-odd miles to the Azores where the owner of the yacht had been awaiting delivery had taken over a week. Then, in fairer weather, they had sailed back as far as Portugal with the owner and his family on board.

Unexpectedly, three of them had been able to get an earlier flight back, returning to Heathrow on Tuesday instead of Wednesday and thus saving themselves a night in a hotel. The fourth crew member had another job waiting in Marseille and had taken a flight to Paris from where he would go on to Provence airport, and Brian, still not feeling one hundred per cent, had opted to stay overnight in Lisbon.

Before he had known what was happening Laurence had been separated from his fellow passengers and escorted into the terminal building.

He now sat in a barely furnished room somewhere

amidst the vast complex which comprised Heathrow airport with only an uncommunicative officer for company
and no idea why he was being held there. The reason had
to be important; very important if someone had taken the
trouble to log his movements and discover that he was
arriving home a day early.

At last the door opened. A ordinary-looking man in his
forties approached Laurence. He wore plain trousers, a
toning jacket and a shirt and tie. His clothes were slightly
rumpled and his face was grim. With him was a second
man.

Inspector Gareth Chambers introduced himself and his
colleague and verified Laurence's identity. 'We need to ask
you some questions, and I'm afraid we shall need to search
your luggage. Is that all you have?' He indicated the
holdall at Peters' feet.

Laurence nodded. Chambers might look tired but so was
Laurence and he was beginning to feel irritable. The yacht
was clean. If he had been held because the police believed
they had been carrying drugs or anything else which
might be illegal he would file a formal complaint. All he
wanted to do was to return to the cottage he had pur-
chased in Dorset after he had left Hannah and get his head
down.

'Am I allowed to know what this is all about?'

'We need to ask you some questions regarding your
son.'

Laurence swallowed nervously. He had arranged main-
tenance through his solicitor. There was a standing order,
for God's sake. Had something gone wrong? No, he
wouldn't have been picked up at the airport if that was all
it was. He listened, still not understanding, as one question
followed another.

'I'd like you to explain your movements over the past
two weeks.'

Laurence did so. He outlined his job and what it entailed
and gave the names of the crew. 'My car's at Southampton
from where we sailed,' he finished. 'I'll go down by train

72

and pick it up then return to my cottage until the next voyage. I suppose you want the address and telephone number? I have a mobile as well.'

'I do.' Watching Peters as he spoke, Gareth had summed him up. As hard as it normally was for a man to assess another man's attraction, he recognized that Hannah's ex-husband had the sort of looks no woman would be able to resist. And the body and the suntan to go with them, probably even in the winter. But the flash of fear which had crossed his face when he first entered the room had been ill disguised. Gareth had already spoken to the company responsible for hiring out crews and knew that Peters had been briefed to sail to the Azores and from there to Portugal. He had certainly disembarked from a Lisbon flight but that did not necessarily mean the yacht had been anywhere near the Azores or Portugal. That was now being checked. Gareth had decided not to have Peters escorted back to Plymouth to be questioned. The length of the journey would allow too much thinking time and, besides, the sooner Gareth could report back to Hannah, the better.

Seated at a table with tea and cigarettes in front of him, Laurence wondered if he ought to ask for a solicitor. But no one had said he was to be charged with anything and he had not even been arrested. 'Look, I've answered all your questions, I think it's only fair you tell me what I'm doing here.'

'I'll come to that in a minute, Mr Peters. We understand you left your wife about fourteen months ago and have since obtained a divorce.'

'Yes.' Hannah was involved? Had something happened to her and was he expected to take on the full-time role as Josh's father? Unsure how he felt about that, he waited.

'And the reason you wanted a divorce was because your wife refused to have an abortion.'

'Not entirely.'

'Oh?' He's uncomfortable, Gareth thought. He won't make eye contact. And he's sweating. It was warm in the room but not unduly so. Misty rain still filmed the sound-proof window through which they could see but not hear the aircraft queuing on a distant runway. Rows of orange lights glowed at ground level and the fluorescent jackets of the ground crew were clearly visible even from where Gareth sat.

'It was symptomatic of our relationship, misunderstandings on both sides. And Hannah knew I never wanted children.'

Gareth doubted the veracity of that statement. 'I understand you've only seen your son on a handful of occasions. Is that correct?'

'Yes. But I have photographs. My mother sends them to me. When I left I decided a clean break was the only way to go about things. I do my share towards Josh's keep, you can check with my solicitor, I've never fallen behind with the payments for him.'

Josh's keep. Not my son's or the child's. The words hinted at feelings Laurence Peters may not know that he had. And had they found Sonia Grant it was highly unlikely that Hannah's ex-husband would be sitting in front of him now. He knew that the Met police had not been successful yet because he had left strict instructions in Plymouth that he was to be contacted the minute they had any information. Already Gareth suspected the man was too selfish to lumber himself with a child and, although he disliked him, he knew he was telling the truth. 'Is it that you don't feel anything for your own child?'

Laurence bowed his head. 'It isn't that simple. I thought that if I saw him too often it might make life complicated.'

Complicated for Laurence Peters, maybe. 'In what way?' But Gareth realized he was being too hard. If Peters saw his son regularly he would want to continue seeing him, he would be unable to help himself and that would have made his ultimatum wrong in his own eyes as well as in Hannah's. Pride had kept him away and, he guessed, fear of commitment. He also guessed how much he must

74

weaken each time he saw Josh, especially now he was crawling. But there was another possibility, if he had the child to himself and no one knew about it then he would not have lost face. 'Go on.'

'You know, visiting rights et cetera. With my job I could never have kept to a routine, to anything the courts might order, and that wouldn't be fair to Josh or Hannah.'

'I'm sure your wife would have made no objections, she would probably have been happy enough to fit your visits in around your work. In fact, I believe your own parents see Josh on a regular basis.'

'Inspector Chambers, I'm exhausted and I want to go home. I'm assuming I'm not under arrest, therefore, if you don't tell me what's going on, I'm leaving.' So far Chambers had only talked of Hannah and Josh. None of it was relevant to his recent movements, the luxury yacht, the *Anna Christina*, or her passengers, all of whom he had delivered to Lisbon.

'Do you have passenger lists when you sail?'

'All my papers are up to date. Always. You may, of course, check them and check with the port authorities. You'll find everything I've told you is the truth.'

'I see. So on this trip, apart from the crew, was there anyone else on board?'

Laurence felt sick. The woman and baby had been noticeably inconspicuous throughout the voyage: she had claimed to be a victim of seasickness. Deliberately inconspicuous? Were they really the owner's wife and child? Could they be illegal immigrants? Was it possible they had kidnapped the child? If so he would never work again. His life would be ruined. 'Yes, the owner's family. His wife and their little boy.'

Gareth sat straighter. A little boy. 'This family, do you know them personally?'

'No.'

'And how old is the son?'

'I'm not sure, maybe about a year old, or a bit younger. I can't be more precise than that.'

75

Peters seemed not to have made the connection and, had he been guilty, would he have mentioned the child with such nonchalance? Gareth sighed. 'And where is the boy now?'

'In Lisbon, I imagine, with his parents.'

'Where did they join the boat?'

'In the Azores.'

'And the rest of the crew can confirm this?'

'Don't be so bloody dense, of course they can. I'm hardly likely to tell you one thing knowing they'd say another.'

'Not unless you all agreed to the same story beforehand. And there's no need to lose your temper, Mr Peters.'

'There's every need when I'm under suspicion.'

'Under suspicion? No one's suggested that. We simply wanted you to help us clear up a few things.'

'Bullshit. You think we were employed to take that child, possibly away from its rightful family.'

'Were you?'

'Good God, this is ridiculous.'

'Mr Peters, were you aware that four days ago your son was taken from his pram in the garden while in the care of his child-minder?' He decided not to mention James Fulford for the moment.

Laurence froze. The horror on his face could not have been simulated. 'What? What do you mean? Where is he? What's happened to him?' He was gripping the arms of the chair.

Gareth refrained from asking why he should care. 'We don't know. We thought that perhaps you might.'

Laurence laughed. It was a sound without mirth. He shook his head, incredulous. 'You think I took him then sailed off with him to a foreign country. And what, may I ask, was I supposed to do with him once he was there?'

'I have no idea.'

'Hannah put you up to this.'

'No, Mr Peters, she did not. We have to investigate every possibility and the circumstances dictated that whoever

76

took Josh had to be someone who knows your ex-wife and the layout of her house and garden. We've also spoken to your parents.'

'My parents?' Laurence did not believe what was happening. It was also hard to believe what he felt for the son he had rarely seen. It was a mixture of regret and guilt and lost chances.

Of course Laurence knew that his parents saw Josh, but they would not dream of taking him from his mother. His own mother had hinted that she'd be happier if he was back with Hannah, or at least went to see her and Josh each time he came home. He had not been able to bring himself to do so. Mostly it was easier to pretend his marriage had never existed.

'We're satisfied Josh isn't with them.'

'Inspector Chambers, I can assure you that I know nothing about Josh's disappearance, nor do any members of the crew. Once you've questioned them and made whatever inquiries you deem necessary, you'll realize that you owe me an apology.' Thank goodness these men could not read his mind: he was guilty. If he had stayed with Hannah she would not have gone back to work and none of this might have happened. 'Am I free to leave now?'

'Yes.'

'Thank you. And if it's any help, you may contact whoever you like as to my actions over the past week or so. I can assure you you won't find anything amiss. And I'd like to know my name's been cleared. Will you please let me know if there's any news?'

Still thinking of himself, Gareth thought as he watched Laurence pick up his holdall and leave. It contained nothing more sinister than dirty washing and a couple of paperbacks. Gareth made one telephone call before setting off back to Plymouth. The Portuguese police would be pleased to assist them and would contact Charles Cross police station when they had verified the movements of the *Anna Christina* and the identity of the passengers who had been on board her.

77

Outside the airport terminal Laurence shivered, not yet acclimatized to a damp June evening in Britain, then made his way to the row of waiting taxis. Josh was missing. It was unbelievable. 'The bitch,' he muttered, forgetting his own guilt feelings and turning the blame on Hannah. 'She wanted that baby but she couldn't even look after him properly.' At least the police must believe him to be alive or they would not have asked the questions they had done.

He flung his holdall in the back of a black cab and folded himself into the seat. 'Paddington station, please,' he said, not caring that it would be an expensive journey all the way from Heathrow. Usually he took the Tube or the airport bus to Reading. He needed to see Hannah, he wanted to let her know he had been right all along. He still had a desire to punish her because, deep down, he still felt something for her. Half of him wished he was still married to her.

He had thought that she knew him, that she understood the sort of life he needed and that children had never been on the agenda. He could not be tied down. Marriage was one thing, but only as long as he still had his freedom. Only now did he realize that he had anticipated their lives continuing in the same way until they were old. There would come a time when he would have to give up sailing, but he refused to think about it, it was in the future. His trips were his reason for living and when he returned from them Hannah had been waiting. A child would have ruined everything. A child, in fact, had ruined everything. Laurence had feared he would become secondary in his wife's eyes. His fears had certainly come true now.

And yet he had demanded commitment from her whilst remaining terrified of it himself. His job as delivery skipper ensured he did not return to the marital home every night but he had known it was always there for him. It had never crossed his mind that he might have to share Hannah. When her parents visited he tried to hide the resentment he felt at the attention she paid them, appar-

78

ently unsuccessfully because they came less and less often when he was at home.

And as for Sonia Grant, he had never been able to stand the woman. Rich, glamorous and oozing confidence, she possessed three of the qualities he found disturbing in a female. She had ditched her husband. Laurence wondered if she had encouraged Hannah to do the same. He shook his head. That was unfair. He had left, Hannah would have had him back.

It was late when the train pulled into Plymouth station, too late to call on his ex-wife. By the time he got another taxi out there it would be after midnight. Laurence's temper had abated. Apart from the anxiety of the job, he had been travelling all day and was desperate for sleep. He couldn't be bothered to dig in his luggage for his mobile so he rang his parents from one of the pay phones at the station.

'Of course you can stay,' Pauline told him, sounding pleased to hear from him. 'Do you know about Josh?' She listened. 'I see. Well, we'll expect you soon. Would you like me to make you something to eat?'

'Thanks, Mum. A sandwich will do, but don't go to any trouble.'

Another black cab conveyed him to his parents' house in Mutley. He closed his eyes against the familiar sights. He wanted to smoke but could not do so in the cab. As he patted his pocket to check for his wallet he realized his mobile phone was not in his bag but in his cream zippered jacket. He switched it on. He had given Inspector Chambers that number too. It might be that he had already tried to reach him on that number and, receiving no reply, suspected him of further treachery.

The taxi rumbled to a halt. Laurence paid the driver and walked up the drive towards the brightly lit house. He was about to let himself in with his own key, a spare one his mother had given him years before, when his phone rang. He pressed a digit and held it to his ear. His mouth was dry, he wanted news of Josh. 'Hello?' But it wasn't the police. It was Marty.

Five minutes later he opened the door and walked into the house with its familiar smells of furniture polish, cut flowers and the back liniment his mother used. She suffered from numerous minor ailments but Laurence suspected they were a way of gaining the attention of his rather vague father.

Later, back in the room which had been his as a boy, Laurence lay in bed. When had he told Marty about this trip? He could not remember. In fact, he wasn't sure he had done so at all. She certainly couldn't have known he'd return early but she'd phoned on the off-chance. It had happened before. But he was glad she had rung. Many times he had vowed not to see her again; each time he had failed. He enjoyed her company and they were good together in bed but there was something lacking on his side. After an hour or so, when he was sated, he always wanted to leave her. Each time she contacted him anew he tended to forget that, because she drew him like a magnet. She was funny and beautiful and pliant and anticipated his needs, but there was something about her, something he couldn't quite fathom, that stopped him getting too close.

In the early hours Laurence came to a decision. He would try to straighten out his life. He had been drifting, too easily swayed. He would go to Marty and tell her it was over. No more procrastination, no more half-excuses. This time he would make it perfectly clear he had no wish to see her again. Then he would speak to Hannah, help her find Josh and come to some more suitable arrangements for seeing him. Nothing but the truth from now on, and he was confident of his reception at the house they had once shared.

His conscience salved a little, Laurence turned over and went to sleep.

Chapter Six

Just before seven on Tuesday morning James Fulford
swung his legs over the side of the bed, walked across the
room and pulled on the short robe which hung on the back
of his door. Unusually, he felt cold but it was emotion not
the weather chilling him. Hannah may have finally spoken
to him but her tone had been less than friendly. He paused
in the doorway and ran a hand through his hair which he
wore cut shorter in the summer. The call had disturbed
him. The initial pleasure at hearing her voice had been
spoiled when he realized she simply wanted information.
And there was still no news of Josh. Almost four days had
passed. James was now convinced that when news did
come it would not be good. He knew the odds, the longer
a child was missing the less chance there was of it being
found alive. At least Hannah had said he could ring later.
It made the thought of the next few hours a little more
bearable but did nothing to alleviate his sense of guilt.
I should've checked the pram, he kept telling himself.

In the bathroom across the landing of his luxury Barbican flat he cleaned his teeth and scrubbed his tongue. It felt
furred. He knew he looked tired although he had slept
deeply. He had drunk too much the previous night. It was
not a regular vice and it had not made him feel any better
or diluted his guilt.

He swallowed some aspirin and made coffee which he
drank standing in the bay of the lounge window. The sun
shone on the craft moored alongside the quays and dis-
persed the gossamer mist which rose from the water. He

had paid a considerable sum for the view and that particular historical Plymouth address. How unimportant they had become over the past few days.

Three times the police had questioned him. There was nothing more he could tell them. Every word he had spoken had been the truth. Inspector Chambers had come to believe him. Hannah Peters had not. He could have stood it better had it been the other way around.

If only he could be sure that Josh had been taken before he had arrived, he might have felt less to blame. But he didn't know and neither did Valerie Mayhew. His worst fear was that no one ever would.

'Oh, Hannah. Let me back into your life. Let me do something to help get your baby back.' It seemed impossible that the police didn't have some lead to follow. And what had Hannah been doing in London? Why did she want George Allison's number? Ought he to ring George and ask? No, there was no point, not until after Hannah had been to see him, the man probably didn't know himself yet.

James showered and shaved and drove across the city to his electronics plant on the outskirts. The noise of machinery and the banter of men helped to deaden his thoughts. He applied himself to orders and invoices and stared at the computer screen, banishing the images of Hannah and Josh which kept coming into his mind. He loved her, he had known that for some time, and he also loved Josh.

He walked the factory floor and made jokes with his manager, he signed his name to cheques and looked at new designs, but mostly he looked at his watch. What time would Hannah get back? When could he ring her?

At four o'clock he put on his jacket, straightened his tie and said he was leaving. Ringing her wasn't good enough, she might change her mind again by this evening. He would go to her house and wait for her. He had to see her face to face.

The sun was now hidden behind grey clouds and a mist was settling over the river, blurring its outline, muffling sounds. The air was damp and moisture glistened on the leaves of the trees. The pleasant day which the morning had promised had failed to materialize, as often happened in June. The tide was rising, flowing silently upstream, stealthily covering the mudbanks whose earthy smell was pungent.

James turned into the lane. The Gregsons' car stood outside the house where it had been parked for the past four days. It was killing them, watching their daughter, missing their grandson. There was an aura about them of grief, a quietness, almost an acceptance, as if they knew that Josh was dead. Without them having said so he knew that they, like Inspector Chambers, did not hold him responsible for their grandson's disappearance. Whatever happened between himself and Hannah, he would always be grateful to them for that.

'James, come in,' Joyce said. 'Have you spoken to Hannah?' She knew he would not have come unless he had had some contact with her.

'Yes.' He wiped the mud from his feet on the mat and followed her into the lounge. 'She rang me first thing this morning from London. She wanted George Allison's number.'

'George Allison? Isn't that one of Sonia's friends?'
'Yes.'

Joyce sighed as she squeezed her forehead between thumb and forefinger. 'That man can't help her. She's going crazy, James, I just don't know what this is doing to her. To all of us. Is it too early for a drink? No, I don't think it is.' Joyce went to the cupboard where Hannah kept bottles of spirits. 'Phillip's gone for a walk. I hope he's back soon, this weather's awful, it won't be long before it's dark. You'd hardly think we were into summer.' I'm talking for the sake of it, Joyce thought, not that James is listening. He was staring at the fire which Joyce had insisted they kept burning. To Hannah, it had become symbolic. Her friends had lit it to welcome her home from the hospital, it would be lit when Josh returned. Superstition, symbolism, what did it matter if it made Hannah feel better?

She handed James a whisky and soda and poured neat whisky for herself, grateful for the brief distraction of having something to do with her hands. She sipped the drink, which burned her throat. The house was warm but the chill of the river mist seemed to have invaded it, to have penetrated her woollen trouser suit and started to seep into her bones. They heard the front door open and close and felt a chilly draught. 'Ah, good, here's Phillip.'

He came across the room and kissed his wife's cheek. She could feel the dampness of his clothes and his face was cold. He looked grey and old and his eyes were dull. He, too, was handed a whisky. He took it without comment. Joyce was aware that his rudeness was unintentional, that his mind, like hers, was elsewhere. 'Will you stay for dinner, James?'

'I think that's up to Hannah.'

No one knew what to say. It was no longer possible to talk about Josh. They sat in silence and listened to the rain as it began to fall in earnest, slanting horizontally across the landscape. Only when the gloom became overwhelming did Joyce get up and turn on some lights.

'A taxi,' she said, with a note of animation. She went to the window. 'Yes, it's Hannah. Pour her a drink, Phillip. She's far later than we anticipated.'

When Hannah let herself in and walked into the lounge three pairs of eyes watched her closely. She had no idea how wild she looked. Beneath her unbrushed hair her face was ashen but her pupils were glittering, either with fury or with madness. 'Sonia's got Josh,' she said then collapsed into a chair. 'She's left London. No one knows where she is, not even George Allison.'

James's stomach lurched. Thank God, he thought. We'll get him back. We will. Had he already reached the stage where he thought of Hannah and Josh as his family? Sonia, of all people, the least maternal woman he could conceive of. Even as he thought it he wondered if it had all been a cover-up for her true feelings.

'Sonia?' Joyce repeated with incredulity. But the telephone rang before she could learn any more.

Hannah ran to answer it. 'Hello?'

'Hannah? It's Gareth. We've spoken to Laurence. He was back a day early.'

'And?' Hannah's hand was at her throat. She could feel her pulse beating erratically. It was odd, the mention of his name still affected her in some way she was unable to define.

'It's very unlikely he's involved. We're double checking just to make sure, the Portuguese authorities should come back to me any time now.'

Hannah sighed. 'Why bother? Sonia's got my baby. Find her, Gareth and find him, too. She can't have disappeared into thin air.'

Gareth did not point out that you *could* disappear, that, in fact, it was easy to do so. Not quite so easy with a child, it was true, but nevertheless possible. 'Keep calm, Hannah. We're acting upon everything you and Marcus Gould told us last night. The Met won't stop searching until they find her, and neither will we. Look, you have to be ready to accept that we might be wrong, that it might not be Sonia.' But Gareth was already aware that no telephone number was listed for her any more, no forwarding address had been given to the Post Office, the letting agency had no idea where she'd gone but had had instructions to collect her mail until further notice when she would either collect or send for it and none of her magazine contacts knew of her whereabouts. It seemed highly likely Sonia Grant had no wish to be found. Yet she had kept that appointment in Edinburgh and that was only a matter of days ago. Something was wrong, something didn't quite fit. 'I'm sorry?' Hannah was speaking again.

'This morning George Allison told me that Sonia ditched him after almost ten years and he doesn't know where she is either. She planned it, Gareth, can't you bloody well see that? She's had months to get everything prepared. She's probably left the country.' I'm hysterical, Hannah thought as her voice rose. I'm exhausted and irrational and I'm no good as a mother or Josh would be here with me now.

'We're checking that aspect, too.' But Sonia Grant would have had to go to great lengths to obtain a passport for the baby.

'Why didn't you know she'd moved? How come I had to find that out for myself?'

'Hannah, please. We're doing all we can. There was no reason to suspect her. She volunteered to go in and make a statement, we had no reason to assume she'd moved.'

'But you're not doing enough, Gareth. Nowhere near enough. I'm sorry,' she added in a quieter voice.

'Are your parents still there?' He realized she was near to breaking point. Now was not the time to tell her of the mistake they had made concerning another of her friends. Not so much a mistake as an omission. There was probably nothing in it, all evidence pointed the other way, but it was still an omission. And nobody knew where the damn girl was. Still, as long as Hannah believed Josh was with Sonia she would be able to maintain some grip on her sanity.

'Yes, they're here. Please find him, Gareth. Please.'

'Hannah, believe me, we're trying. We're not about to give up now. Look, see if you can get some rest, have a doctor prescribe something.'

But Hannah had rung off. No doctor could help her. She turned to look at James. Like her parents, and no doubt herself, he looked ill. She had been unfair in blaming him, or in blaming him more than Valerie. She had to accept that Josh might have been taken even if she had been at home with him. And there were Laurence's parents to think of. They were waiting as anxiously for news as her own were. The police were completely satisfied that Pauline and Andrew Peters had not abducted their grandson, but so much time had been wasted in checking when Hannah could have told them that herself.

'Hannah, why don't you go and soak in the bath?' Joyce took her glass from her hand.

'No. Later, maybe. I'm fine, Mum. You look tired, James,' she said, realizing she had hardly acknowledged his presence.

'I am. Hannah, I keep thinking that if I'd only looked in the pram, if I'd checked . . .'

She held up a hand. 'Don't. Please, James, don't. It's no good. There are so many ifs. I'm going to find Sonia if it's the last thing I do.' But in the back of her mind there was still some doubt. Until Laurence was totally cleared he was still a possible suspect.

On that first terrible evening Gareth had questioned her at length about Laurence's job and how it worked. 'Companies advertise for crews,' she had told him. 'They have lists of them on stand-by. Laurence, as a delivery skipper, is never short of work. It's a big responsibility but he loves the sea.'

'And he sails all over the world?'

'Yes.' Hannah had paused. 'And these yachts can sail without informing anyone, just as they can moor off the coast in the same way. It would be easy for him to have taken Josh out of the country.'

Yes, it would be easy, but why would Laurence Peters wish to do so? Perhaps he had come to regret his decision and wanted the boy for himself, maybe he was the type of man who simply took what he wanted, Gareth had thought. But that was before he had met him.

Hannah had known what he was thinking and reiterated her mother's initial response, that she was being punished for going against his wishes. On that first evening everyone believed that Josh was with his father.

'If you don't want a bath, then I insist that you eat,' Joyce said firmly. 'We must all eat.'

Half an hour later the four of them sat at the table in the kitchen alcove and pushed food around their plates. 'Have you heard from Jenny?' Joyce asked, trying to initiate conversation which did not involve what was really on their minds.

'No, not since . . . not since her last letter.' They had corresponded regularly and Jenny had telephoned once or twice. She had promised to come and stay when she got a long weekend off.

'So she doesn't know about Josh.' Joyce put her head in her hands. 'I'm sorry, darling.' Hannah had stopped herself from saying not since Josh was taken, but Joyce had not been able to stop herself from saying his name.

'I know. It all comes back to Josh in the end, doesn't it? I wrote her a postcard asking her to telephone me. Ringing Jenny's a waste of time, all the nurses share a phone on the ground floor of the nurses' home and you can never get through.'

'But surely . . .'

'I didn't go into detail, Mum. I couldn't, not in writing. I just asked her to ring as soon as she could, said it was urgent. She might be on days off and hasn't received it yet.' Hannah had not thought of that before.

It was over two months since Jenny had left. The time had passed so quickly. Sonia and Jenny. The two people she had believed to be her friends. One had betrayed her, the other had moved out of her life. Thank heavens for Lorna, Lorna who rang every day and offered use of her services or her shoulder to cry on. But Hannah had not been able to face anyone outside the family until Monday.

Phillip poured some wine and drew James into the conversation. His feelings for Hannah were obvious but circumstances may have ruined any chance he might have had with her. It would be a shame. He seemed a decent man and, if the worst happened, a fear Phillip would not formulate even silently, James might have been the one to help Hannah recover. If recovery was possible.

James insisted upon helping Hannah with the washing up. He wanted to be near her but he also wanted to be doing something useful, no matter how trivial the action and despite the fact that Joyce had whispered that it was better for Hannah to have something to do.

'Thank you,' Hannah said. She hesitated before adding, 'Look, would you like to stay the night, James? You've had several drinks and you look shattered. And in the morning I'd like to ask you about George Allison.'

'If it isn't inconvenient – I'd rather not drive.' He leaned against the sink and folded his arms. A week ago and they would each have known instinctively what the other was thinking. If Hannah was tired he kissed her goodnight and went home. He understood it was hard work teaching and caring for Josh on her own. But now? What did her invitation mean? How did he ask her? I won't ask, he decided. 'Do I need to make up the bed?' With Hannah's parents in the house there was only one spare room.

'No. It's ready and aired. Thanks, James.'

'For what?'

'For being so understanding.'

He kissed the top of her head, allowing himself no more contact than that. But he felt happier, he felt if things worked out he might still be in with a chance. Her hair smelled smoky, which surprised him, but he did not comment, nor could he tell her that she was still lovely despite what she was suffering. It was not appropriate now. 'I'll go on up then.' He did so, knowing that he would sleep now that he was under Hannah's roof again.

Upstairs, Josh's bedroom door remained firmly closed. That room was out of bounds.

Hannah sat at the table, which was still damp from where she had wiped it. Jenny. Why had her mother's question formed one in her own head? But she was too exhausted to work out what it was. Heavy-limbed she went upstairs and crept into Josh's room. She had not meant to, it was instinctive, something she did every night before she went to bed. Before he was taken. His empty cot made her want to scream. Five days tomorrow, she thought, how many more can I endure? Picking up his sleeping suit where it still hung over the radiator she buried her face in it. Her tears burned as they ran down her face. It still retained Josh's special scent.

She carried it through to her own room and laid it on her pillow where she slept with her face in its folds.

'I need to make a call,' Laurence said as he left the break-fast table.

'Go ahead.'

His resolve was still strong where Marty was concerned but he must rearrange the time of their meeting. There were more important things to attend to first.

'Look, I'm going to see Hannah,' he said when he returned to the kitchen.

'That's a very good idea,' Pauline said with a rueful smile. 'She's been going through hell. Well, we all have.'

'And not before time,' Andrew said from behind the newspaper. He was carrying on as normal, terrified not to, suspiciously believing that if he behaved any differently they would never see Josh again.

Laurence borrowed his mother's car as his own was still in Southampton. It was early when he left the house, a little after eight. It had stopped raining. The pavements were drying, steam rising, and the sky brightened as he left the city. When he turned off the main road he realized he was trembling. At the end of the lane was the house he had once shared with Hannah, where they had had four years of happy marriage until he had ruined everything. Did he have any justification in visiting it now that his son wasn't there? Did he have any right at all to speak to Hannah after what he had done to her? But they would have heard the car, he would have to go through with it.

Apart from Hannah's car there were two others parked outside, neither of which he recognized. They blocked the entrance so he pulled up on the rough grass verge of the lane, two wheels in the mud of the shallow ditch alongside it.

90

'Laurence!' It was Joyce Gregson who opened the door. She stood in the hall, smartly dressed, well made-up but looking years older than when he had last seen her.

'I had to come, Joyce. Is Hannah in?'

Joyce hesitated. What would seeing Laurence do to her daughter now? But Hannah had heard the doorbell. 'Yes,' she said. 'Yes, she is. You'd better come in.' Formally, as if he was a stranger, she showed him into the lounge.

Phillip, seated in an armchair, glared at him. His lips were pressed together in disapproval. 'I take it you're here because of Josh? It's rather late to show concern, don't you think?' he asked coldly.

'Yes. Because of Josh, but Hannah too. The police picked me up when I came off the plane. I didn't know, Phillip, I really had no idea. It shook me, I can tell you, and I can't imagine why anyone thought I might have taken him.' The door opened. Laurence swallowed. He had been totally unprepared for the effect seeing his ex-wife in these circumstances would have upon him. Hollow-eyed and thinner, she was still lovely. 'Hello, Hannah,' he said quietly.

She stood by the door, gripping its handle. Her face was ashen, her brown eyes wide with surprise. 'What do you want, Laurence?'

'I came to find out what happened and to offer any help you feel I might be able to provide.' He knew how stilted he sounded but he had hoped to see Hannah alone. 'I want to try to find my son.'

'Your son? Your son? How fucking dare you? How dare you come here and use those words to me?' She had come further into the room, her arms rigid at her sides, fists closed tightly, colour spreading across her face. 'You never wanted him, you made that very clear on the day you walked out. You'd have had him murdered if you'd had your way. You've shown up here a few times, laden with presents as if you can buy him. Or maybe us. You have no idea what it is to be a father. None whatsoever. So don't try and pretend you care now.'

'Hannah!' Phillip was on his feet, but it was too late. His gentle, loving daughter had swung back her arm and hit Laurence with every ounce of the strength she had left. Livid red streaks stood out on his face.

'Get out of here, you bastard, and don't ever come back,' she screamed.

Phillip went to her and held her, feeling the shudders through her thin shoulders. Joyce was right, she was going crazy. She looked wild and dangerous, there was no knowing what she might do next. 'Hannah's right, Laurence. I think it would be best if you do as she says.'

'My God. I can't believe you. If she'd gone along with what I'd said, this situation wouldn't have arisen. So much for wanting a baby when she can't even look after it. What were you doing, Hannah, entertaining your lover?' God, why am I doing this? Laurence thought, unable to stop himself. He was hurt, no longer a part of anything. How foolish he had been to think he could make it all right after such a long absence. He could see how much Hannah was suffering and he was making it worse. What he was accusing her of was a reflection of his own guilt. He had been the one to take lovers, not Hannah.

'No.' Phillip spoke quietly, only Hannah could hear. He had felt her muscles stiffen and kept his arms around her tightly to prevent her attacking Laurence again.

Laurence, defeated, turned to go. The lounge door had remained open and the raised voices had alerted Joyce. She came into the room, James at her side. 'Yes, well, I see I've hit the proverbial nail,' he said with a sneer, glancing at James.

James glanced from Laurence to Hannah and did not need telling who the man was. 'I believe I heard Hannah ask you to leave,' he said pleasantly, but firmly, keeping his hands in his jacket pockets because he wanted to hit this man with bluster written all over his self-righteous face.

'I don't know who you are but there's no way a stranger's going to order me out of my own house.'

'Those days are long over, Laurence.' Joyce was the only

person able to display some control over her emotions. 'This has always been Hannah's house, you contributed nothing to it. You are divorced, at your own instigation. If you don't get out immediately I'll ring the police and have you removed.'

'You're crazy, all of you. You've always made me out to be the villain of the piece.' He stopped and shook his head, ashamed of the words which came unbidden. He *was* the villain, he knew that, he had always known that. He had come to try to make amends without taking into account, and allowing for, the permanent damage he had inflicted. He had avoided commitment; his punishment was to be left out. He would never be included in this family tragedy, no one would ever believe how sorry he was and that, even though he had never had a chance to get to know Josh, he felt his loss keenly. He sensed that his own parents disliked him for the way in which he had treated Hannah.

'I'm sorry,' he said, facing each of them in turn. 'Hannah, I'm truly sorry.'

The wildness had left her face. All Laurence saw was the young woman who had once been his wife, still beautiful but so tragic. He understood why he wanted to hurt her. It was because he had not been able to possess her totally. Maybe he had also known that in almost every way she was better than him.

'I realize it must've been a shock for you. The police told us they had questioned you, but it doesn't excuse your behaviour either today or in the past. And, Laurence, if I ever find out you've had anything to do with this, I will kill you.' Hannah's voice was level but he knew she meant what she said. She, too, had had a shock, she had not expected to see him.

Gareth had rung that morning. Laurence was in the clear. The Portuguese police had confirmed that the party aboard the yacht were genuine but she would not give him the satisfaction of telling him so. Besides, Hannah was convinced that Josh was with Sonia. Let the phone ring, she prayed, let them have found her. Let Josh be safe.

'I'll go now. I really didn't come here to cause a scene. Believe it or not, when I heard about Josh – no, I'd better leave it at that.' He left the room. Seconds later the front door opened and closed. He had gone. No one spoke for quite a while.

Laurence had initially walked back into Hannah's life without warning, and now again, at a time when she was most vulnerable, and he had thrown accusations at her. All those months of yearning, of longing for his touch, when she would have taken him back, were in the past. What a waste they had been. Even up to six months ago she would have accepted his apology and tried to make a go of it, if only for Josh's sake. Now she saw only the shell of the man, the good looks and charm behind which he hid. It was far too late for Laurence. For a split second the aching emptiness she felt without her son was replaced with a sense of freedom. She could look at her ex-husband and feel pity, even a little compassion, but never again love, or even liking.

'Hannah? Are you okay?' James was staring at her, afraid she might pass out, her face was so white.

'Yes. I'm fine now. I just didn't expect to see him, not now.'

'I'll put the kettle on. Come and give me a hand, Phillip,' Joyce offered diplomatically. Having seen Laurence again, seeing him for what he was, Hannah might find it within herself to forgive James.

The postman came in a van but he had been and gone without anyone hearing the clatter of the letter-box because of the scene with Laurence. On the way to the kitchen Joyce picked up the two envelopes from the mat and placed them on the kitchen table. She would give them to Hannah when she took in the coffee.

From the window she saw the the rising ground behind the house. Everything was green now. A warm May followed by the rains of June had provided ideal growing

94

conditions. 'I once read that a house built on the side of a hill and near to water ensured good things.'

'Whoever wrote that couldn't have been more wrong in this case,' Phillip said, touching his wife's face.

Joyce took his hand and held it. There seemed nothing to say, no way of offering comfort. Without Josh the house seemed as barren as trees in winter. Joyce had tidied away his toys. It was painful enough for her, let alone Hannah to see them lying around. How many more days would they have to wait for news? It could not go on for ever, could it? But Joyce knew the answer to that. Yes, it could. Out there were parents whose children had been missing for years and who were still waiting for news, good or bad, either way, that would never come. She bit down hard on her lower lip. Do not cry, do not give up yet, be strong for Hannah, she told herself.

It was an effort, but she prepared a tray and carried it through to the lounge, Hannah's post resting against the coffee pot.

'Thanks, Mum.' Hannah was sitting on the squashy settee, her body limp, as if with that final act of aggression towards Laurence she had exhausted her strength. She had been amazed at the violence she was capable of feeling. Reaching for a cup she frowned at the envelopes and picked them up. One was a bill. The other was addressed in familiar handwriting. Jenny's? No. 'My God.' Her vision blurred and the room began to swim. She inhaled deeply.

'Hannah? What is it?' Phillip wondered if it was time to call a doctor.

She shook her head, staring at the envelope. No, not Jenny's writing, but Sonia's.

She ripped open the envelope. The letter shook in her hands as she stared at it, uncomprehending.

'Hannah? What is it?' Joyce stepped towards her, the coffee forgotten.

'It's from Sonia. Sonia's written to me.'

'For God's sake, read it,' Phillip said, abrupt with anxiety.

Hannah stared at the scrawling loops and wondered if she was sane.

Joyce clasped her hands tightly in front of her, an indication of her own suspense as her daughter scanned the letter.

Finally Hannah ran a hand through her hair, cleared her throat and began to read. Her voice was flat and without emotion.

'"Dear Hannah, I had to write. I couldn't just leave things. I am more sorry than you'll ever know that I can't be with you at the moment, although I'm sure James will take care of you, and so will your parents, of course.

'"Until today I felt it was impossible to contact anyone. For reasons I cannot explain just yet I have left London. I had hoped to be able to tell you my news as soon as I moved but circumstances have intervened.

'"I am desolate over Josh but only recently have I understood just what you must be going through. My life has taken a totally unexpected turn and I find I am not as well equipped to deal with it as I imagined, but only because this is something I cannot bring myself to share just yet. Typical, selfish Sonia, no doubt you are thinking.

'"Above is my new telephone number. I have been without a phone for a few days, some technical hitch about not enough lines, but by the time this reaches you it should have been connected. I would welcome a call if you feel you are able to talk to me. I'm sure I don't need to ask you, but please, Hannah, do not give this number to anyone else for the moment.

'"My thoughts are with you, and never forget I am always your friend no matter how it seems at the moment. How drastically life has treated us both. However, we must both be strong, as I know you already are, and optimistic. Believe me, you and Josh are in my thoughts every minute of the day. With love, Sonia."'

There was no address, only the phone number. '. . . no

matter how it seems at the moment,' Sonia had written. It was almost an admission of guilt. Hannah turned the envelope over. It was postmarked Exeter, date-stamped yesterday. Sonia was in Devon. Or had been. Or had someone else posted it for her? Hannah wondered if Sonia had actually written it. The tone and sentiments were so uncharacteristic of her.

'I don't understand,' Joyce said, sagging into a chair. She pulled her skirt over her knees in such a schoolmarmish way that Hannah almost smiled. Her mother had taken compassionate leave; as Phillip had opted to become a figurehead of his business some years ago, his time was his own if he chose. Naturally, as soon as the college where Hannah taught learned of Josh's disappearance they had immediately made alternative arrangements for Hannah's classes.

'If Josh is with her, if it's a baby she wants, why do this? Why contact you and in such an enigmatic way? It doesn't make sense,' Phillip said.

'Guilty conscience?' James supplied, taking a seat beside Hannah on the settee. 'Or maybe she's decided she can't actually cope and wants to hand him back. Perhaps she's relying on your past friendship not to take matters further.'

'I must ring Gareth.' Hannah went to the phone and dialled his number but slammed the receiver down when she got the engaged signal. 'I'll find her,' she said. 'If she's still got Josh or if she's hurt him in any way then it'll be me that deals with her, not the police.'

Joyce raised her eyebrows. Having seen her daughter in action with Laurence earlier she did not think much of Sonia's chances of survival. 'Just ring the police, Hannah. You know it's the quickest way to find her.'

'Wait.' James got up and fetched the directory which lay on the shelf under the telephone table.

'If you're thinking of looking for her address, James, forget it. She's always been ex-directory and there hasn't been time for her to have the number included even if she isn't this time.'

'I know that, but I can check the dialling codes. If I look under the heading for local and regional calls and find it, we'll at least know she's within a thirty-five mile radius. It won't take more than a couple of seconds, there'll be less than twenty numbers.'

'Look, if you won't phone Gareth, I will. But wouldn't it be easier just to ring Sonia as she suggested?'

'I don't want to do that, Mum. How can I ask her over the phone? And if she has got Josh, she isn't likely to tell me where she is.'

'Unless she does want to hand him back.'

'Calm down, everyone. We're wasting time. Get on to Gareth right away. He can check something like that in minutes,' Phillip said, but no one seemed to be listening. He turned to gaze out of the window, his back to the room, unable to agree with the general opinion. Sonia Grant was not the sort of woman to admit defeat. If she had taken Josh, which he doubted, she would not have made contact with Hannah. Sonia had had other reasons for keeping her head down.

James ran his finger downs the page quickly. The frown of concentration bisecting his brow smoothed out as he smiled. 'Got it. 01647. It's regional. But it doesn't give the town.' He turned to the back of the directory and started running his finger down the list of national dialling codes.

Phillip shook his head and turned back to face them, his hands in the pockets of his cord trousers. 'It doesn't work like that. Even if you find it there will be several places with the same code.'

'Yes, but don't you see? It has to be in a certain area. It's a starting point,' James argued, desperate to be of some use to Hannah. 'Yes. Here's the first. Chagford.'

'I'm going there.' Hannah was on her feet.

'Darling, don't be so impulsive. You'll be in for such a disappointment if she isn't there. It could be any village.

Just let Gareth know. You can't take this on yourself.'
Stubborn, stubborn daughter, Joyce was thinking. It's as if
this has become some sort of game to her, and not one
she's playing for fun. Inspector Chambers would be able to
find Sonia within a very short time once he was in possession of the telephone number.

'You're right. But you ring him. Do it now, but I'm going
there anyway, and tell him I've done so.'

'Or Cheriton Bishop,' James called after her, still studying the directory. 'Wait, I'll come with you. I'll bring the
phone book and look on the way.'

'Thank you. I appreciate it, but I have to see her alone.
I'll find her.'

Hannah was already in the hall. She grabbed her handbag and car keys and was out of the door before anyone
could stop her. Pulling out into the lane she wished she
was better dressed, that she had at least brushed her hair.
Not that Josh would notice her jeans and T-shirt and linen
jacket. To hold him again was all that she wanted. To hear
his chuckle and to kiss his soft cheek. Soon she would do
so, she knew it, she could feel he was close.

Phillip was already on the phone, relating the latest
development to Gareth.

'I see,' was all Gareth said when Phillip had explained.
'And I'm inclined to agree with Mr Fulford. If Mrs Grant
does have Josh she may have decided to hand him back.
I won't be far behind Hannah. I'll get the number traced
immediately, they can radio through the address as I'm
driving.'

'Give him my mobile number,' James said as Phillip was
about to hang up. 'In case we're out. It might be an idea for
us all to get some fresh air.'

How practical he is, Joyce thought. We do all need to get
out of the house. Laurence would never have been so
solicitous. Even James looks exhausted. What is this doing
to us all?

'Thank you. That's all sorted,' Phillip said when he had
hung up. 'He'll use your number if necessary, James. Do

you need a coat, Joyce? James is right. We're going to walk until we're damn certain we'll get some sleep tonight.' Whichever way it goes, he added silently.

She sighed. 'I just hope they get to Sonia before Hannah does.'

'So do I.' His daughter was at the end of her tether, there was no knowing what she might do. Phillip felt old and tired and, like Joyce and James, longed to get out of the house for a while. It was stupid to feel it was an act of disloyalty to want to do so.

'She wasn't always like this.'

Phillip stroked his wife's face with his fingertip. 'Don't worry. She'll be back to her old self once Josh is back with us again.'

James looked away, envying them their closeness. Whatever else happened, they had each other. 'I'm in the way, Joyce. I'll take myself off to work but I'll leave you the phone. I know Hannah has yours.'

'Good heavens, there's no need for that, not unless you have to be there.' She wanted him to stay. If Hannah returned disappointed it might take more than herself and Phillip to deal with her. And she liked the man with his considerate ways.

'If you're sure.' He was pleased to be included. Work would not have distracted him.

'And maybe . . .'

'Sh. Don't build your hopes up yet,' Phillip warned his wife sternly.

Watching him hold Joyce's lightweight jacket, James could see that they had become attuned to one another's thoughts during the passage of time. He wanted to be like that with Hannah, had, in fact, started to be until Sonia Grant had ruined it.

They locked the door behind them. It was the first time in five days that the house had been empty.

The sky was a pale blue, a few clouds hung in the distance but there was no threat of rain. Already it seemed like an age rather than hours since Laurence had put in his unwelcome appearance. They walked in silence, carefully watching their feet on the riverside path which was still muddy. The sky began to brighten further, its arc higher. Joyce felt the warmth through her jacket and was grateful for it.

Their muscles began to ache as the path ascended, the gradient increasing with every step. James held back some straggling brambles with their hard green berries which had caught at Joyce's sleeve. She smiled her thanks. Soon those berries would ripen. Autumn would follow, then winter and Christmas. Josh's second Christmas, one he would appreciate more than the first. To Joyce the idea of him not sharing it with them was unbearable. She blew her nose to disguise her tears then, with her chin high, she forced herself to walk faster over the uneven terrain, unmindful of the ruts where the higher ground had dried.

No one mentioned Hannah or what she or Gareth might discover. It was too much like tempting fate. The air was still. No birds sang in the mid-afternoon. Only the occasional breaking twig or the rustle of wildlife in the undergrowth broke the silence.

At the brow of the hill they turned in unison. Way below them lay the house. It looked diminished, vulnerable, from that height. A thin curl of smoke rose from the chimney. Don't let the fire go out, Joyce prayed as she crossed her fingers superstitiously. It had become as symbolic for her as it was for Hannah.

'Jesus!' Phillip almost lost his footing. None of them had really expected James's phone to ring. The shrillness of its tone cut through the air. It had startled them all.

'It might not be Gareth,' James warned as he answered the call. But it was.

'We've located the address. It is in Chagford. We're on our way as I speak.'

'Thanks for letting us know.'

'Is it bad news?' Joyce asked fearfully, noticing James's grim expression.

'No. They've located the address. It is in Chagford. Hannah's first stop.'

No one knew what to say. No one dared hope.

Joyce pulled out a handkerchief. Her face was hot and her legs felt weak. It was time to turn back. Phillip took his wife's arm for the descent, which would be hazardous because of the tree roots pushing up through the ground. James walked carefully behind them.

Upon their return Joyce made tea, her actions automatic. Preparing the British antidote to everything was all she ever seemed to do lately. Phillip laced his with whisky. They sat in the kitchen, away from the heat of the fire which had not gone out although only glowing embers were left in the grate. One of the dry logs, stored in the basket in the alcove beside the chimney breast, had crackled into life when Phillip threw it on to the red hot ash before he left the room. Once more they braced themselves and settled down to wait.

They tried to make conversation but failed. The sound of the ticking kitchen clock filled the room. 'I think I'll put my feet up,' Joyce said.

Half an hour later Phillip and James joined her in the lounge. Phillip glanced at James and smiled. James smiled back. On the settee, Joyce, her head at an awkward angle, had finally fallen asleep.

Once Hannah had turned left off the A38 the road wound through the countryside. She passed the occasional solitary house and slowed, looking for signs of life, for a pram, for nursery curtains. She crossed a bridge over the River Bovey and drove into Chagford where she stopped the car. The prettiness of the village, of the thatched, pastel-washed houses on a summer afternoon escaped her. Nothing mattered but Josh, nothing was as beautiful as her eight-month-old son. She pulled out her phone, took a deep breath then tapped out the number on the top of Sonia's letter.

'Hello?' The voice that answered was wary.

'It's me, Hannah.'

'Hannah! I'm so glad you rang. They only connected the phone this morning. I was terrified you wouldn't want anything more to do with me for not being with you right now. How are you? Is there any news?' She was gabbling.

Cut the bullshit, Sonia, Hannah wanted to say, but she did not dare antagonize her. She had to get into the house. 'I'd like to talk to you.'

'You are talking to me, you know you can always talk to me. I'm just so pleased to hear from you. Oh, Hannah, I'm still not sure why I've done what I have done.'

'In person.' Her voice was cold. She steadied herself against the steering wheel. An admission. She had been right about Sonia. But Sonia seemed not to notice her coldness or to find her request a strange one.

There was a long pause before Sonia answered. 'Oh, God. I didn't intend anyone to know where I was. It's so stupid of me when I know I can trust you completely. Look, Hannah, I'm in a place called Chagford. It's not that far from you. About forty miles, I'd imagine.'

'I know where it is. What's your address?'

Sonia recited it. 'When can you come?'

'Tomorrow? About two?'

'That's fine. I'll look forward to it. There's so much I want to tell you. I just hope it won't upset you.'

Clever me, Hannah thought. I'll be there within minutes. She won't have a chance to do anything rash such as make a run for it or hide Josh. Upset me? My God, how the hell does she think I feel?

She stopped a pedestrian walking a dog, presumably local, and asked directions. 'It's a row of timbered cottages. Turn left down there. You can't miss it,' the elderly man told her, raising his cap as he walked away.

Hannah thanked him. Her heart was thumping. She could almost feel the adrenalin pumping through her veins. Sonia knew the car. She parked it out of sight of the cottages and began to walk. The sun beat down on her head as she walked past the pretty gardens where roses bloomed, their petals scattered on the small patches of grass. Hannah peered at the names and numbers of the cottages. This was the place. It had a tiny overgrown garden at the front where old-fashioned plants had seeded themselves. The wooden gate creaked as she pushed it open. She approached the door feeling sick with excitement. Her first, weak knock went unanswered. She banged harder. The heavy oak door was pulled open without warning. One of the cats slithered out.

'Hannah!' Sonia's hand flew to her throat. Her rings glittered as sunlight caught the stones.

'You might've told me you were moving. Especially as you're living so close.'

Sonia shook her head, puzzled. 'How did you get here so quickly?'

'It wasn't difficult. May I come in?' She had not yet spoken Josh's name. She was afraid to do so in case it broke the spell. She needed to believe he was here but her certainty was wavering.

'God, yes. Of course.'

Hannah stepped into the narrow hallway. Its walls were white, the ceiling low. It was a typical Devon cottage. She breathed deeply. Above Sonia's perfume she could smell – what? Something familiar, the same baby foam she used in Josh's bath. Her heart thudded loudly. Oh, God, she thought, oh, thank you, God. She had found Josh.

'In here. Have a seat. I'll make us some tea.' Sonia opened a door to the right. The newest cat sat washing itself in a corner.

Hannah saw only one thing: not the lovely old furniture, the original low beams or the modern television set in the corner but a teddy bear, propped in an armchair, a blue bow tied around its neck. A blue bow. She swung around, triumphant. Her linen jacket flew open and her eyes glittered. Sonia took a step backwards. Hannah looked crazy, almost deranged. 'You've got him. I knew it.'

'Of course I've . . . Oh, no. Oh, Hannah, no. You can't possibly mean –'

'Where is he?' She tore at the door handle and was out of the room, opening other doors, leaving them open when they revealed nothing she wanted to find.

'Wait!' Realizing exactly what Hannah had thought, Sonia was terrified of what she might do when she learned the truth. She followed her up the stairs, taking them two at a time. She had misjudged the situation. It was a mistake to have made contact so soon.

Hannah stood in a doorway, completely motionless, her arms hanging limply by her sides. She stared unblinkingly at the pine cot. The sleeping baby, dressed in pale turquoise towelling, was clean and comfortable, his cheeks flushed with sleep. But he was tiny. It wasn't Josh.

'Hannah?' Sonia began tentatively, touching her arm.

Hannah turned slowly, all colour drained from her face. 'Just what exactly is going on here?' she hissed. Even in her sickening disappointment, which she had not had time to register fully, she was mindful of the sleeping infant.

'Come back downstairs, please. I'd like to explain. I owe you an explanation.'

'Where's Josh?'

'I don't know. I honestly don't know. I wish I did.' Tears filled Sonia's eyes. 'Oh, Hannah, did you really believe I'd taken him?'

Hannah nodded but could not answer. She had been ready to believe anything of anyone. Her legs gave way and she stumbled down the last few stairs. Sonia took her arm and led her back to the room with the teddy bear. 'What's that noise?'

'My bleeper. The police are trying to contact me. I need to make a phone call.'

'It's there.' Sonia pointed towards the cushioned window-seat where the telephone sat.

Hannah dialled Gareth's number. Her mouth was dry. Then, without warning, it filled with saliva and she thought she might vomit. There were several clicks before she heard Gareth's voice. Her call had been patched through to the car. 'Are you all right, Hannah?'

'Yes. I'm with Sonia.' She swallowed. It had come out as a whisper. 'I'm with Sonia. Josh isn't here.' Speaking the words made it real. She started to shake. 'He isn't here, Gareth. Goddammit, he isn't here. You can check for yourself. You've got to find him.' Her voice rose hysterically. She dropped the phone and sank to her knees, her head resting on the window-seat, her body heaving with dry sobs. All hope had evaporated.

'It's all right. We will find him. Take it easy, Hannah.' But she did not hear him, or the doubt in his voice. Sonia picked up the receiver and began to speak.

Gareth and a female officer had arrived minutes after Hannah in an unmarked car and had seen her enter the house. Gareth had not wanted to barge in and startle one of the women into doing something they would regret, not when a baby's life might be at stake.

'Hello, who is this?' Sonia asked.

'Inspector Chambers, Devon and Cornwall police. Is that Mrs Grant? Mrs Sonia Grant?'

'It is.'

'Is Hannah all right?'

'Far from it. She thought I'd got Josh.'

'Yes.'

'Ah, I see. So did you.'

'Not an unnatural conclusion when you disappeared without telling anyone.'

'I had my reasons, Inspector, but I can assure you, they are nothing whatsoever to do with Josh. I take it you're in Chagford. You're quite welcome to come and search the house.' She had almost added, Or dig up the garden, but it would have been unthinkable in front of Hannah. 'Do you want to speak to Hannah again?'

'No. Just ask her if she'd like us to take her home. One of us can drive her car. I'm sending someone in to have a word with you, Mrs Grant.' Gareth knew that his presence was more useful back at headquarters. The local police

106

could make the search and ask the questions. If Hannah said Josh wasn't there, then he wasn't, but Sonia Grant still needed to be interviewed.

Hannah, now on her feet, was able to hear both sides of the conversation. She shook her head. She could not go home. She could not face another night of seeing that empty cot. But could she cope with the knowledge of the occupied one upstairs? And whose baby was it? Suddenly she wanted to hear what Sonia had to say. 'Can I stay?' she asked. She had no fight left, not even enough energy for the journey home.

'Of course,' Sonia said quietly. Then she spoke into the receiver: 'She's staying with me, Inspector. Would you let her parents know, please?'

'Of course.' He disconnected the line. This is going to be the end for Hannah, he thought. And where did they start looking next?

Once two local officers had been despatched to Sonia's house Gareth sat, deep in thought, beside his driver as they made their way back to Plymouth. Trees in full leaf overhung the narrow roads in places and, at times, they had to pull in to let other traffic pass. He had given instructions for the house and garden to be searched thoroughly and for Mrs Grant's strange behaviour to be accounted for. That Hannah was prepared to stay there seemed to prove the woman hadn't taken Josh.

And the Avon police had been in touch that morning. They had interviewed Jenny Greene. Gareth was furious, with himself as well as with them. Yes, the hospital where she was training had been contacted. Jennifer Greene was a student nurse, aged twenty-eight. She lived in the nurses' home now but her home address was in Plymouth. She had sub-let her flat. She had, as Hannah had told them, previously been an airline stewardess. This had all been verified by administration as had the shifts she had worked over the previous week by the ward sister. There was no way in which she could have concealed a baby on the premises. But no one had spoken to Jennifer herself.

107

There had seemed no need, not when Hannah had produced the letters she had written and posted from the post-box outside the hospital gates, not when the woman was registered as a student nurse there and had had no opportunity to snatch the baby.

By the time they got back to Plymouth Jennifer Greene, supposed friend of Hannah's, should have arrived from Bristol.

Having returned from her days off, which she had spent with her boyfriend, she had been picked up that morning and interviewed by the local police. But the result of that interview was not at all what anyone had expected. Jennifer Greene had a lot of explaining to do.

Chapter Seven

Laurence had blown it. But he had been hurt, badly so, seeing that other man in what had once been his home. Humiliation and anger had rendered him less than articulate. All the things he had planned to say to Hannah had escaped him when unexpectedly confronted with Phillip then Joyce and Hannah's boyfriend.

He had driven away from the house unsure of where to go. Anywhere was preferable to facing his mother who would want an account of his visit. His father still worked but Pauline had taken early retirement and gave her time to housework and various groups, and she would be at home that day.

The weather was fine and maybe this influenced his choice of route. Without being aware of it he found he was on the Tavistock road, heading towards Dartmoor.

The colours were magnificent; heather and gorse and lichen competed with the shadowy blues and purples of the tors and the occasional banks of bracken, the brown stalks of winter now threaded with the bright green ferns of summer. He parked in a lay-by, one where there was no ice-cream van, and stared into the distance. I'll try again with Hannah. When this is all over and she's on her own, she'll listen to me. But she would need time to forgive him for what he had done that morning.

More than half an hour elapsed as Laurence thought of his marriage and what he had given up. And Josh, his son, whose existence he had mainly ignored and who suddenly meant so much to him. Despite the sun the moors seemed foreboding. Mist and rain would have suited him better. Laurence started the engine. He needed to be amongst people, strangers who would not judge him, who could not know the recent drama of his life.

Coming to a pub he pulled into the small car-park and ordered a beer and a sandwich. It was still early, not yet twelve, and he was the only customer. The man serving leaned his elbows on the counter and started up a conversation, asking if he was on holiday. Laurence said yes, it was easier than giving any other explanation and therefore encouraging a more personal exchange.

The interlude had been welcome. Laurence decided to put the morning behind him and work out what he would say to Marty later. It would be one complication out of the way and he could face Hannah with a clearer conscience. I'll just state my case, he thought, just tell her the truth. I will not allow her to manipulate me again. But there were several hours to fill until the time he was due to arrive at the farm. He had previously imagined spending them with Hannah.

He took the same road back to Plymouth and parked on the Hoe. There, amongst early holidaymakers, he sat on the wide expanse of grass and watched the naval shipping in the Sound. Silver-grey frigates sat proudly alongside the barrier; an occasional power-boat sped past, the sound of its engine half a beat behind it, a twin furrow of spume in its wake. Everyone stopped to watch as one of the massive cross-Channel ferries made its leisurely turn into Millbay Docks. Laurence had always found water restful. His whole life had been lived near or on it.

At half-past three he bought a cup of tea at the café and drank it sitting beneath the shade of an umbrella. In the sunshine, in the presence of strangers, he was certain he knew his own mind and that he would at least achieve one thing that day.

When people started to make their way home Laurence went back to the car and checked the directions Marty had given him. She had mentioned she was moving but he had not seen her new place. Sometimes they had met at her flat but mostly they used hotels. Laurence had never taken her to his own place in Dorset.

It took him some time to locate the farmhouse because the country lanes were mainly unsignposted and Marty's directions were barely adequate, but she probably knew the area better than he did.

He whistled in surprise when he finally pulled into the courtyard. The house was far larger than he had anticipated and everything was in excellent repair. The paint-work was fresh and the roof tiles new. The stable-door at the front opened before he had killed the engine. He got out of the car and walked quickly towards Marty who stood there waiting for him.

'Laurence,' she said, her voice low and seductive as she lifted her head to kiss him. 'It's seemed like such a long time. Come in, let me show you around.'

He followed her into the house, noticing how tastefully it was furnished and decorated, how new everything was. A rich meaty garlic aroma permeated the air but did not override Marty's expensive perfume. Her hair hung loosely, a soft cloud of red curls, which always made Laurence want to touch it. He'd have to be very careful if he wasn't to be drawn in by her again.

'What do you think, Laurence?' she asked with a satisfied smile when he had been shown every room.

'It's terrific.'

'I know. There's still that one bedroom to furnish, but that can wait. Sit down, I'll get us some wine.'

He pulled out one of the heavy wooden kitchen chairs and watched her sensual movements. Unlike Hannah who was slim, thin now, Marty had more curves and exuded sexuality. Her eyes were bright and sparkled with laughter as if she was always enjoying a private joke. There was something about her other women lacked, or maybe were not able to display so easily. A love of life, perhaps. But how alluring she was as she skirted his chair with the wine bottle in her hand, her knee brushing his thigh, a wisp of hair touching his cheek as she leaned forward to fill his glass. Be careful, Laurence, an inner voice warned him. Don't let her get to you again. But he still accepted the large glass of red wine she handed him. Had he, he wondered, already subconsciously decided to stay, to enjoy what she had to offer one more time before finishing it for ever? He wanted Hannah, he knew that now, and he also wanted Josh. But why miss out on this final opportunity? Hannah didn't seem to have wasted much time in finding a replacement.

'Was it a bad trip, Laurence? You look a bit tired.' Marty circled her glass on the table. The meal was in the oven, there were only vegetables to cook and it was too early to eat yet.

'Not one of the best. We had a man sick.' He paused, unsure what Marty would think of him if he expressed his concern for the child in whom he had once claimed he had no interest. 'Why do you see him, then?' she had asked at the time.

'I feel obliged to,' he had answered although that wasn't the truth. He didn't know, or didn't want to admit why he felt compelled to visit his son.

Her company and the wine had relaxed him. It had been a stressful day and Laurence needed someone in whom to confide. 'Josh is missing,' he said, not meeting her eyes.

'Josh missing? What're you talking about?' She frowned at him, her face a little flushed from the heat of cooking.

'Josh. My son. Someone's taken him.'

Marty turned away. 'God, how awful. Oh, Laurence, I don't know what to say. I know you went through a bad time with your divorce but this seems too much for someone to have to cope with.' He needs me now, she thought as she turned to adjust the oven temperature. But at least I know it was Josh he went to see and not Hannah.

'I really didn't expect to feel like this.'

'You didn't fool me, you know. It was obvious you cared about him, you just wouldn't admit it to yourself.'

So Marty had known. How odd, then, that Hannah

112

hadn't spotted how he felt. 'It must sound crazy, but I wish there was something I could do to get him back.'

'For Hannah's sake?'

It seemed a strange question. 'For everyone's sake. I can't bear to think of him out there somewhere with a stranger.' Laurence bit his lip. He felt near to tears. What if Josh was cold or hungry or hurt and frightened? He couldn't bear the thought of the expression that would be in his trusting brown eyes.

'The police will be doing all they can.'

'Yes. I know that, but it's five days now. Anything could've happened in that time.'

For everyone's sake. It was not the answer Marty had wanted to hear. Yes, find the boy and return him to his mother then Hannah would be happy and she'd leave Laurence alone. Laurence didn't know that she knew Hannah, that Hannah had once said she would take Laurence back. Marty hated the idea of his visits to his old marital home, hated the pull Hannah might still have. It would have been better if he'd ignored the birth of the child altogether. If it wasn't for Josh they would have been together long ago. No, if it wasn't for Hannah, she reminded herself. The bitch. The bitch who had everything and who had tried to trick Laurence by becoming pregnant against his wishes. Well now she, Marty, could provide a lovely home and everything else in competition with his ex-wife. And this time he would not be leaving.

'You never said, how did you come by this house?'

Marty laughed her throaty laugh. 'My mother died and left it to me. It needed a lot of work so I didn't move in at first. It took quite a while to get it straight. I own it outright.' She hesitated before adding, 'She also left me quite a lot of money so I've given up work.'

'Really?' Laurence was surprised. Marty had made an excellent air stewardess and he had assumed she loved the job. She was attentive to customers' needs and made them feel good. It was on one of her flights he had met her. That

113

very same night they had shared a hotel room. 'So you've known about this for some time?'

She nodded. 'Yes, since last August. But I wanted it to be a surprise.'

'It's certainly that.'

'I'm really glad you like it.' Because you're going to be living here, she added silently. You can't procrastinate any longer, Laurence, we are finally going to be together. She was fully aware of the power she had over him when she was in his company and she knew exactly the right way in which to exert it.

Before they ate Marty said she must shut in the hens. 'Help yourself to more wine. I won't be a minute.' She left by the back door.

Laurence could hear her calling, 'Chucky, chucky,' in the old farmers' way. Then there was silence. Five minutes later Marty returned. She was smiling enigmatically.

'You're hardly dressed like a farmer's wife,' Laurence commented when she returned, the soft material of her dress swirling around her hips.

'Ah, but I'm not anybody's wife yet,' she whispered, her lips brushing his ear as she placed cutlery in front of him.

Laurence shivered. Too late, he knew he should have said his piece and left.

They ate in the kitchen. She had decided that the dining-room was too formal for what she had in mind for later and Laurence still needed a little loosening up. His face had that closed-in look again.

After the meal she poured two small brandies and led him by the hand to the three-seater sofa in the lounge. Sunlight flowed into the room through the glass doors although the sun was much lower in the sky and there was a slight chill in the air. Marty placed the glasses on the surface of the solid, varnished coffee-table hewn from a section of a tree trunk. She bent over and switched on the gas fire. Flames flickered over the artificial logs behind the glass panel. Never again would she clean out ashes.

She turned and, very slowly, began to remove her clothes. Her pale skin was touched with pink from the rays of the sun and the glow of the fire.

Laurence gasped. He had forgotten how beautiful she was naked. As she lowered herself to her knees in front of him he reached for her full breasts and took one hazel nipple in his mouth. He groaned, unaware of Marty's knowing grin. There would be no further discussion of Josh and Hannah now.

Laurence knew then that he stood no chance of leaving that night. What he wanted to say would have to wait until the morning.

Even knowing Josh wasn't there, both women were tense as the police searched the house and garden methodically, tramping mud across the kitchen floor when they had finished outside. They interviewed Sonia out of Hannah's hearing and, satisfied that the sleeping baby was hers and that she knew nothing about Josh's disappearance, they soon left.

Sonia was shaking. Until that afternoon she had had no idea she was under suspicion and Hannah had displayed such violence upon her arrival that she had been terrified she was going to harm Anthony. 'I think we both need a stiff drink,' she told Hannah who had been waiting in the sitting-room, too stunned to move, unable to take in all that was happening, too heartbroken to even think straight.

Needing some time to get over her own shock, Sonia returned to the kitchen, fed the cats then poured two large glasses of chilled white wine, the damp bottle almost slipping from her trembling hands. She smiled wanly as she handed one of them to Hannah. 'I'm not breast-feeding. I can't.' She sat down. Hannah was calm now, utterly calm and defeated. She looked dreadful, ill and lifeless, her spirit crushed.

'Hannah, please forgive me. I couldn't tell you,

115

I couldn't tell anyone. I just wanted to keep him to myself. You'll never know how much I've wanted this, how many years I've suffered and how very much I envied you. Then, when I heard the news about Josh it was impossible to let you know, I was sure it would hurt you too much. How could I flaunt such happiness in the face of your misery? But I really didn't imagine you'd think I'd taken him. Oh, Hannah, how could you have thought that? I've always been your friend. I love you like a sister.'

Hannah, white-faced, said nothing. She waited, hardly caring what came next or that Sonia had declared her feelings so strongly.

'Ever since I can remember I've wanted a baby. Brian's baby initially. I assumed he wanted one as badly as me. Gradually it became an obsession. Any man would have done as the father. I've lost count of the miscarriages I've had. Marcus Gould has been fantastic, he tried everything possible for me and then, when I was due to leave for a fashion shoot overseas, I discovered I was pregnant again and cancelled it. But I miscarried once more. I was so ill, depressed rather than ill really, I didn't think I'd make it that time. It was the closest I've ever been to suicide. He got me through that, too, just as he had done on every other occasion.

'I had to pretend children didn't interest me, Hannah, but I was only trying to fool myself. As I approached forty I knew it was too late. I gave up.' She smiled. 'And that's when it happened. Maybe that's why it happened. Although I didn't know it I was already pregnant when I visited you back in January. Almost five months, would you believe?'

'You didn't know? Surely if you'd had all those miscarriages you would have recognized the signs.' Hannah bit her lip. 'I'm sorry. Forgive me.' It was a spiteful thing to have said. It was not Sonia's fault Josh was missing.

'No, strangely enough I didn't. Having given up altogether I had stopped looking for signs. However, someone said I was putting on weight. Well, you know me, I dieted

116

like crazy. My periods have never been regular. Marcus said it was because of the way I treated my body, that although he didn't class me as anoreetic, I wasn't far off it. I was over five months pregnant before I knew it for certain.'

'And the father?'

'Ah.' Sonia flicked back her hair. It was a little longer now and softened the sharp contours of her face. 'That was the problem. I couldn't tell him. And if I'd stayed in London as I intended at first, he would have known. I don't want to share my baby, not with anyone, not even with his own father. I couldn't even share my pregnancy, Hannah, hard as you might find that to believe. I wanted every minute of it to myself. It was my one and only chance. If anything had gone wrong it would have been the end of me. Five months was longer than I'd ever got before. I didn't even tell my mother until after he was born. It was a hell of a shock to her, poor dear.'

'But you went to Scotland last week. Where was the baby?'

'I left him with my mother. It terrified me but I saw by the way she handled him that I needn't have worried. God, how I hated to leave him, but I'd given my word on the job. Fortunately it was only in an advisory capacity. I've never got through anything so quickly. I'd already found a replacement photographer. Stupid, maybe, but I wanted to finish with a clear conscience. I'd turned down any other assignments.'

Hannah recalled that Sonia's mother lived in Middlesex. She would have driven up and caught a flight from Heathrow. 'And before that, how did you conceal the fact?'

'I didn't get very big. He only weighed five and a half pounds. I took to wearing baggy clothes and capes. Then, towards the end I bought this place and got out of London. I'd already had the spare bedroom done before I realized I couldn't stay at the flat, that if I did it would soon be common knowledge I'd had a baby. No one knew, apart from my GP and the hospital staff down here. Once I suspected the truth I dare not let Marcus know, even after all he'd done for me. I've actually only been living here for two weeks. After the birth I booked into a private place the local hospital recommended, not exactly for convalescence, but to ensure there were experts around for Anthony's sake. I still dread something happening to him but we're coping.'

'So you've been here two weeks.'

'Yes. Once I knew I'd passed the dangerous stage I began to hope I'd go full term. I started looking for places. I knew whichever way it went I couldn't go back to work. You won't believe me, Hannah, but I wanted to be nearer you. I was going to tell you, I really was. I'd decided to get the Scottish job out of the way then turn up and surprise you. But then you rang and the police contacted me and I couldn't, not under those circumstances. That's why I probably sounded a bit off. I just didn't know what to say and I knew it could only cause you extra pain if I gave you my news.'

'I wondered why the police didn't know you'd moved. Timing, I suppose.'

'They rang me on the mobile. I'd returned from Scotland and was at my mother's at the time. I said that naturally I was willing to make a statement and went to the local police station. I even told them I was with my mother. I can see how it must've appeared, but it was coincidence, my being in London at the time. It wasn't that I had anything to hide.'

'I wish you'd told me. I wish I hadn't had to believe it was you. What's he called?' Hannah asked quietly. 'The baby?'

'His name's Anthony. It means priceless – at least, that's one meaning. And that's what he is to me. And now I wouldn't dream of going back to work. Amazing, isn't it, when my whole life has centred around my career.'

'I did.'

'You had to, Hannah.'

'Yes, but look what happened. It was my fault.'

' No. You mustn't think that. Not ever.' She had almost said, Whatever happens to Josh.

'I try not to, Sonia, but it's hard. I blamed James and Val to start with. It was wrong of me. I'm his mother, the fault's mine.'

'You won't get anywhere with that attitude. Drink up. You look as if you need another. I know I do.'

Hannah smiled weakly. The old Sonia was still there. Little Anthony hadn't altered her totally. 'Am I allowed to know who the father is?'

Sonia's back stiffened, then she relented. 'I've kept too much from you already and I'll never forgive myself for what I've put you through. Yes, you have a right to know. It's George Allison, as you've probably guessed. Hannah . . .?'

'You have my word, Sonia. I won't tell anyone. But do you know how much he loves you? I met him, he's going crazy not knowing where you are. He'd marry you in an instant, and he'd make a wonderful father.'

'You met George?' Sonia placed her glass on the floor, wondering just what sort of conversation had taken place between her two friends.

'I was trying to find you. I went to the flat but it was empty.' Hannah explained all that she had achieved whilst she was in London.

'My God, you didn't miss a trick,' Sonia said with admiration when she mentioned the interview with Marcus Gould. 'And Marcus agreed to speak to you?'

'Yes. But only because he thought initially that I was a potential patient. He obviously doesn't know about the baby. What did you mean when you said you couldn't go to him?'

'He met George when he came with me to the clinic and he knows of my relationship with him. Okay, I'm certain Marcus wouldn't have discussed my medical history with him but he would have automatically assumed that George knew about the baby. I went to my GP once I realized for certain what was causing the changes in my body. Anthony was born down here in the local hospital. He's a Devon boy.' She smiled. 'Hannah, can you forgive me?'

'Of course I can.' Sonia believed in private health care. It was a measure of how much she wanted the birth kept secret that she had renounced it.

'No wonder the police suspected me. Don't they have any leads at all?'

'None. Laurence is in the clear, as are his parents. I think they believe James and Val are innocent but they're not prepared to confirm that to me yet. And there's me, of course.' Hannah sighed. Although nothing had been said they would have checked her movements that day. Sometimes she knew she was going crazy when she asked herself if it was possible she had harmed Josh but was now in a state of denial. It had happened to other women.

'Don't even think it. They know it's not you. Look, Hannah, what you said about George, I know you're right, I know what he feels but I can't divide my love. Every bit of it is for Anthony. I had to get away, somewhere where George would never think of looking for me. The more time that passes, the less likelihood there is of him pursuing me. He'll forget, maybe find someone else and I won't have to blame myself for hurting him.'

'I understand, although he loves you too much to want someone else. Will you tell Anthony when he's older?'

'I'm not sure. If I did he might want to make contact and all this would have been in vain. I'm taking one day at a time at the moment, but it's not to say I won't change my mind. However, George would never think of looking for me in the country.'

'No. Rustic scenes were never your thing.'

'They are now.' Sonia smiled. She had not lost Hannah's friendship after all. It was probably the two drinks, but Hannah looked a little better than when she had arrived. 'What're you thinking?'

'It's odd. I was sick with disappointment that it wasn't Josh upstairs in that cot, but I'm also glad it wasn't you who took him. And Sonia, I am glad about Anthony. Listen, is that him?'

'Oh, dear. It's feeding time. Hannah, will it . . .?'

'No. Bring him down. I shan't mind, honestly.'

But seeing the tiny little boy in Sonia's gentle arms was almost too much to bear. They had to find Josh, life was not worth living without him, she or Gareth Chambers must do something quickly.

Once Anthony was fed and winded Sonia put him on a rug in front of the sitting-room fire and changed his nappy. His tiny knuckles found his mouth, he sucked at them as if he was still hungry, then fell asleep almost as soon as Sonia picked him up. She laid him in his carry-cot and sighed. 'I didn't know it could be this good,' she said. 'Now, let's do something about eating,' she added more briskly, aware how close to the edge Hannah was, how hard she was struggling not to cry as she gently touched the baby's cheek with her fingertips.

In the kitchen they prepared a meal between them and talked of old times, carefully avoiding the subject uppermost in Hannah's mind.

'Have you heard from your friend Jenny? She must've settled in by now. She's been gone a few months now, hasn't she?'

Hannah frowned and stopped slicing carrots. 'Yes. But I haven't heard recently. It's odd. We were so close, even after such a short time. Or so I thought. I saw her at least once a week until she left and we've kept in touch by post. I wrote and asked her to telephone urgently but –' Hannah stopped, mid-sentence, as the realization hit her. 'She hasn't been in touch since Josh disappeared. I gave the police her name, along with everyone else's. They said the hospital had confirmed that they had a student nurse by the name of Jenny Greene but Gareth hasn't come back to me on that. Why hasn't she rung, I wonder?'

Sonia, who had been coating pork chops in herbs and breadcrumbs, also stood still. 'When did you write?'

'Over the weekend.'

'Well, then, she mightn't have got your letter yet. If you posted it on Sunday then she wouldn't have received it until yesterday at the earliest. Besides, you can't possibly think Jenny's taken him?' But she saw by her face that Hannah was seriously considering it.

'It's possible, isn't it? I mean, that might be why she hasn't been in touch.'

'Get on the phone immediately. Ring Inspector Chambers and tell him exactly what you've just told me.'

Hannah sighed. 'No, there's no point. If she's training as a nurse she couldn't possibly have an eight-month-old baby in tow, especially as she lives in the nurses' home. The police have already checked. She was on duty during the relevant time. And you're right, she's probably only just received my card.'

'Ring him, Hannah, do it now, for God's sake. You have to, just in case.'

Sonia had a point. Anything, no matter how insignificant, was worth reporting. Unless Jenny was away somewhere she would have been on the phone immediately she received that postcard.

She rang Charles Cross but was put through to one of Gareth's team of detectives. 'Inspector Chambers is having a word with Miss Greene at this very moment,' she was told. 'He said if you rang to tell you that he'll contact you first thing in the morning.'

'Not tonight?'

There was a slight hesitation. 'No. In the morning.'

'Thank you,' Hannah said, wondering if Gareth finally had a lead.

Neither of them ate much of the meal they had taken so much trouble in preparing. Sonia tried to be cheerful but it was obvious Hannah could not take much more. Sonia knew the signs. Hannah was as close to a breakdown as she had once been herself.

'Come on, let's go to bed,' she suggested at eleven

fifteen. 'You've got your bleeper thing, haven't you? Just come down and use the phone if it goes off.'

'Thanks, Sonia. And I'm truly sorry I thought the worst.'

'Forget it. Try and get some sleep.' Sonia embraced her, wishing there was something she could do to help.

Hannah, in a borrowed nightdress, lay in bed staring at the ceiling. Jenny. She had been thinking of her recently. But what was it about her that she couldn't recall? Something she had said or hinted at? Or was it some small action she had tried to disguise? But the harder she tried to remember the more elusive it became. More puzzling was why Jenny was being questioned in Plymouth. Gareth was ringing in the morning, she would just have to wait. Hannah swallowed and fought off the panic. Was he waiting until then to deliver bad news? Her mother's words came into her head: 'If there was bad news the police would come in person.'

Just after two she heard Sonia get up to feed Anthony. I'd go through all that again, ten times over, a thousand times over, Hannah thought, if I could only have Josh back again. Hot tears ran down her face and into her hair and ears. The irony of the situation was too painful to contemplate. Sonia, her friend, was nursing a baby she had always claimed never to want. Hannah, who had lost a husband in order to keep hers, had now also lost her child.

Finally, sometime around three o'clock, with no more tears left to shed, she turned on her side and closed her eyes.

Chapter Eight

Gareth was exhausted. Like Hannah, he had built his hopes on Sonia having abducted Josh. They hit the outskirts of Plymouth just as the rush-hour traffic was at its peak although most of it was heading in the opposite direction. The streets were full of people leaving work and the bus queues were at their longest.

The driver turned in at Charles Cross police station, a modern building of smoked glass and blue steel. Inside it, waiting for their return, was Jennifer Greene.

Gareth could not wait to hear what she had to say. The brief fax from the Avon police said that she had returned from her days off and that they had spoken to her. However, she claimed never to have met Hannah Peters. Obviously something was very wrong. He went straight to the interview room where she had been seated for over an hour. She was attractive and looked younger than her age but she was displaying the classic signs of anxiety. She sat twisting her hands, her pupils flickering unsteadily as she looked from Gareth to the female detective accompanying him and back again. Anxiety or guilt, he wondered as he smiled to try to put her at ease.

'I'm Detective Inspector Chambers,' he began. Having introduced WDC Ferris, he explained the procedure the interview would follow, that everything they said in that room would be recorded. She said that she understood.

'Miss Greene, you're here because we believe you might be able to help us locate a missing child. His name is Josh, his mother's name is Hannah Peters.'

'I told the police in Bristol, I don't know anyone of that name, except because of the letters.'

This was the part which puzzled Gareth. Jenny Greene had admitted that she received and sent letters to a Hannah Peters but maintained she had never met her.

'Mrs Peters told us that she had a friend with the same name as yourself who used to live in Plymouth but who went to Bristol to train as a nurse earlier this year. Was that person you?'

Jenny sighed. 'Look, I don't know what's going on but I did live here, in my own flat which I now rent out, and I have started my training but I was accepted for the September intake last year. I swear I've never actually met anyone called Mrs Peters.'

'All right. Then how do you explain the letters?'

Jennifer Greene bit her full lip then shrugged in resignation. 'I'd better start from the beginning. I was a stewardess for one of the local airlines. I'd been working for them for several years and I fancied a change. I really thought nursing would suit me, but I'm not so certain now. Anyway, before that I was friendly with a girl called Marty. Our paths crossed now and again and we'd chat. She's one of those vibrant people, someone you feel good to be with. We had the occasional drink together but we weren't exactly friends.

'Anyway, we kept in touch after I left then she wrote and told me she'd left, too, although she didn't say what she was doing.'

'When was this?'

'Sometime in the early New Year. I hadn't heard from her for quite a while before that. She wrote to ask me a favour. She said she was seeing a married man and would I be prepared to act as a sort of Box Number.'

'And you saw nothing wrong in this?'

'No, not really. She explained that he was going through a divorce and didn't want her dragged into it and that for the moment the only way they could keep in touch was through the post. Obviously she couldn't write to him at home.'

'Is Marty married?'

'No. At least, she wasn't when I last saw her.'

So if this married man existed there was nothing to stop him writing to Marty direct, Gareth realized. 'Please explain what happened with these letters.'

'I would receive an envelope addressed to me in Marty's writing. This I would open. Inside was another envelope, stamped and addressed to Hannah Peters. All I had to do was to post it from Bristol. After a while I'd receive another letter, postmarked Plymouth. These I'd send on to Marty, unopened, in another envelope.'

'But this doesn't make sense. This married man could have written directly to Marty, and what does Hannah Peters have to do with any of it?'

'I assumed she was someone from whom the boyfriend collected his mail, someone who was in the same position as me, helping two people who couldn't be together yet.'

No, Gareth, thought, that's far too complicated and it doesn't ring true. 'To whom did you address Marty's mail?'

'Just Marty.' Jenny shrugged. 'It's strange, I never did find out her surname.'

'So you didn't know her well?'

'No, not well, but for several years. Our paths crossed now and again. I liked her. I wanted to help her.'

'Yet you agreed to this even though you say you hardly knew her?'

'Yes. I mean, it was only going to be for a few months, until the divorce came through.'

'All right, Miss Greene, but this still doesn't bring us any closer to tracing Josh Peters.'

She frowned, genuinely bewildered. 'But I don't know anything about a missing baby.'

'Tell me what you do know – Marty's address, for instance.'

Jenny reached over the side of the chair and picked up her handbag from which she removed a small address book. She handed it to Gareth, open at the relevant page. It was a Plymouth address in a good area. 'Thank you. Do you know how long she's lived there?'

'Ever since I've known her. Oh, I almost forgot. There was a postcard. I sent that on, too, in an envelope. It said to telephone urgently.' She paused. 'It's awful, I felt so sorry for Marty, I know what it's like, you see. I was involved with a married man myself once.'

'Oh?'

'Someone who worked at the airline. It's over now. It wasn't important, and it's got nothing to do with any of all this.'

Gareth nodded. Except, being in the same boat, or thinking she had been, Jenny was more inclined to help this Marty. The postcard would be in their possession very shortly. Someone would go to that address to retrieve it. It was the one Hannah said she had written to Jenny, her so-called friend, because she was desperate. 'But you never forwarded anything to any other address?'

'No.'

Gareth left the room and sent two officers to Marty's Plymouth address. 'Bring her in,' he instructed. Then he found someone to get on to the airline for which Marty had worked. He needed a few minutes to think before he returned to the interview room. Marty, whoever she was, had gone to a lot of trouble. It was obvious she knew Hannah if they were in correspondence even if Hannah believed her to be called Jenny Greene. But what was the purpose of the correspondence and had it any relevance to Josh? Perhaps they would know by the end of the day.

It was an hour later that Gareth asked, 'Miss Greene, did you know Marty had moved? Did she ever mention somewhere else she had to go to?'

'No.'

'Okay. I want you to tell me anything you can remember about Marty, no matter how trivial it may seem. What

127

she looks like, how she speaks, friends, boyfriends, anything.'

Jennifer Greene began to speak but it was apparent from the start that she had little of use to tell them. Marty's conversation, apart from when she had asked the favour, had never included personal details. But at least they had a good description. Jenny might not have much solid information but she was certainly very observant, even down to the tiny mole over Marty's top lip. Marty had moved the previous October; presumably she had paid to have her mail forwarded, hopefully for as long as a year. The next task was to find out the new address. 'All right, Miss Greene, unless you can think of anything else, you're free to go.' Gareth had already been told that she was staying with her parents that night and returning to Bristol in the morning.

She stood and pulled on her coat. 'Is there any chance of me being asked to leave the hospital because of this?'

She may have expressed doubts about her new career but he saw how much this fresh start meant to her. It was a shame she had marred it herself. 'No. You've been helping us in the course of an investigation – that's what we'll say if we're asked. But please don't ever make the same mistake again. If anything else comes to mind make sure you give me a ring.'

It was too late to contact the relevant Post Office department; instead, officers were sent to question Marty's old neighbours. Someone must have known her. It would not be easy to find her if she had deliberately chosen to disappear. But they would. In the end they would. A photograph might help.

Hannah was with Sonia and it was too soon to build up her hopes. Instead, he sent an officer to Hannah's house where, along with Phillip and Joyce who had met the girl known as Jenny, he went through her personal things. There were photographs: family groups, plenty of Josh, several of Sonia, but none of Marty.

While Gareth waited he reread the little they knew about

Marty. She had worked for an airline but had quitted the job. They had tapped into the computer. As far as the National Insurance people were concerned, she no longer worked. Before he could read much further he learned that June Hoffman, Marty's superior, had confirmed she had left the previous October, not January as Jenny Greene had believed. She was excellent with customers but not easy to know. There had never been any complaints about her work but she had no particular friends. 'And then her mother died suddenly,' June had added. 'She gave in her notice soon afterwards.' June Hoffman only had the address in Plymouth where Marty had previously lived. Marty Rowland. They now had a surname but it meant little. The people who had bought her flat had no forwarding address and the janitor who worked on a part-time basis in the building wasn't of much help. 'She told me she'd informed almost everyone that she'd moved,' he said, 'but a few straggling letters might come through for a month or so. She told me it wasn't worth paying the Post Office change of address fees and would I mind keeping anything that came for her. It was no hardship. All the mail comes through one box and I sort it anyway. She calls in occasionally but, as I said, she gets very little post.'

Utility bills would automatically be sent to her new address, so maybe it was only Hannah's letters she was collecting from her old flat. There was no point in contacting the Post Office now.

A search of the electoral roll proved fruitless but maybe she had not yet been sent a form to fill in. There was no number listed in the telephone directory for the area and by mid-evening it had been confirmed that no unlisted number existed either. But she probably had a mobile phone, would certainly do so if she wanted to cover her tracks. If she had a telephone at all.

He wanted to go home and see little Gabrielle, who would now be in bed, and listen to his wife as she talked of the normal events of her day, but he would carry on for a while. And what should they do about Sonia Grant?

Probably nothing. Moving house without telling anyone was thoughtless but it was not a crime even though it had put the woman under suspicion. And Sonia didn't have Josh.

He read through the Peters file, thick now with detail and information though none of it pointed to where baby Josh might be. Then he jotted down all they knew.

Marty had befriended Hannah, possibly deliberately, using the name of Jenny Greene. She had known Hannah only since January but a friendship had formed quickly. Hannah said they had met by chance, walking by the river. Which may or may not be true. Josh was about three months old at the time.

No one knew where Marty lived or if she worked now because she might be paid cash in hand to avoid any dealings with the authorities. But that left the problem of what she did with Josh. If she had him. She had led Hannah to believe she had gone to train as a nurse and used someone she knew to establish this. But why? Had she intended to take Josh from the start?

Something's wrong, Gareth thought. Women who have lost babies or can't have them, if they are very disturbed, do not make such complicated plans. They snatch a child; from a pram outside a shop, from an unwary mother in a supermarket, from a garden, yes, but not one in the middle of nowhere and they do not wait until that child is eight months old. They were on the wrong track again, just as they had been with Laurence and Sonia. Even so he instigated inquiries at hospitals and clinics in case anyone by the name of Marty Rowland had had such a problem. Yet Gareth was suddenly certain that Marty's involvement, if she was involved, centred around Laurence. There was nothing to indicate she had taken the child, no reason to arrest her even if they found her. It was not illegal to use any name you wanted, even without changing it by deed poll, as long as it wasn't for fraudulent purposes, and Miss Greene had been sure a married man was involved, a married man awaiting a divorce. Except Laurence and Hannah were already divorced.

For the next couple of hours every name on the computer would be checked, starting locally at first, then spreading farther afield. If there was another female called Jennifer Greene in its memory she would be traced; if there was anyone named Marty Rowland they would find her. Unless, of course, her name was not Marty Rowland at all, Gareth thought with resignation. But it wasn't a common name. Why choose one which would be noticed if it wasn't hers?

He ran a hand through his hair. If only they'd got on to it earlier, so much time would have been saved. They had committed the worst sin, that of omission. They had not checked thoroughly on Jennifer Greene on the very first day. They had taken all this at face value. They had not confirmed that the student nurse was the same Jenny Greene that Hannah had known.

He knew he was being harsh, that in normal circumstances their questions, answered by hospital administration and ward staff, would have been sufficient, but these were not normal circumstances and six days had been wasted.

Never was he so pleased to see the plump and cheerful face of his wife Judy when he arrived home just after ten. He held her for several minutes before going upstairs to kiss Gabrielle. 'Tomorrow,' he whispered to his sleeping daughter. 'We'll find this Marty tomorrow.'

Only as he fell asleep did he remember that June Hoffman had said that Marty's mother had recently died.

Chapter Nine

Towards the end of Wednesday afternoon Joyce replaced the telephone receiver as if it was fragile and turned to face Phillip and James. 'That was Gareth. Sonia doesn't have him,' she said very quietly. 'Josh isn't with Sonia.' There was no hint of the dread she was feeling in her voice. 'Hannah's staying there tonight.' She walked from the room, her head held high, her shoulders stiff. James and Phillip said nothing and continued to sit in silence, listening to Joyce's footsteps as she climbed the stairs slowly.

Silently, almost reverently, she opened Josh's bedroom door. Hannah had touched nothing. It was Joyce who had placed his bunny on his thin, baby pillow knowing that downstairs it was a constant reminder. She gripped the rails of the cot, her knuckles white and, agnostic or not, she began to pray. Bring him home safely, bring him home soon, was her litany. It had been the longest five days of her life, how much longer they must have seemed for her daughter, yet somehow they'd managed to keep going. Just.

'Joyce?'

Only when Phillip took her by the arms and turned her to face him was she aware of his presence and the fact that her face was wet with tears. 'I'm sorry,' she sobbed into his shoulder. 'I've tried so hard to be strong for Hannah. I love that little boy so much, Phillip. I just don't know what I'll do if anything's happened to him. Look what it's doing to all of us. I'd pay any ransom to get him back. I'd give up my life if I had to.'

'So would I. So would I.' Phillip pulled her wet face closer to his warm chest and stroked the back of her neck. He had been thinking along the same lines. No one was immune. There was James, sitting downstairs, his kind face tortured as if the worst had already happened and he was entirely to blame. And Valerie Mayhew who rang every day but refused to see Hannah or even speak to her because her sense of guilt was so great. Valerie's parents would be affected too, living with her would not be easy And Pauline and Andrew, Josh's other grandparents, who loved him and who were also suffering deeply. Even Gareth Chambers would be marked, Phillip thought, and his men. If Josh never came home it would live with them, too, even if only as a case they had lost. 'Let's go down. I'll make us some tea.'

Joyce tried to smile. 'That's all we ever seem to do nowadays, make endless cups of tea and coffee. But thank you anyway.' She went to the bathroom and splashed cold water on her face. 'God, I look so damn old,' she told her reflection. She combed her hair and applied some lipstick then went to join the men.

Somehow they got through another desperate night.

'It's six days now,' James said dismally when they were assembled in the kitchen the following morning. None of them had slept well, it was only six thirty. At Joyce's invitation he had agreed to stay again the previous night. There was some comfort in numbers and with a guest in the house it was easier not to give in, to put on a brave face.

Neither of the Gregsons answered. They knew exactly how long it had been. 'Is that the phone?' Joyce jumped up. She was normally light on her feet like her daughter but anxiety made her movements jerky and she almost knocked over her chair. 'Hello?' she said breathlessly.

'Is Hannah there, Joyce?'

'Good gracious. Pauline! How are you? Sorry, that was a stupid question to ask. But no, she stayed with Sonia last night. We're expecting her back sometime this morning.'

Joyce offered no further explanation. It would have been redundant now that they knew Josh wasn't with Sonia.

'Oh. Then Laurence isn't there either.' She sounded disappointed and a little worried. 'I was hoping – well, it was foolish, I know, but he told me he was going to see Hannah and I thought this might have brought them together again.'

Joyce ignored the remark. If Hannah wanted Laurence back, it was her choice, she would do nothing to influence her either way and she would try to conceal her dislike if he did return to the marital home. 'No. He did call in yesterday morning. There was a bit of a scene, I'm afraid, but none of us are at our best at the moment. He didn't stay long, it was all a bit awkward.'

'I see.' Pauline sighed.

'What is it? Is something the matter?'

'It sounds ridiculous, worrying about a grown man, but he hasn't come home and he's still got my car, you see. I tried his place in Dorset and left a message there but he hasn't come back to me and his mobile's switched off.'

'Where do you think he's gone?' Was I right all along? Joyce wondered. Is Laurence involved?

'I've no idea. Yesterday morning he said he had to make a telephone call, I assumed it was to Hannah, then he asked to borrow my car because his was in Southampton and that was the last we've heard from him. It's almost twenty-four hours. It's unlike Laurence not to give us a ring.'

Despite Pauline's garbled account, Joyce had to give him that. No matter what other faults he might have, in the years she had known him Laurence had always let Hannah know if he was going to be late. Even on the fatal night when he had struck Hannah he had made sure that Pauline let her know where he was and that he had not been involved in an accident. 'He didn't ring here before he arrived yesterday,' Joyce said. 'But if he does contact us we'll let you know immediately. Has he got a girlfriend? Or someone he might have stayed the night with?'

'That's just it, we don't know. If I had any idea who he telephoned yesterday I might know where to start looking. You must think me neurotic, but with everything that's going on, well, it isn't easy to think straight.'

'I know. You never stop worrying about them. Did you try the redial button?'

'No. I never thought of it, there was no reason to until now and we've used the phone since.'

Joyce began to worry a little herself. Laurence had been at sea on the day Josh was taken but maybe he had got someone else to snatch him and had now gone to collect him. Her theory did not fit in with Laurence's reaction yesterday morning but Gareth Chambers would have to know. On the other hand, something may have happened to Laurence. Paranoid though she knew it to be, Joyce wondered if someone had it in for the whole family. 'Try not to worry, Pauline. We'll keep in touch.'

Joyce disconnected the line then immediately rang the police. Gareth Chambers was otherwise engaged but a female detective took the message. 'Do you happen to know the registration number of Mrs Peters' car?' she asked.

'No, I'm afraid I don't.'

'It doesn't matter, we'll soon have it. Look, Mrs Gregson, please don't raise your hopes too high, but we think we might have a lead, it's a bit tenuous so I think it's best not to mention it to Hannah yet. Not until Gareth's spoken to her. And it might be wise for you to stay by the phone. Hello? Are you still there?'

Joyce nodded. Her throat was constricted, she was unable to speak. 'Yes,' she finally whispered, 'yes, I'm still here. Thank you. Thank you so much.'

When she returned to the kitchen both Phillip and James saw at once that something had changed. The years had slipped from Joyce's face. Both men stood up simultaneously, expecting to have to take some form of action, if only to catch Joyce who stumbled towards a seat. 'We're not to . . . we're not to build up our hopes,' she began, but

135

got no further because she was crying and both men were talking at once.

When Laurence opened his eyes daylight was penetrating the curtains but he did not immediately recognize his surroundings. He groaned. Marty. Of course. He had visited her on her own territory before, at her flat in Plymouth, but had not felt comfortable. Sharing her living space was too intimate, her sharing his, even more so. Mostly he had booked them into an hotel. He felt hot with shame. Despite all his good intentions he had been unable to resist Marty and had stayed overnight.

Beside him Marty stirred. Her coppery curls lay on the pillow, the skin of her visible arm and shoulder was pale and freckled, beneath the covers she was naked, as was he.

It had been a mistake but Laurence had not seen that at the time, not once she had removed her clothes and started to unbutton his shirt. He sat up and brushed the lock of hair from his eyes knowing what he must tell her.

'Good morning, darling. Did you sleep well?' Marty's hand slid across his thigh, caressing it, moving higher.

Laurence pulled away. 'I've got to go. I've got a lot of things to see to. And there's something we need to get straight.'

'Go? So early?' Marty sat up, letting the bedclothes fall from her, deliberately exposing her well-shaped breasts.

'Yes.'

'Coffee first, at least.'

'Okay.

She got out of bed and pulled on the rust-coloured silky robe which hung behind the door. The ruffles around the neck were like an extension of her hair and followed the V to her cleavage. 'Don't rush, stay in bed, I'll bring it up to you,' she said as she tied the belt around her waist.

As soon as he heard the water running to fill the kettle, Laurence got up and pulled on his clothes. He wanted a shower, he wanted to wash away the smell of Marty and sex and his own guilt. It would have to wait until later.

'You should've stayed in bed,' Marty said when he went downstairs. Her smile was warm, seductive, but did not quite reach her eyes. Something was troubling him, she sensed it. 'Why do you have to leave so soon? You could stay here, you know, you can stay for as long as you want, until your next trip, if you like.' She saw him flinch and bit her lip, turning her back to get out the cups.

Something's wrong here, Laurence thought. All this, the way she is, the house, the furnishings, her clothes. Did she really inherit the money? He sat at the table and waited until his coffee was in front of him before he spoke. 'Marty,' he began, stirring in sugar, not meeting her eyes, 'I haven't been strictly fair with you. I should not have come here last night. I should have said as much over the phone.'

'Why ever not? You know you're always welcome. More than welcome. I think by now you know what I feel for you. It's been more than three years, Laurence. I always believed that we had an understanding, that you were just waiting until everything was sorted out properly and then we'd be together. You always said your marriage was a mistake.'

'No, I didn't. It was you who always said that, and that's one of the reasons it isn't fair for me to keep on seeing you. You've been under a misapprehension. It's my fault. I should've disabused you of it ages ago.'

Marty stood in front of the cooker, perfectly steady. The cup and saucer in her hands did not rattle, the steaming liquid did not spill. 'Why not, Laurence? Why isn't it fair when I'm so very happy?'

Her voice was light and deceptively calm. Laurence, imagining she was being reasonable, decided he would answer her honestly. 'Because I don't love you.'

'I see. Is it Hannah?'

'Yes. It's Hannah, but it's also Josh. Especially now.'

Marty put down her cup and saucer. She needed time to

137

think. Crossing the kitchen she stared out of the window. Sunlight now flooded the room. The slaughterhouse was visible, its heavy padlock glistening, still damp from the early morning dew.

'I knew you'd understand, Marty. I didn't want to hurt you, we've had some good times and I think too much of you for that.'

I didn't want to hurt you, Marty, she mimicked silently. Well, it's too late, you bastard. You have already done so. 'Of course I understand. I always suspected you'd never got over Hannah. Help yourself to some more coffee, I'm going to get dressed.' She smiled wanly. 'I don't want to say goodbye to you in a state of undress.'

With a sense of relief Laurence got up and refilled his cup. He would do the right thing by staying for a little while longer. He could hardly just walk out on her having delivered the bombshell. She had taken it better than he had imagined, although it was hardly flattering that she hadn't made a fuss, hadn't, as usual, begged him to stay.

Marty went into one of the bedrooms. It would never be used and was therefore furnished simply but only because she could not live with an empty room in the house. The only people to inhabit her four walls would be herself and Laurence. Or so she had thought. But since Laurence had shown such interest in the baby she had made sure the second spare bedroom was adequately furnished. There, in that spartan room on a rack screwed to the wall in the built-in cupboard, was her mother's shotgun. Once she had found it was still there she had cleaned and oiled it. No one but herself now knew of its existence. There was a box of ammunition on the shelf above the rack. She took some out, loaded both barrels then she went to her own room to get dressed.

Downstairs, she propped the gun against the hall wall on its butt. 'Where did you go yesterday?' she asked.

'I went to see Hannah. We had a row. Then I drove around for a while.'

And you came here later. I was the substitute, second

best to your ex-wife, Marty was thinking. How very charming of you to have pointed that out.

Laurence was hardly listening, he was thinking about Josh, about the innocence of the child he had disclaimed and what he might be going through. Was he hurt, miserable, starving or worse? Was he dead? And Hannah. Never had he witnessed a person carrying so much pain. 'Pardon?' Marty had spoken.

'I asked you if James was there. Is that why you argued, because of him?'

'Yes, he was there actually.' Laurence looked up, frowning. Marty didn't know Hannah, she knew nothing of his family except the little he had told her. 'How did you know about James?'

Marty was smiling. 'Does it matter? Oh, Laurence, there's an awful lot I could surprise you with.'

'Yes, it bloody well does matter.' Laurence was on his feet. Something was definitely wrong. For the first time since he had known her he felt afraid of her.

'Calm down, lover. I know you, remember? You don't want Hannah, you simply want what you can't have. She's with James now, she isn't yours any longer. You were the one that left, don't ever forget that. You should never have married her in the first place. Not when you could have had me.'

'No. You're wrong. You don't understand.' He no longer understood himself. He wanted only to walk out and never set eyes upon her again.

'I understand perfectly. It's your powers of reasoning which are diminished. This,' she said, gesturing wildly, 'all this was for you. The farm, the land, all of it. A ready-made home just as you had before. With her. You can't possibly know what I've been through to get it. But I earned it. Every single penny of it.' She was panting, sweat broke out across her brow. She mustn't go too far, not yet. Catching her breath she swept back her hair and leaned against the table. She felt weak but the effect must not be ruined now. She had dressed with care, wanting to look her best. The evening dress she had bought in Debenham's had been a success last night, the emerald linen one she wore now with strappy sandals was meant to have completed Laurence's capitulation. It had failed. But she was in possession of an alternative. 'What if I helped you find Josh? If he was safely returned to Hannah would you stay with me then? You could still see him, I wouldn't object.'

'Are you crazy?' Laurence was on his feet. 'How on earth can you help to find Josh? And, no, Marty, it's over. You have to understand that. You won't be seeing me again.' He would get his mobile number changed immediately.

Marty smiled. 'Wait there. There's something I want to show you.'

From outside the door she picked up the gun and raised it to her shoulder just as her father had taught her, just as she did when she shot rabbits. She aimed it into the kitchen. 'Laurence,' she said, 'go to the front door and open it.'

Laurence took three steps backwards. The heavy chair clattered to the floor behind him. 'Jesus Christ, Marty, what're you playing at?'

'This isn't a game, Laurence. You're the one who plays games. This gun is real and I know how to use it. Go to the door and open it.'

White-faced, he did as she had asked. Keeping her distance she threw him a key. 'Now go and unlock the slaughterhouse doors.'

'The what?'

'That building to the left of the house. There's no one for miles. If you try anything I'll kill you.'

Her voice was too level, too calm. He suddenly realized two things: that she was insane and that she meant what she said. Despite the remnants of mist rising from the fields he was sweating. His shaking fingers dropped the padlock key. He bent to retrieve it, fumbling on the ground, conscious of the twin barrels levelled at his shoulder blades.

'Open the door and throw down the key then go inside.'

Laurence blinked in the relative darkness of the interior. There was one tiny window, high up, out of reach. 'Wait.' The metal doors clanged shut. Over the reverberation he heard the smooth click as Marty secured the prong of the padlock and the rattle as she tested it. Taking a deep breath he tried to adjust to his surroundings and discover a way out. The window was set in one of the longer walls; opposite it was a plain wooden ladder leading to what was once an open-sided storage area. It was now bare. The ladder was fixed, but had it not been it was still too short to have reached the window.

Laurence froze. He had heard a small sound. He was not alone. There was also an unpleasant smell. Were there rats? He turned slowly. In the corner was some straw with a bundle of something lighter in colour on top of it.

Nearing the corner bile filled his throat. He swallowed hard. On the straw was a baby in a dirty white sleeping suit decorated with red fire engines. It was hardly breathing and covered in scratches from the straw. Beside it lay bread, dirt and dust embedded in the butter, and a beaker half full of milk. He knew with utter certainty even in the half-light that this was Josh, that this was his son and that Marty had taken him.

Never before had he experienced such uncontrollable rage, a desire to lash out and really hurt, to kill. What he had occasionally felt towards Hannah was nothing compared with this. But his rage left him as quickly as it had come. For now Josh was more important than Marty. Kneeling on the floor he studied the little face so like his own. He wanted to touch Josh, to hold him, but he wasn't sure if it was wise in case he was injured. 'How could she, the bitch? How could she do this to a baby?' And how did she know about Hannah and James?

He stood up, his knees cold from the cement floor. Of course, he could use his phone. But it wasn't in his jacket pocket. Nor was his key ring. Just as he did at his Dorset cottage, he had placed them on the worktop in Marty's kitchen because of the bulge they made in his clothes. They hadn't been there when he'd drunk his coffee. Marty had hidden them.

He had to think, he had to get them out of there before Josh died. You're a shit, an absolute shit, Laurence Peters, he told himself. How could I ever have believed I did not want this child to be born? His throat narrowed, there was a stinging sensation behind his nose. Because it was so long since he had felt such things he thought he was choking. But he was crying, his shoulders heaving as hot tears ran down his face. He lay on the hard floor next to his son and reached for his hand. It was ice-cold.

Marty's breath was ragged as she backed away from the slaughterhouse. How dare he treat her like that. Three years of her life she had given him. It had been a last resort to take the child but she hadn't harmed him.

When her breathing returned to normal she went back to the kitchen and sat at the table. Since she had moved into the farmhouse she had started to sleep properly, not waking every hour or so, troubled by nightmares or unfounded fears. Free-floating anxiety, the psychiatrist had called it. But what did he know? He had also told her her father's love was unnatural then, later, that he didn't believe she had been abused at all. She had not seen him again after that session.

I'm tired, she thought, tired of waiting, tired of the past. She thought back to that morning during the Easter holiday, the last day before she had to return to school, when she was sent to the field at the back to hoe between the rows of vegetables. She had not seen her father at breakfast. After an hour she was tired and thirsty and decided to stop and get a drink. On the way to the house she saw that the slaughterhouse doors stood open. She went to see why.

Gloria Rowland was standing, feet apart, a pick-axe held

high over her head. Marty watched in fascination as Gloria Rowland struck the second blow. 'Go back to the field, Marty,' her mother had said.

Mid-morning Marty and Gloria were in the kitchen when the post van arrived. Gloria went out to meet it. 'Nothing for you, Mrs Rowland. Couple of feed bills for your husband, by the look of it,' the postman commented as he always did.

'It'll be me that pays them. The bugger's run off with a woman from the village,' Gloria had told him, unaware that Marty had followed her outside and heard what she said. 'He won't be coming back, not this time.'

'I'm sorry to hear that, Mrs Rowland,' he had replied, too embarrassed to meet her eyes but revelling in this latest piece of gossip.

Even Marty knew the postman would not hesitate in spreading the news in the village, and farther afield around the farms as he went on his rounds. She had also witnessed the satisfaction on Gloria's face as the red van had bumped off down the path. Gloria stood watching its retreat, arms folded, a smug smile on her lips. It was frightening because Gloria never smiled. But no one would question what she said, Edward Rowland would not be missed. He was disliked in the village, the whole family was considered odd and to be avoided.

When Marty returned from school the next evening, tired because she had had to walk to and from the bus-stop now that her father had gone, the slaughterhouse doors stood wide open and Marty knew for certain what her mother had done.

Inside the house Gloria sat at the kitchen table, for once idle. Her hands and arms shook as she sipped her tea, the nerves quivering from the effects of strenuous exercise. When she replaced the mug in front of her Marty saw that her palms were raw, blistered from wielding the pick-axe she had used to loosen the earth of the slaughterhouse floor, to mix sand with the earth.

The following day she returned from school to find her

143

mother powdered in dust. She had used the bags of ready-mixed cement, delivered a week before, to cover the slaughterhouse floor. It was not very evenly spread, and it was still setting which was why the doors were left open again.

From that day on Marty hated her mother more than ever. It had not been Gloria's hands that had caressed her as a mother's should have done, but her father's. But she must have known. How could she not have done? Which meant that although she had silently colluded with her husband she had always been jealous and had therefore killed him.

Nothing was said, not about her father nor the concrete floor. Gloria knew her child would remain silent, had always remained silent, that everyone had already accepted the fact of Edward's disappearance with a woman from the village.

Gloria had worked as hard as Edward. There was no transitionary phase, she simply took over the running of the farm as if her husband had never existed. And she continued to remain silent, refusing to answer any questions Marty asked about him.

Marty was not streetwise like other girls her age and they had no television from which she might have learned what really went on in the world. She had been trained for obedience, sheltered so much from reality that nothing that happened at the farmhouse seemed out of the ordinary.

Despite her lack of friends Marty worked hard at school and when a careers officer came to talk to them she knew where her future lay. It meant living at home a while longer but it would be worth it.

The job made her happy but even after a flight proper sleep continued to elude her. In the sanctuary of hotel rooms, behind the locked doors, nightmares would wake her or sleep refused to come as she pictured the concrete floor of the slaughterhouse. She had told the psychiatrist and, later, the police what had happened but no one believed her.

Marty was hungry. She got up and refilled the kettle. 'I must feed the hens in a minute,' she muttered, 'they mustn't suffer because of Laurence.' Give him time and he'll come round, she thought as she placed two fresh eggs in a saucepan and lit the gas.

She looked out over the rolling countryside towards the edge of Dartmoor then she dropped her gaze to her own land. There were already vegetables ready for pulling.

I will forget Laurence and his brat for a whole hour, she decided. By lunchtime he'll have come to his senses. Having washed up and done the routine chores, she took coffee into what used to be called the front room. Marty had decided against carpet and had had the boards stripped, polished and varnished. There were rugs on the floor and matching curtains at the tall windows. The furniture was pale, all the upholstery was in shades of brown and green, peaceful, soothing colours, chosen to make the house seem like a continuation of what lay outside.

She ran a hand along surfaces, checking for dust. There was none. Central heating had been installed, and the gas fire – never again would she rake out fires or get coal grime beneath her nails.

Marty had suffered, now others would too. 'You mustn't judge your life against other people's, Marty, and you mustn't blame everyone else for your own shortcomings,' the psychiatrist had told her. 'There comes a time when we must put the past behind us and take responsibility for our own lives. Once that has been accomplished then you know you have reached adulthood.'

It was around that time that she had stopped going to see him. They had both known it was a futile exercise. Marty only accepted the things which fitted in with her own concept of herself. But on one thing she had taken him at his word. She was taking responsibility for her own life and she did not care what effect it had on anyone else. But he was wrong about blame. Only her mother was to blame.

She would not think of her parents. Not today, not when

she would soon have everything she wanted. Laurence would make up for the past. 'He will not get away,' she said loudly. No matter what he might be thinking he would not be able to stay away either. Marty could read his mind. He wasn't able to stay away when he was married, why should he do so now?

Only now, as she thought of Laurence and the child she had taken, did Marty wonder whether she had been wrong, whether Gloria Rowland had only discovered what her husband was like on the day she killed him and that the reason she did so was to protect her daughter from further abuse.

Chapter Ten

Gareth was back in the incident room by 7 a.m. Officers were already in the process of tracing the address of Marty's mother, who they knew had died within the last year. They had to hope that she had not remarried and changed her name.

If there was some sort of legacy it would explain how Marty was able to give up her job, Gareth thought, and why she was able to disappear. The hospitals had no record of the mother being admitted, in which case she had either been nursed at home or had died suddenly. And someone must know about it.

Don't build your hopes up, Gareth told himself, even though he had given the go-ahead for Hannah's parents to be informed that they had a new lead. What bothered him now was that he might be counting his chickens. Just because Marty had taken on someone else's identity did not mean she had also taken baby Josh. 'Jesus Christ,' he swore. 'If it's not her, then who is it?' And the longer they spent looking for Josh, the less chance they had of finding him alive.

At eight Gareth picked up the phone and rang Sonia Grant's number. She answered almost immediately. In the background a baby was crying, Sonia's baby. What was that sound doing to Hannah? 'Is Hannah still there?' He hoped so. She might take the news better in Sonia's company. The two women had obviously been reconciled.

'Yes. Hold on.'

'Hannah, we've been in touch with a Jennifer Greene, a

student nurse at the address you gave, but she isn't your friend. She's never met you.'

'What?'

'I know, it's hard to take in. Just listen to me for a moment, please.'

Hannah sat down, pulling Sonia's borrowed dressing-gown tightly around her body as Gareth began to speak. She felt tired and beaten. Marty. The name meant nothing to her. How badly she had been deceived. She had invited an impostor into her house, made her welcome, trusted her, and all the time her intentions had been evil.

'What we need is a photograph. Your parents have searched and can't find one. Do you have one, no matter how old?'

'No. No, I don't think I do.'

'It can't be helped. Did she ever mention her mother?'

Hannah thought for a moment. 'Not that I can remember. Wait, yes, she said her parents lived in Plymouth.'

But that would be in the guise of Jennifer Greene, Gareth realized. 'Did she ever meet Laurence?'

'No. We were already divorced by the time I met Jenn . . . I mean Marty.'

'Could they have met elsewhere?'

'It's possible. She was an air hostess and Laurence flies all over the place. Why?'

'Would she have known when he'd be away?'

'Well, I may have mentioned it in conversation. She knew he existed and my position, and Laurence usually managed to let me know in advance of his visits. Are you trying to tell me that Laurence might have told her when he'd be away?'

Anthony had stopped crying now that his bottle was ready. He sucked greedily on the teat, taking in air until Sonia tilted it. She kissed the top of his head, her hair falling over her face. Hannah felt such a pang of longing for Josh it seemed to envelop her. She sank back into the chair as if she was falling through a cloud. What if Josh never came home? What if he was already dead? Don't,

148

her brain screamed. Don't, don't, don't. Just listen to what Gareth has to say.

'It's only a possibility. You see, according to Pauline Peters, Laurence seems to have disappeared as well.'

'My God. Then he is involved?'

Gareth did not answer because he couldn't. He just did not know. 'Are you going to stay at Sonia's?' he said instead.

'No. I'm leaving as soon as I'm dressed.'

'Okay. I'll get back to you later, one way or another.'

'Thanks, Gareth.' Hannah replaced the receiver and sat without speaking for several minutes. Laurence and Marty, or Jenny as she had known her . . . Was it possible? She had never allowed herself to think about how he might spend his nights when he was away from her. But so close to home, and with a so-called friend – that was despicable. If it was true. Everything was still so uncertain. And had Marty befriended her deliberately, had she already known where Hannah lived and contrived that meeting on the footpath? Did she want both Hannah's husband and her son? Bile rose in her throat. She swallowed hard. I must not give in, whatever happens I must not do that, she vowed.

'What did he say?' Sonia pulled the bottle from Anthony's mouth and lifted him to her shoulder, rubbing his back in circular movements. He burped loudly and a dribble of milk ran down the sleeve of her silk kimono. At one time the mess would have horrified her.

Hannah repeated what Gareth had told her.

'Christ, the bitch. All that time pretending she was your friend. How could she do that to you?'

'They don't know for certain that she has done anything.'

'Come off it, Hannah, who else can it be? Who else knows their way around your house and garden? And look at the lies she's told.'

'You're right. But they don't know where to start looking. They don't even know where her mother lived.' Marty

149

had lied, Marty had taken her in. A pain shot through her chest. Marty was an evil bitch and Josh might be dead. 'Look, Sonia, thanks for putting me up but I need to go home.'

'Of course you do. Shall I come with you?' She stood up, Anthony's head lolling sleepily, still glamorous in her designer nightclothes but softer, the contentment that had always been missing now apparent in her face.

'No, really, I'll be fine.' Hannah reached out and hugged her, avoiding squashing the baby just as Sonia had once done with her and Josh.

Within fifteen minutes she was on her way. The return drive seemed to take for ever. Twice she checked her bleeper was on but no call came. She was restless, furious, and wanted to be out searching but there was nothing she could do, nowhere she could start looking, not when she had believed Jenny was in Bristol. What good was there in thinking at all? The pain and the waiting had become part of her, there seemed never to have been a time when that state had not existed.

Nothing had altered. The potholes in the lane still jolted the car, smoke rose from the chimney and the last few wisps of morning mist floated on the river. Hannah felt she had been away for days.

Joyce had heard the car and stood in the doorway, offering her arms to her daughter as she approached. Hannah did not respond, her body was rigid. 'I'll make you some coffee,' Joyce said, unsure how much her daughter knew. They had almost run out of supplies. No one had shopped. All they had eaten was the odd sandwich or something from the freezer. And no one had touched the sealed plastic containers in the fridge which contained food Hannah had cooked for Josh, mashed up adult food. Inedible now, but no one had the heart throw out the contents; it would seem too much like tempting fate.

It was warm outside but Hannah went to the fire and held out her hands. The iciness of fear remained in her veins. Her father looked haggard, James more so as he had

150

not shaved. He had now become accepted as part of the group, one of those who waited, sometimes in despair, at other times with hope.

They sipped the coffee that nobody wanted as Hannah repeated her conversation with Gareth. Disgust and shock were obvious in all three faces.

'And to think I liked the girl!' Joyce said. 'She was always so friendly.' But if that was the lead the female detective had mentioned she didn't think it would get them very far.

James wasn't listening. He rubbed the side of his nose with a finger, something he did when he was thinking. 'Marty. It's an unusual name, but I've got a feeling I've heard it somewhere before.'

'Think, James,' Phillip said sharply, standing up as if this action might encourage him to do so.

He shook his head and sighed. 'No, sorry. It escapes me at the moment.'

Sonia had been as horrified as Hannah when she learned the real identity of Jenny, so it was not from her that James had heard the name Marty. 'Or maybe I read it.' His head jerked up. What on earth had made him say that? The memory was near the surface. He closed his eyes, willing it to surface completely.

'The newspaper. Do you think you might have read it in the newspaper, James?' Hannah had grabbed his arm. 'I mean, if her mother died suddenly, an accident, say, it might've been reported.'

'Calm down, darling.' Joyce believed she was clutching at straws. Hannah's eyes had the dangerous glitter of a fanatic. Before long her daughter would be in need of psychiatric treatment. Maybe they all would.

'That's it.' James grinned. 'You've got it. There was a report in the *Evening Herald*. There had been an accident, I can't recall exactly what, and they were able to release the name of the deceased because the next of kin had been contacted.'

'Can you remember roughly when this was?' Hannah

had not relinquished her grip. Her nails bit into James's flesh.

'Last year sometime. The daughter's name was definitely Marty, but whether it was Rowland I couldn't say.' Within seconds James was speaking to Inspector Chambers, repeating what he hoped he had recalled accurately. He was filled with relief. He was doing something, he was being useful, what he had remembered might help to bring Josh back. If it did, would Hannah still want him? Make it all right, he prayed. Let him be safe. Let Hannah love me again. 'Yes, it was definitely the *Evening Herald*,' he repeated. 'God, let me think . . . Sometime in the summer it would've been.

'They're already looking into it,' James said, returning to his armchair. 'The police in Exeter have come up with similar information because it was them who had the task of tracing Marty. And it all fits in with what they already know. Apparently no one knew where the daughter was because she hadn't kept in touch with her mother since the day she left home. However, the officers trying to trace her at the time inquired in the village and discovered she worked for an airline. It's got to be the same person.' He paused. 'They now have an address for the mother.'

'Thank God.' Joyce seemed to sag a little. Was it possible the waiting was over?

'If she came into money or property, that would explain everything. She'd be able to disappear without having to worry about a job,' Hannah said excitedly. The girl she had known as Jenny Greene had been good with Josh. He might still be safe and well, especially if Laurence was with them, too.

'If she did inherit she may well have sold up and used the money to go elsewhere.' Phillip knew it was far too early for the optimism which had affected them all. He must play the devil's advocate. The girl might have left the country, she might not have Josh, Josh might be dead. He knew how radically things had altered, that now almost a week had passed they were allowing themselves to think the unthinkable; that Josh might not be found. Hannah would collapse if she had to face another disappointment. And if Josh was dead he and Joyce would also lose their only child because Hannah would never recover.

But they could talk of nothing else. No one left the lounge that morning. They watched as the few remaining clouds drifted away exposing a bright blue sky. It seemed like an omen.

Two hours later they had still heard nothing. The waiting had dispirited them and a mood of depression settled over the room once more. The police had an address for a farmhouse in Devon. They must have reached it by now. No one dared to think how they would feel if it was discovered to be empty.

'That's where the money came from, her mother's estate,' Gareth said with satisfaction immediately the information was faxed through from the offices of the local press. The address of the property was named in the paper. Lower Denntiscombe Farm. Better still, they had spoken to John Lavant, the family solicitor, who had confirmed a considerable sum of money had been involved as well as the property.

'If she's not at the farm find out everything you can about this woman, where she went to school, friends, talk to the people she worked with at the airline, medical records, anything.' Gareth was already on his feet. Having checked a large-scale map of the area they were on their way to Lower Denntiscombe Farm.

He thought as they drove, his car followed by two others. As yet, there had been no sighting of Laurence Peters' mother's car. He and Marty might have taken Josh away to some other hiding place. They might have killed him, his little body never to be found. This was what they always dreaded most in such cases.

'Damn it.'

'What?' He turned to the driver, who was muttering under his breath.

'I've missed the turning.'

'Oh, Christ.' Gareth shook his head. He must remain calm, they must all remain calm. They had no idea what they might find at Lower Denntiscombe Farm.

There was nowhere to back up, not with two cars following. They had to go on, to waste precious minutes while they found a gateway wide enough in which to make a three-point turn before retracing their route.

What sort of a woman was Marty Rowland? he wondered. Just how much was she capable of? Clever, clever Marty Rowland. But, hopefully, not clever enough, because they had tracked her down. Or hoped they had. Let her be there, please let her be there. And let Josh be safe, he thought as they wound their way through the country lanes, three cars in a grim procession.

Marty had placed Laurence's phone and car keys in the cutlery drawer. She now removed the keys and went back outside. She unlocked the car and got in, adjusting the driver's seat until her feet were able to reach the pedals. The engine started first time. The car could not be seen from the road and it was too late for the postman, his van had passed earlier, but it was better to be safe and park it somewhere out of sight.

At the rear of the house was a tangled hedge of bramble overhung by a row of trees. It would suffice as a temporary hiding place. If things didn't work out she would need a permanent one. She could, of course, drive up to the flooded gravel-pit and push it over the side. The water was deep and milky green and children were forbidden to play anywhere near it. As a small girl Marty was the only one who had dared to go up there. She had often wondered what lay at the bottom of it, what secrets it held. One more wouldn't matter; if she had to kill Laurence, that is. She laughed. How strange to have thought of digging him a

154

grave and wasting all that energy. How much simpler to strap him into the driving seat and push the car over the side. If there were fish in those murky depths they would be well fed for quite a long time.

Give him a bit of time and he'll come round, she thought, as the off-side wheels slid into the damp grass in the narrow ditch beneath the hedge. The ambiguity of her feelings did not strike her as odd. That he would take exception to being locked up at gunpoint did not cross her mind, nor had she allowed for his feelings for the child. All that she thought and did seemed rational. She had come so close to having all she had wanted that nothing must now stand in her way.

Swinging the car keys she walked back past the hen-house, avoiding the muddy patches, amused at the busy clucking and hustling around her ankles. 'He knows I've got the child, therefore he knows the power I've got over both of them,' she told the unheeding birds. Her original plan had backfired. Laurence was supposed to have jumped at the chance of moving in. Maybe she ought to talk to him right away and get things straight.

But I don't have to kill the baby, she realized. If it starves to death it isn't murder. The same applied to Laurence. The slaughterhouse was safe, he could not escape however hard he tried, and in a few days he would be too weak even to attempt it. 'You're very clever, Marty, you think of everything,' she said. Daddy, Mummy, Hannah's baby and Laurence. All of them would have come to an end in the place that had been special to her.

The soft wind blew her hair around her shoulders. She could smell the lemon-scented shampoo she had used yesterday and a hint of Laurence's sweat. It was a beautiful day. Only good things could happen on such a day.

The sun glinted on her nails, which were painted a greeny gold. She had done them yesterday to tone in with the soft folds of the shimmering bronze silk and chiffon evening dress, the dress she had slipped off her shoulders and let fall to the floor. How could Laurence not love her when he had looked at her like that? She admired her nails as she went around to the kitchen entrance; fingers splayed, she held her hand this way and that. No outside work today, no washing-up without gloves on. She must not chip the polish because Laurence would come to his senses and she wanted to look her very best for him.

She hung his car keys next to her own. There was no one to miss Laurence, not now that he lived alone in Dorset. She didn't know quite where, he had never said. She frowned, angry with him again. He hadn't told her he'd bought a new car either. How long shall I give him? Another hour? No, that was too long. She picked up the gun and the slaughterhouse keys and went outside.

'I'm opening the door,' she shouted. 'Get to the back with the child and don't move. I've got the gun.' There was no response, no sound at all. Marty unlocked the door and pushed it open slowly to allow her eyes to adjust. 'That's good,' she said, seeing Laurence sitting next to his son. 'I need to talk to you.'

'I can't imagine we've got anything left to say. Josh is barely alive, Marty. Haven't you got a heart? You'll go to prison for murder.' There was desperation in his voice. How could he have thought he knew this woman?

'Oh, I don't think so. Only you know he's here and if you don't do as I want you won't be in a position to tell anyone.' She remained in the doorway, her figure silhouetted against the sunlight, the gun aimed at the corner. 'You said your next job isn't for several weeks, who's going to miss you? Certainly not Hannah.'

My parents, he thought. Surely they'll begin to wonder when I don't return the car. But they would have no idea where to look, nor would anyone else.

'My father died in here. So did my mother. She killed him and I killed her. For you, Laurence, for all this.' She did not lower the gun to gesticulate. 'What do you think about that? We both, as they say, got away with murder. And I can do it again.'

He did not answer. He believed her and recognized in

those seconds that she was truly insane. Instead he asked, 'Why did you take him? Why did you take my son?'

'Your son? Since when has he been yours, my darling? You wanted him aborted. You told me. Think back, Laurence, think back to the night we met. Do you know what you've put me through, seeing me on and off over three years, letting me believe we'd be together one day? I'll never forget the day you showed me Hannah's photograph and said she was your wife. And you ask me if I've got a heart. I could shoot you both right now and no one would be any the wiser.' Her finger tightened on the trigger. Laurence held his breath.

'Why shoot me if you want me to stay with you? I'll stay, Marty, if you let Josh go. I'll do anything you say.'

'I can't let him go now, can I? I'll still be arrested. He'll starve to death, he won't feel a thing. Look at him, it's like he's asleep.'

'But you've kept him alive so far. That'll go in your favour.'

Marty laughed. 'Oh, sure. Then the minute I'm arrested you'll be running back to Hannah. I'll bury him somewhere. We could plant something, a tree in his memory.' She imagined its roots sinking deeper, seeking nourishment which they would find in the decomposing flesh and then, replete, those roots would twine themselves around the bones of Hannah's baby. He wouldn't go into the gravel-pit with his father, if she decided to kill him, she wouldn't give either of them that satisfaction.

'Marty, just tell me why you took him. If I can understand that, maybe we can work something out.'

She frowned because she didn't know the answer. Insurance, maybe, for just such a situation as this.

'Did you hate Hannah that much? Is that it?'

'Partly.' Yes, she had wanted to punish her because of Laurence, because she thought Hannah still had a hold over him, but she wasn't sure what had prompted her to go to the house that day. Laurence had been due back at any time. Perhaps, deep down, she had known he

157

wouldn't live with her, perhaps she had intended using the child as blackmail, as she was actually doing.

'Or was it to make sure I stayed? Make a phone call, Marty, just one, to anyone you like. Anonymously. Use my mobile then you won't need to go anywhere where there are people. Leave Josh somewhere and tell them where he can be found. You can leave me locked in here, but just do it, please.'

'Maybe.' The gun had not wavered, it remained steady in her hands, pointing at a spot between Laurence and Josh.

'I thought I knew you, Marty. I was wrong. How did you meet Hannah?' He wanted to keep her talking, to watch for a second when her guard might come down. He needed time to think of a way out for himself and Josh, but he did not doubt she would use the gun if he tried to get it off her.

'That was down to you. You boasted about your lovely house and where it was, and, of course, you'd shown me that picture. It wasn't hard to find her. I wanted to meet her, I wanted to see where you had lived. I was often at your house, Laurence. I know all about you and your wife and her friends. I've touched your things, Laurence, the things you used when you lived with her. I've waited all this time for you and this is how you repay me.

'I was so happy when you said you were getting divorced. I thought once it was all sorted out you'd come to me.' She stopped. She had said too much. 'I'll be back. Just think what you've done, just think about your part in all this.' She turned and in one quick movement had shut the door and locked it.

I'll make the bed, she decided. Everything'll be ready for later, when he realizes his mistake. We'll have another night like last night. She went upstairs and leaned on the windowsill. Everything was going to be all right.

For three years she had wanted him and lived in the hope he would leave Hannah. But when he had told her that his wife was pregnant Marty believed she had lost him for ever, until he mentioned the abortion. He had left his wife, divorced her, but made no move to live with Marty, so she decided to arrange a meeting, to hear Hannah's side. How Marty had laughed listening to Hannah when, in the early days, she said she missed Laurence and wanted him back. But all that had changed. It was the child Hannah wanted back now.

She had seen through Laurence almost immediately. He enjoyed the good things in life. Despite his well-paid job he would not come to her unless, like Hannah, she was able to provide them. To do so she had had to kill her mother, the means to money and property. It had been so very easy.

But what to do about the child? Laurence was right. She could dump it somewhere then telephone to say where it was. And it might die before anyone reached it, she would have gained nothing then. 'You bastard.' Her teeth were grinding. Laurence had tried to trick her. He had wanted her to do that, to take the child somewhere isolated and ring the police from his mobile phone. They would be able to trace the call to within a radius of a couple of miles, they would know whose phone it was and then they would come for her. She would never have risked using her own. No. It was too late. She would not do it. Laurence would soon get over the death of his son. And Hannah would forget Laurence once she knew her baby was never coming home. 'Let him stew a bit longer,' she said as she turned to smooth out the sheets and shake the duvet.

The bedroom window, like all the others, was open. She had been brought up used to plenty of fresh air. In the distance she heard a car. The driver dropped a gear to negotiate the narrow lanes with their sharp bends. Then she heard a second car. She frowned. It was unusual, little traffic used the road at the end of the farmhouse lane. Opening the window wider, she leaned out over the sill and listened. The breeze blew from the south, carrying the sounds clearly towards her, rippling the crops in the fields. There were more than two cars. She held her breath. Something was wrong. Something was very wrong indeed.

She ran down the stairs and picked up the gun. The key to the slaughterhouse hung on a hook by the front door. She grabbed it. The cars were approaching the entrance to the farm lane. She could see the tops of them over the hedge. If they passed by, all would be well. She stood still listening, holding her breath again. They did not pass by.

She sprinted across the cobbles and screamed through the door, 'Don't move, don't say a word. You make one sound and you're both dead. And I'll kill the baby first.'

The cars were coming closer. She had to hide the gun. The first car was already in sight now, it was turning in at the gate. There was only one place she could think of. Marty stepped to the side of the building and rested the shotgun against the wall behind the water barrel. She moved away quickly, breathing deeply, flexing her fingers, trying to compose herself. She fixed a smile on her face just as the first car drew to a halt and four men got out and approached her.

Laurence had heard the cars. He stroked Josh's head and talked to him in whispers. He did not believe that his son would live, or himself for that matter. 'It's a reprieve,' he whispered, stroking Josh's dirty hair. 'That's all this is.'

But was it the police? Were they looking for him and Josh, or was it someone entirely different, builders, maybe, coming to do more work on the place? It hardly seemed to matter. His whole life had been a mess and he had made it so. If he could somehow save Josh then maybe it wouldn't have all been in vain,

He was lying on the straw, his body against the tiny one next to him, trying to instil some heat into it. Josh was unnaturally cold and his breathing was very shallow. Once or twice his eyelids fluttered. Several times Laurence had pushed the spout of the beaker containing milk into Josh's mouth, very gently, sniffing it first in case it was sour. He wasn't sure if he'd swallowed any but at least his lips were wet.

'Where did it start to go wrong, Josh?' he whispered. Way back, he realized.

He cursed himself for giving Marty his mobile phone number. She'd ring and beg him to see her, just one last time. He would give in and they'd end up in bed. The cycle kept repeating itself. They were as bad as one another. But what a mistake it had been, letting her know that he and Hannah had separated. What a scene she had made. He really ought to have ended it then.

'Look, I can't just walk out of one relationship straight into another,' he had said as his excuse. 'Give it time and we'll see how we go.' He had known, even then, that he could not live with her on a permanent basis, but her temper was such that he had taken the easy way out. And this situation was his fault entirely, he ought to have refused to see her last night. 'But I wouldn't have known you were here, would I, Josh. Oh, God.' Saying his name brought more tears to his eyes. He wiped them on the back of his now dirty hand.

Sounds filtered through to him. Outside, people were talking but their voices were too indistinct and muffled for him to hear what they were saying. Did Marty still have the gun? Was she aiming it at someone else now? Dare he risk calling out? Yes, he could protect Josh with his own body if necessary.

He stood up and walked towards the heavy metal doors knowing that he had nothing more to lose. The son he had hardly known was dying, the wife he had undervalued had found someone else, someone better. Even as he walked towards the doors, even in this single heroic action in what might be the last seconds of his life, Laurence admitted that Hannah would not have had to look far to find someone better.

Gareth got out of the car. Other officers followed from the cars behind.

'Marty Rowland?' he asked.

She was smiling, smiling at this medium-sized man with greying hair who wasn't a patch on Laurence. 'Yes. That's me.'

'I'm Inspector Chambers.' Jennifer Greene had given a description of Marty. It was accurate but she had not made it clear quite how strikingly beautiful the woman was. Unexpectedly, she was wearing an expensive emerald linen dress which accentuated her shapeliness. Her nails were painted a sort of gold and her amber necklace and ear-rings were the same rich colour as her sandals. Hardly the gear for working a farm.

'We're investigating the disappearance of a baby. Josh Peters, Hannah's baby. We know you and Hannah were friends so we thought you might be able to help.' Go in gently if you find her, his superintendent had advised. Get her co-operation if you can. Don't do anything to make her act rashly, to make her harm the child or somebody else, or refuse to tell them his whereabouts. But they didn't know if Josh was alive.

'What on earth made you think that?' Her eyes widened and she directed her smile towards the man beside Gareth, who looked more susceptible to female charm than the stern-faced inspector.

'You told Mrs Peters that you were going to Bristol to become a nurse. You also lied to her about your identity, using the name of a woman you'd worked with, and now her baby is missing. This is the obvious place to start looking, wouldn't you say?'

'Look, this is all a stupid mistake. Yes, I did lie, but only about my name.' You're a fucking bitch, Jenny Greene, you told them, she thought. When I get out of this I'll kill you, too. 'I wanted her to think I'd gone away because, if you must know, my life has been shit up until now. When I heard that my mother had died I saw my chance, I could come back here and live by myself just as I've always wanted to do if ever I had enough money. I thought it was easier to let everyone think I'd moved away. Hannah would only have tried to keep in touch, she'd have wanted to come here, you see. No one can come here except me. And Laurence.' Too late she realized what she'd said.

Laurence Peters. Was he there as they spoke? In the house, maybe, or running across the fields, trying to hide his son? Had they planned all this between them? 'Your mother died last year, didn't she?'

'Yes.' Her throat tightened. They know, she thought, somehow they've guessed. But she was cremated, they can't do much about it now. If I left any marks on her they won't find them. Not won't, didn't. There must have been a post-mortem.

'May we take a look around, Miss Rowland?'

'Of course.' She started to walk towards the house. Thank God she'd hidden Laurence's car and his phone. There were no outbuildings behind the house, only at the side of it. If they went up to the back bedroom there would be nothing in the view to interest them and they'd probably think the car was hers. She'd come into money, they knew that, she could afford two. But how had they found her? No one but John Lavant knew where she was, not even Laurence until yesterday.

'Outside first, I think.' Gareth was testing her. He had seen the padlock on the concrete building. They had a search warrant anyway.

'Outside. If you're telling me you think I've got Hannah's child and that I'd keep him outside then you're dafter than I thought you were. Besides, you'll disturb the hens and they'll stop laying.'

'Break down the door.' Gareth nodded towards the slaughterhouse. Three men came from behind him; one of them held a crowbar in his hand. The other two approached Marty.

'There's no need for that.' Marty handed over the key then took several steps backwards. As soon as the door was open she reached for the gun and picked it up. Pushing one of the approaching officers to one side she aimed the gun at Gareth. 'They're mine. To do what I like with. Don't you understand that? They belong to me. Laurence and I are going to get married. Now go.'

As if in a trance, she watched the officers close in on her. Hadn't they heard what she said?

'Put down the gun,' Gareth said quietly, feeling the knot of fear in his stomach. They had got this all wrong. They had not taken into account the possibility that she might be armed. He might even die. They all might. 'For everyone's sake, put down the gun, please, Marty.'

Gareth held his breath. They, she had said. She and Laurence were going to get married. Then Peters was definitely here and so was Josh.

Marty spun round and aimed the gun towards the interior of the slaughterhouse. 'Go away,' she shouted over her shoulder. 'Leave now or I'll kill the baby.'

'Miss Rowland, please put down the gun.' There was a note of desperation in Gareth's voice. She meant what she said. To lose Josh now would be devastating. 'You know we can't leave. Don't make things harder for yourself.'

'Don't make things harder for yourself,' she mimicked. As if they could be.

Marty lowered the muzzle of the gun but she did not put it down. Instead she aimed it into the corner where Josh lay.

From inside the building her shape was clearly outlined, as were those of the figures behind her. Laurence, who had staggered back in relief when the doors were flung open, had seen the police. Now he saw where the shotgun was pointing. Directly at Josh. He ran towards Marty, using his own body as cover for the ice-cold one of his child as she fired. He heard shouting and running footsteps followed

164

by an explosion. But he felt nothing more than a jolt as the cartridge sank into his flesh. A second shot followed immediately.

Marty laughed, a high, insane laugh. Afterwards, no one could say with any accuracy what had taken place during the preceding seconds.

Chapter Eleven

Hannah was incoherent, laughing and crying at the same time. They had found Josh. Josh was on his way to hospital as they spoke. And Laurence. They both needed urgent treatment but they were safe. 'No,' Gareth said from his mobile phone, 'we don't know the extent of Laurence's injuries yet.'

Hannah hung up but her hand still gripped the receiver. Suddenly she was unable to move. But Josh was ill, very ill. Children are resilient, she told herself. They recover quickly. And he hadn't been harmed, only mistreated; half-starved, dehydrated and filthy. Could he survive?

As they made their way outside, Hannah could not recall what Gareth had said about Marty.

Phillip realized that only he was capable of handling a car and no one wanted to waste time waiting for a taxi to come. His daughter was on the verge of collapse, his wife was barely controlling herself and James looked as though he might pass out.

Derriford Hospital lay on the outskirts of the city, a vast complex which served a wide area. Hannah's limbs shuddered throughout the journey but she remained silent, her lips pressed tightly together. Joyce in the back seat beside her held her hand.

Phillip parked and they walked towards the building. Gareth and a WPC waited at the main entrance for them. Wordlessly, they were escorted to intensive care. Heads turned at the sight of the uniform as they walked down the corridors.

Another deputation awaited them outside the IT unit. It consisted of two doctors with grim faces. One approached Hannah, removing his hands from deep in the pockets of his white coat as he did so. 'Mrs Peters?' he inquired softly.

Hannah nodded, her expectant smile fading. She was dissolving. If she didn't see Josh within the next thirty seconds she would be nothing but a pool of water on the floor. She gripped her mother's arm to stop herself from fainting.

'Mrs Peters, we did everything we could but . . .'

The corridor lights spun wildly overhead and there was a buzzing in Hannah's ears.

'I'm very sorry, he died five minutes ago, it . . .'

They were the only words which registered, Hannah had not heard the rest of the sentence. She sank to the ground before anyone could catch her.

They were seated on opposite sides of the desk, Gareth Chambers and Detective Sergeant Angela Horsefall on one side, Marty Rowland on the other. To Marty's left sat her lawyer, not John Lavant, but Alastair Greenaway, a criminal lawyer from the same firm. He had had a few minutes alone with his client to introduce himself and advise her. This accomplished and the formal pre-interview procedure over, Gareth began.

'Why did you take Josh Peters?' he asked.

Marty shrugged. 'I don't know.'

'But you admit you took him.'

'You know that I did.'

'Was it planned, is that why you befriended Hannah?'

'No. We met by chance. I don't know why it happened.'

She's lying, he thought, but there's no way to prove it. Already he sensed that her solicitor had advised her that she might get away with a plea of insanity. 'How long have you known Laurence Peters?'

'About three years. We were having an affair.'

'An affair. But didn't you hope it would develop into rather more than that?'

'Yes.'

'But Laurence didn't want to know so you held him at gunpoint and locked him in the shed.'

'The slaughterhouse. It's called the slaughterhouse.'

'Because you intended to kill people there?'

Marty laughed. Even under the harsh light in the windowless room and despite the circumstances, she was still beautiful. 'Of course not. My great-grandfather used to kill pigs there.'

'And your mother died there.'

'Yes.' Marty lowered her head.

'Do you miss her, your mother?'

'I don't see where these questions are leading,' Alastair Greenaway interrupted. He had not met Marty until that day and had been surprised at her determination. 'I see no reason not to answer their questions,' she'd told him. 'They'll probably be easier on me if I do.' Then she had smiled and he had capitulated. Miss Rowland seemed to know exactly what she was doing.

'It might be relevant,' Gareth replied. It might even be in your client's interests, he thought but did not say.

'Not miss her, no. We never really got on and we lost touch after I left home.'

'Why was that?'

'She was a cold woman. She was jealous of me. My father loved me more than her and she knew it. That's why she killed him. She buried him in the slaughterhouse beneath the concrete.'

Alastair met Gareth's eyes. They were both thinking the same thing. Marty Rowland was out to prove she was insane.

'What makes you say that?'

'I was there. I was fifteen at the time. It was the last day of the Easter holidays and Dad didn't appear for breakfast. My mother told the postman he'd run off with a woman from the village but I saw her with that pick-axe and she started cementing that floor the very next day.'

'Did you tell anyone about this?'

'Yes. My psychiatrist, and, later, the police. No one believed me. No one believed how much Dad loved me. That stupid shrink said I was fantasizing about my father. How can that be when all I did was to love him back?' She took a deep breath. 'I'm sorry, I didn't mean to shout. I just wish there was someone who understood me.'

'Interview halted at 15.11 hours. Detective Sergeant Horsefall is leaving the room.' Gareth switched off the tape.

Angela Horsefall shut the door behind her quietly. She knew exactly what was expected of her, she must check the records for March and April of 1986 to see if there had been any report of a murder or a missing person and then she would get on to Marty's old school. If she was fifteen a child psychiatrist would probably have been involved.

The interview was resumed at ten to six; by which time they had read the initial notes taken by the psychiatrist and the police report in which Marty had claimed her father had been murdered by her mother. How on earth had Gloria Rowland coped with that? What a thing for a child to do. No wonder they had grown apart. Unless, he thought, it was true. Maybe killing ran in the family. But the police had seemed satisfied at the time even if they hadn't, at Marty's suggestion, dug up that concrete floor.

'She'll get away with it,' Gareth said before Marty was brought back into the room. 'She knows exactly what she's doing.'

'All right, Marty. You've admitted you took Josh, tell us how you did it.'

'I was going to see Hannah but I was almost at her house before I realized she'd be at work. I thought I could see Josh anyway. I parked at the end of the lane and walked around the back way. It was a lovely afternoon. Josh was in his pram in the garden. He was just lying there, asleep.' She paused and shook her head. 'He looked so beautiful. I picked him up. I – well, I don't remember anything after that until I got home.'

'You had a car seat?'

'No. I might have put him on the floor or strapped him into the seat-belt. I really don't know.'

'And when you got him home?'

'I put him in the slaughterhouse. It's my favourite place, you see. I thought he'd be happy there like I was with Dad. I fed him and gave him milk and I changed him a couple of times. I thought he'd be all right, I thought he'd like living with me. I'd look after him like Dad looked after me.'

You're a lying bitch, was Gareth's instinctive reaction. You took him to spite Hannah, to cause her maximum pain because you couldn't have her husband. And then you turned the whole thing around and used Josh to try to keep Laurence. But what jury would think as he did? They didn't know Hannah, they had no idea what she'd been through and when they saw Marty, especially if she filled her eyes with tears as she was now doing, how could they ever think ill of her?

But there was a second subject to deal with, one of which Marty was still unaware. It was time to introduce it and to see what reaction it provoked.

After stoppages for drinks and food, all of which Marty accepted, it was nearly midnight before they had a complete statement. Everything had been covered, there were no loopholes. And Marty was still smiling. What she had done seemed not to have affected her either mentally or physically. In her green linen dress she might have been going out for the evening. In the morning she would be questioned again by another team of detectives and then she would undergo psychiatric assessment.

'If she isn't mad she can certainly play the part,' Gareth said to Angela as they prepared to go home.

'There's no remorse, sir, or, at least, no outward sign of it. And all that stuff about the past – no psychiatrist will be able to say she's normal.'

170

Treatment, not prison, Gareth thought. And for how long? Until it was considered she was no longer a danger to herself or others, and if Marty Rowland was the actress he believed her to be, if she could convince people it was some sort of a crime of passion and never likely to happen again, what then? How did Hannah's future look? Not that Hannah would care for the moment.

Chapter Twelve

James had been given a key to Hannah's house and had gone on ahead of the others. His standing with Hannah was no longer clear. She might have reason to despise him. Now that Laurence had proved himself, one desperately brave action wiping out the sins of the past, he would be forgiven, maybe reinstated in Hannah's heart. It was Laurence who had saved Josh, James who had, in a way, been responsible for losing him. Time, he thought, that old adage about time being on your side, but I've got plenty of that, I can wait. Hannah was worth waiting for. She would not want Josh out of her sight. James, indeed everyone, would be very much in second place for a long time. She had already said she would not be going back to work but there was the question of how she was to live. Even if Laurence had made a will during the time of their marriage, he had probably altered it upon their divorce. Not that it mattered, he had nothing much to leave apart from the property in Dorset and his car which someone had arranged to collect from Southampton. Money had run through his hands.

They had stayed by Josh's side throughout the first night. All of them, silently praying to whatever divinity they might or might not have believed in. Pauline and Andrew had arrived soon after them. Pauline, her lips clamped together to stop herself from crying, had simply reached out to Hannah and held her. No words were spoken, there had been no need. Later, sometime during the early hours, she had taken Hannah's hand. 'It was better this way, it had to be this way. Laurence lived his life the way he wanted to. It may not have been the right way, but it was his choice. Josh was never given any choice.'

Hannah had stayed for the next two nights, wishing to be on her own with her son. It had been touch and go but Josh was tough and had been well taken care of before Marty abducted him. And now he was coming home. He was lucky, he would never remember anything of all this. The rest of them would have to live with it. Pauline and Andrew especially.

The previous day James had left the family at the hospital and returned to his own flat. It had felt cold, unlived-in and unwelcoming. From there he had telephoned all the people who were waiting for news: Sonia, the college where Hannah taught, Lorna and her husband, Joyce's school where the staff had also been anxiously waiting, Phillip's company, Valerie Mayhew who had broken down in relief over the phone and, lastly, George Allison.

'Thank God,' George had said. 'That poor woman was distraught. I've never seen anyone in such a state, I thought she was heading for a breakdown.' He had hesitated before asking, 'James, it wasn't Sonia, was it?'

'No. Not Sonia.' James was very fond of George, he was like an older brother, but he had to respect Sonia's wishes even if he only knew of them through Hannah. For the moment, Sonia did not want to be found. He hung up, relieved that George hadn't questioned him further. He would have hated to have had to lie.

James opened Hannah's front door. The first thing he did was to light the fire. It had gone out but that was all right. Josh was safe now, it was no longer a talisman. Outside, the rain was sweeping across the river and hitting the windows in violent bursts. Long snakes of water slid down the glass. The ground was sodden, puddles lying on its surface where it had reached saturation point. As if in relief, the heavens had opened an hour after Josh was pronounced out of danger. It had rained ever since.

James watched the trees swaying as showers of raindrops fell from their leaves. Hannah's house was isolated but it wasn't lonely. It felt like a home, she had made it one. He boiled the kettle although he was not expecting them for at least another half-hour then he set out a tray. There were no biscuits for Josh but there was jam and fresh bread and butter which he had bought on the way from his flat, and a packet of chocolate buttons.

It seemed an eternity before he did hear the car, the sound of its engine barely discernible over the hissing of rain.

'This reminds me of the last time I drove you back from hospital,' Phillip said as he glanced yet again in the rear-view mirror after they had turned into the lane. He had seen the smoke rising from the chimney and smiled because it was James who was there to welcome them this time. Not Sonia and Lorna but a man who loved his daughter. Joyce was beside him, Hannah was in the back and Josh was strapped into his car-seat, his mother's hand on his chubby leg. She could feel his warmth, his living being through the thick cord of his dungarees.

'He was a bit smaller then,' Hannah replied, stroking his hair back from his face. She had not stopped touching him since she was led, trembling and tearful, to his cot in intensive care. It's not Josh who is dead, was the refrain which had run through her mind during that seemingly endless walk to his bedside. They had found him just in time; starving and dehydrated and filthy, his bottom raw, but not injured, no bruises other than those he might have inflicted upon himself crawling about in the straw. Hannah could not bear to picture him in that lonely outhouse. I'll be able to tell him his daddy was a hero, she thought, sadly. Because no matter what Laurence had been like, no matter how many other women there had been, he had tried to keep Josh alive by giving him milk and in the end he had sacrificed his own life for that of his son.

The gun had gone off. No one was certain who it had finally been aimed at, if at anyone, but Laurence, only a yard from Marty, had taken the full impact of the blast. He had lived long enough to reach the hospital, to mutter a few phrases, to hear that his son was alive and then, as if he was tired of the world, or himself, he had closed his eyes and died. Hannah had not had the chance to thank him, to say goodbye to him. Nor had his parents who had arrived fifteen minutes too late.

The car doors slammed and they went inside, Hannah hurrying, protecting Josh from the rain with her body in the same way in which Laurence had protected him from gunfire. He struggled in her arms, anxious to re-explore his home. Water dripped from her hair and ran down her face.

'Bloody hell,' Phillip said, wiping his feet on the mat. 'It's a deluge.'

The sky had darkened and the rain fell in torrents, splashing back up off the ground, obscuring their view of the river. But no one cared. Josh was safe. They were safe. They were home.

Hannah put Josh on the floor in the lounge, having smiled her thanks at James who had already fixed the big guard around the fire. Josh was immediately on all fours, as if he was marking out his territory. He crawled across the carpet and pulled himself to his feet by means of the seat of an armchair. His face was still pale but he seemed otherwise all right. He slapped the cushion and looked back at Hannah over his shoulder, making indecipherable noises, sounding vaguely annoyed.

'Bunny,' Joyce said. 'He remembered. That's where he left Bunny.' She went upstairs to fetch it. The tears that threatened now were of relief and exhaustion, a release of the build-up of tension.

James, as if he was no more than a family retainer yet still feeling like an intruder, made the tea and brought it in. He had filled Josh's beaker, his own beaker, not the one Marty had bought, and handed it to him. Josh burbled at him, repeating the same sounds several times and pointing, making them all aware he was telling them something important even if they could not understand what it was.

Hannah watched her son, her eyes never leaving his face. He was like Laurence, and now, she noticed, also a little like her. Her hands still shook, she wondered if they would ever stop. And she was sad, sad that Laurence had died and sad for Pauline and Andrew. At least they have you, Josh, she thought, their grandson, a living reminder of their own dead child.

There was an awkward silence. Now it was over no one knew what to say, what topics were safe or if it was better for Hannah to talk about what had happened. Instead, they all watched Josh, amazed at his resilience.

It was Joyce who decided she would cook them dinner while Hannah gave Josh his tea and put him to bed. Hannah had wanted to put the cot in her room but knew it was an overreaction, that it was not in Josh's best interests to do so. She tucked the small duvet around his shoulders, slipped Bunny in with him and stood by the cot until his thumb slipped from his mouth and he was sleeping as soundly as if he had never spent a night away from the house.

It was an effort not to keep checking on him every ten minutes, to ensure he was there, that she wasn't dreaming. 'It's a terrible night, I think you'd all better stay,' Hannah said after they had eaten and had taken coffee into the lounge. The rain continued to fall, the wind rattled the window frames and once or twice a down-draught blew smoke into the room. And she didn't want to be alone, not this first night now that it was over, even though Josh was back, even though Marty was safely locked up. Her recovery would take a lot longer than her son's. The scar from that long, long week would probably never heal over.

James went to bed first, straight to the second spare bedroom. He would not have dreamed of sharing Hannah's bed with her parents under the same roof, even if nothing had happened. And he still had no idea how she

176

felt or if he had been forgiven. It was far too soon to ask.

Hannah lay awake for a long time, her hands clasped across her middle, feeling the bones poking through her skin. Apart from tonight, had she eaten all week? She could not remember. She could not remember anything other than the pain and longing and the waiting. It doesn't matter now, she told herself. Josh has come home.

She got up at six, woken by dreams, her heart racing. Josh was still there, sleeping peacefully. She could hardly wait until he woke and she could hold him again.

Sonia arrived mid-morning just as Joyce and Phillip were leaving to go back to their own home and respective jobs. The rain had eased to a misty drizzle, the air smelled of damp vegetation. Anthony was crying, a loud, insistent lusty cry instantly recognizable as that of hunger. 'God, I'm sorry. I thought he'd last another hour, at least,' Sonia said. 'I can't seem to fill him up at all lately.'

Hannah kissed the top of his head. Josh was resting on her hip, her left arm holding him tightly against her body. She took Anthony in the other arm and smiled as she watched Sonia struggling with all the baby's paraphernalia, so many things for such a short trip, just as Sonia had watched her last January on the day she had introduced her to James Fulford.

Later, James, Hannah and Sonia were in the kitchen, a bottle of wine on the table between them. They had had an indoor picnic lunch provided by Sonia. 'It was the least I could do, I wasn't invited,' she had said, unpacking delicatessen food which needed no preparation. Josh was on the floor playing with a saucepan and a wooden spoon; Anthony was being fed.

'What'll happen to her? Marty?' It was typical of Sonia to be the first one to mention Marty Rowland, the girl Hannah had known as Jenny.

'We're not sure. There'll be psychiatric reports first. Gareth said she'll get some sort of custodial sentence but not necessarily prison.' Hannah was still too euphoric to envisage the future.

'For how long?' Sonia, like all mothers, managed to hold a conversation as she went through the process of wiping and winding and offering the bottle again, not looking at the speaker but taking in what was said.

'No one's prepared to guess. If it isn't prison, then she'll be released as soon as she's stable on medication. She didn't harm Josh, although she neglected him – that goes in her favour.'

'And what about Laurence? She killed him, for God's sake.' Sonia was disgusted. She had not liked the man but he had not deserved to be murdered. No one deserved that.

'They seem to think it wasn't deliberate. They believe Laurence went for her at the same time as the police did and tried to get the gun off her. She says it went off accidentally in the confusion, that she had no intention of using it, and they can't prove otherwise. Apparently, it was all a bit of a muddle.' Gareth had told Hannah all this at the hospital. She had seen how relieved he was to have found Josh but the outcome had not been as satisfactory as he would have wished. Someone had died and they could not prove it was murder or even manslaughter. And, he had added, there was now the question of Marty's mother, of whether her death was accidental in view of the circumstances, but that, too, could never be proved. No one had seen Marty in the area, nobody had known where she was other than that she hadn't been flying at the time, and the pathologist had been certain it was an accident. And if she had done it, she had been clever, she had waited for the money, she had not given herself away by coming forward too soon. There were not even the threads of a case to present to the Crown Prosecution Service. Unless a psychiatrist got to the bottom of it, only Marty herself would ever know the truth.

'What'll you do, Hannah, if they let her out in a couple of years, or even sooner? Will you move away?'

'I can't think about that yet, it's hard enough trying to forget the last week. Anyway, have you had any more thoughts about George?' This was safer ground.

'I spoke to him yesterday,' James interrupted. 'He was delighted to hear about Josh.'

'You didn't . . .?'

James grinned and shook his head. 'No, I didn't. But I should have done. He just wanted reassurance that it wasn't you who had taken Josh. He didn't ask me if I knew where you were.' In retrospect he could see that this had been deliberate on George's part. He was that sort of man. If James knew Sonia was not involved he might also have known where she was. George would not have put James in a position where he might have to lie.

Sonia leant her head against Anthony's, her pale hair in contrast with his which was brown like his father's. He sighed a long, shuddering contented sigh prior to falling asleep on her shoulder. 'It's a hard one, isn't it. I've had the baby to myself so far, do you think I owe him a father?'

'You shouldn't think like that, Sonia. Thousands of women bring up children on their own and you're fortunate enough not to have to worry about money. You've got to think of yourself, and there's George to consider. Could you live with him, spend the rest of your life with him, or would you get bored and hurt him again? You told me some months ago he was becoming a nuisance. Would it be fair to him if you don't love him?'

'I wasn't strictly honest, Hannah. That's what it felt like but it was because I was scared. I felt strange, disorientated, but I didn't know then that I was pregnant. He'd asked me to marry him. I was terrified of the commitment. I thought I was bound to let him down. I always seem to let people down.'

'That's rubbish. And he loves you.'

Sonia blushed. 'Yes, well, I am fairly irresistible,' she said with a laugh.

James watched the two women, close friends, able to say exactly what they thought, both mothers. He felt he was probably in the way and decided he ought to leave, that there were things they needed to talk about unhindered by the presence of a male. Hannah had not yet had a chance to talk about her feelings for Laurence. When she did it would not be with James.

He kissed the top of Hannah's head and said he was going home.

'And he loves you,' Sonia said, nodding in the direction of the kitchen door through which James had exited. 'How do you feel about him now?'

'I'm not sure. There's still a tiny part of me which can't forgive him. Or Val. And it's wrong of me, I know. I suppose it's because I can't forgive myself for leaving Josh with someone in the first place.'

'Listen, Hannah, it wasn't your fault. Thousands of mothers work, and you have to stop blaming Val and James. The fault lies with one person only and, if you think of it, a little bit with Laurence. If he hadn't kept on seeing her this mightn't have happened.' She held up a hand. 'Okay. End of lecture.'

Hannah smiled. Sonia was right.

When the babies were asleep, Josh in his cot, Anthony in his travelling cot in the lounge, Hannah opened some more wine. At last she had something to celebrate. She and Sonia talked all evening, as they cooked, as they ate and as they washed up and then into the early hours. Hannah began to feel better, to gain strength, as the torrent of words eased her guilt and torment. It was like ridding an abscess of poison. Laurence was forgiven. He belonged in another area of her life, not the present, but he would not be forgotten.

'Oh, bugger it,' Sonia said suddenly, throwing down the tea towel. 'Can I use the phone?'

'Of course you can, but it's after midnight. Who on earth do you need to . . .? Ah, of course, George Allison?' She recalled he had trouble sleeping and he certainly wouldn't mind being disturbed by Sonia.

'Yes. Bloody George Allison.'

When she returned to the kitchen she picked up a dish-cloth with nonchalance but Hannah saw the faint flush colouring her enviable cheekbones.

Hannah's GP came to the house regularly. Satisfied with Josh's progress he warned Hannah that she might have a reaction, that depression and grief might follow euphoria, especially as Laurence had died. It did not happen.

She saw Pauline and Andrew twice a week but knew it was a struggle for them to appear cheerful. 'Would you prefer not to see Josh for a while?' she asked, aware of the reminder he presented.

'Oh, no, Hannah. Please don't stop bringing him.'

October arrived and Josh was walking. Hannah invited James and both sets of parents for Christmas. 'Just us,' she said. 'It'll be very quiet.'

James called in every day and sometimes stayed for a meal. He made no demands and asked no questions. He would leave all the running to Hannah. By mid-December he saw signs of recovery but he was uncertain who was being tested when she left Josh with him whilst she drove to the village for some forgotten item. There was a sense of unfinished business, a hiatus, because they did not know what would happen to Marty.

On 23rd December, as Hannah was making the final preparations for Christmas, Gareth drove up and knocked on the door. Under his arm was a parcel.

'Come in,' Hannah said with a smile. 'You're just in time for tea or coffee.'

They sat in the kitchen. Josh was asleep. The house was quiet apart from the tick of a clock. Hannah took mince pies from the oven and offered him one. 'Okay,' she said, hands on her hips. 'You'd better tell me.' She knew that grim expression.

'By the way things are going it looks as if they'll decide she's unfit to plead.'

'Meaning what?'

'Meaning psychiatric care and enforced treatment, not prison. There're records going back to her schooldays. These things take months, Hannah, we won't know one way or another until the New Year. I just wanted you to know, to be prepared.'

Hannah sat down. She understood the difference. A prison sentence had a beginning and an end, a sooner end if the prisoner behaved well, but at least you knew where you were. Marty denied killing Laurence, she claimed the gun had gone off when everyone converged on her. That it was loaded and had been pointed at Gareth, then at Laurence and Josh, seemed not to matter because intent to kill could not be proved, especially when Marty claimed she had not known it was loaded. Psychiatric hospitals were able to release patients as and when they felt they were fit to return to the community. Marty was clever. She would not be there long. 'What about her mother, have you found out anything more?'

Gareth shook his head. His mouth was full of mince pie. It was nearly as good as the ones his wife made. 'The result of the inquest stands. The post-mortem showed no injuries or trauma other than what would reasonably be incurred from falling. There's absolutely nothing to say Marty Rowland was ever near the place. Look, she's got other things on her side. She bought a beaker and nappies for Josh, she kept him alive even if she stopped changing him.'

'Just,' Hannah said, spitting the word. 'Only just alive. Another day and he might not have been.'

'Hannah, he's safe, that's the main thing. Look, I must go.'

'You'll let me know, Gareth, won't you, what they decide?'

'Of course I will. Oh, this is for Josh for Christmas. It isn't much.'

Hannah was touched. She had come to like Gareth Chambers a lot. He had explained that for victims a case wasn't over once the culprit was arrested. They needed to have results, to know the outcome of a trial and what could be expected of the future. Hannah's future was still uncertain.

She watched Gareth leave then sat down, pushing pastry crumbs around the kitchen table. Laurence's funeral was behind them. It had been a quiet affair, just herself and Josh, Pauline and Andrew and half a dozen people with whom he had worked. With the New Year to come it might be a little easier for his parents to try to rebuild their lives.

Josh was awake. She could hear him gurgling. For now she must think of him and not Marty or Laurence.

Christmas was not as quiet as Hannah intended. Sonia and Anthony had been added as guests and, at the last minute, George Allison. With two babies in the house it was a happier time than they had anticipated. George proved to be a natural with children and Sonia watched proudly when he changed his son.

Spring arrived early. Daffodil tips pushed through the damp earth before the crocuses had finished flowering. A haze of green was on the trees before the middle of April. Josh was steady on his feet now, and he could speak, making himself understood through his own special phrases. Anthony had started walking. And Marty's lawyers spoke up for her in court. She could afford a good barrister.

Hannah, terrified, had taken her place in the witness box. 'It wasn't so bad,' she told Sonia. 'I just had to tell them how we met and how she'd pretended to be someone else.'

Gareth had believed this to be a point in favour of the prosecution, that by doing so Marty had proved her actions were premeditated. But Marty had claimed she loved Laurence so much she just wanted to see where he had lived.

'She's going to Oakhaven for treatment,' Gareth told Hannah the following day. 'It has a secure unit.'

It was less than Hannah had hoped for. Oakhaven was

an ordinary psychiatric hospital, nothing like Broadmoor or Rampton. Marty Rowland had been judged mentally ill, not criminally insane, and the jury had accepted that the gun going off had been a tragic accident.

'We were made to look like idiots,' Gareth said to James when Hannah went upstairs to change Josh's nappy. 'That's what money can do, it can buy top lawyers who can twist words. If we hadn't charged in like bulls at a gate Laurence would still be alive, or so they would have it. And the damn shrinks were on her side, independent or not.'

'How did they testify?'

'Oh, Josh wasn't injured, Marty was just repeating the pattern of her own childhood. Not that there's any proof she was abused. She wanted Laurence and his baby but, because of her mental state, she had acted in an inappropriate way to get them.'

'Inappropriate?' James ran a hand through his hair. 'Jesus Christ. How long will they keep her there?' he asked quietly, hearing Hannah's footsteps on the stairs.

'How long's a piece of string? Here's the boy,' Gareth said in a normal voice as he leaned forward, his elbows on his knees, and began to exchange some baby talk with Josh.

From an earlier conversation with Gareth James had gained a little relief. Marty had admitted it had been around two when she had taken Josh. Valerie Mayhew had been at the house, not James. Valerie had gone to train as a children's nurse. She had rung Hannah to say that as much as she loved children, and Josh especially, she would feel safer in a hospital where there was plenty of support. She would never trust herself alone in a house with a child again even though she could hardly be blamed for what happened.

May was warm and turned into June. The days passed quickly for Hannah. She was recovering and starting to look better. She had put on a little weight and the gauntness had disappeared, but there was still a wariness in her eyes. A long hot summer would be very good for her.

James waited patiently, taking her and Josh to the beach or the country, biding his time, knowing he had to get it right. In August he went to see Sonia, now entrenched in her country cottage with Anthony. 'I need your advice.'

'Mine?' Sonia, slender and cool in a yellow sundress, stared at James in surprise. Her hair had grown even longer and was held at the back of her head with a butterfly clip. Several strands had escaped. She looks younger, James thought, and happy.

'Gone are the days when I was a fount of all knowledge, my dear. It's all playgroups and toilet training these days.' She smiled at the disappointment in his face. 'Anyway, the answer's yes. Ask her.'

James laughed, unaware his feelings and intentions had been that obvious. If Sonia knew, had Hannah guessed?

He bought champagne but left it in the car in case the answer was no.

At the end of August Gareth called in. Someone he knew at Oakhaven had told him that Marty Rowland was responding to treatment and taking her drugs as and when directed. Hannah did not seem as disappointed as he had expected.

'I've got some good news, Gareth,' she said. 'I'm getting married. James will live here with us, his flat's too small and there's no garden. We might eventually sell, but we'll see what happens first. And it means I don't have to worry about going back to work.'

He looked at her closely, unsure whether she had made the decision for that very reason, so that she never need leave Josh with anyone, or because she really loved James Fulford. He hoped it was the latter, but either way he was glad there would be someone around to take care of Hannah and Josh. She was still more vulnerable than she realized.

George Allison rang Hannah from London in a state of overjoyed disbelief. Finally convinced that Sonia meant what she said, he had put his house on the market and was in the process of buying a sturdy stone house in Chagford in order to be near her and his son. 'I've already got a buyer so I'm moving in immediately,' he said.

From Sonia Hannah learned that George saw them both every day and lived in hopes that she would eventually marry him; for the moment he had settled for the status quo and was happier than he had ever been. He ran his business from home, much as he had done in London.

To Sonia's amusement the rather military-looking man could often be seen steering the pushchair along the village streets with a proud smile on his face. She still wasn't sure about marriage but it seemed less of an issue between them. Most nights they ate dinner together and sometimes George stayed. Sonia's cameras did not gather dust; Anthony became her main subject before other mothers demanded her services. 'It looks as if I've started my own cottage industry,' she told George as autumn closed in.

'Nothing's ever been able to hold you back,' he replied as he handed her a glass of champagne, which was still her favourite drink. 'Here's to us,' he said more quietly.

'And to Hannah and James.'

Chapter Thirteen

She quite enjoyed playing their games although, as the months passed, it became easier and easier to win. 'I don't know why, honestly I don't. No, it wasn't because I hated Hannah, I just wanted a baby. Laurence's baby. Someone to love.'

'Why did you lock him in the shed, Marty?' Angus Pearson asked as he had asked during each of the previous two sessions.

'Not the shed, The slaughterhouse.'

'Okay, the slaughterhouse. Why did you do that?'

She shrugged and sucked a finger, a gesture of childhood innocence she had acquired since being at Oakhaven. That, and the artless, open smile. 'Because I thought he'd be as happy there as I was. I'd never have hurt him and I never meant to hurt Laurence. I loved him.' I loved him but I couldn't have him so he had to die. Besides, he knew too much. I should never have said I killed my mother. One answer for you, Angus, but the truth for me.

'Your parents, how did you view them as a child?' Angus Pearson studied his patient as she talked. This was his third session with her and he had come to no conclusions. According to the nursing staff she had settled in, behaved herself and took her medication on cue. Articulate, intelligent, certainly, for she had asked what each of the drugs did, what side effects she could expect and how long before they could be reduced. But how clever was she? She was giving all the right answers, the answers that confirmed the psychiatrists' opinions that had brought her to Oakhaven instead of prison, but Angus had his doubts. Time would tell, but he suspected Marty had a personality disorder rather than a mental illness. Which meant intelligence combined with cunning, an ability to manipulate and an inordinate capacity for lying. 'Do you always follow the examples your parents set?'

'My mother was a cold woman, she was never tactile in the way my dad was.'

'Would you care to explain that statement?'

Not really, but if it makes you happy. 'She never kissed or cuddled me but Dad did. We'd go to the slaughterhouse and he'd touch me all over.'

'*All* over?'

'Yes.'

'Didn't you object?'

'No. It proved how much he loved me.'

'Is that what he told you?'

Marty shook her head. Her hair was lank now and she hoped it was only her imagination which made it seem thinner. 'He didn't tell me anything. He didn't have to, I just knew.'

'Were you confused when you took baby Josh away from his mother?'

'Yes.' Marty lowered her eyes. Now and then she answered truthfully. But she had to be careful. Angus had a way of changing tack unexpectedly. She still wasn't sure what had prompted her to drive over there and take him from his pram, knowing that Hannah would be at work and Valerie somewhere in the house. 'I didn't hurt him, I never meant to hurt him.' Starve him to death, maybe, but not hurt him.

'And Laurence Peters? Did you mean to hurt him?'

'I've already told you that. Why do you keep asking me the same things? They happened. It's over. Can't we get on to the future, to my treatment?'

'You admit you need treatment?'

Jesus Christ, Marty thought, biting the side of her mouth to keep from screaming at him. Of course I don't need fucking treatment, I need to get out of here, and I want to know the quickest way about it. 'I must do if I'm here and not in prison. About Laurence, they all rushed at me. The gun went off. I didn't know it was loaded, I had no idea it even worked. I just wanted to make him stay.'

And so it went on for another half-hour. Yes, she had wanted Laurence, no, she hadn't meant to kill him, she hadn't wanted anyone to be harmed, she hadn't meant to take Josh. She could not bear to think of Hannah, smug and comfortable with her child and James Fulford.

'What happened to your mother, Marty?'

Back to that again, she thought. 'She had an accident. Apparently she fell off the storage space in the slaughterhouse.'

'Did you kill her?'

Marty laughed. 'Of course not. She was my mother.'

'But you never went to see her.'

'No. I loved her in my own way, but after what she did I couldn't go back there.' Marty hesitated. Until now she had been unsure whether her father's death would be useful in proving she could not help acting as she had done. Naturally Angus would have heard all about that. Shrinks loved to hark back to childhood and the influence past events exercised on the present. If she gave him this one, solid reason for what they considered to be her inappropriate behaviour, she could let him believe he could exorcise it and then he would consider her to be cured. That was the way they worked.

'What did she do, Marty?'

'She killed my father.'

Angus Pearson allowed himself a few unnecessary seconds to digest this information which was supposed to be new to him and decide what to do with it. 'How do you know?'

'I saw her. I saw her in the slaughterhouse. There was blood everywhere.'

He revised his half-formed opinion from personality disorder to psychotic; possibly delusional, possibly schizophrenic. But then, he had revised it on each occasion he had spoken to Marty Rowland. That was the problem with his work, there were no definites, no real rules and no way of getting to the truth. She might simply be playing games with him. 'You say you loved your father?'

'Yes.'

'Despite what you told me he did to you?'

'Yes. He'd never have left me.'

Me, not us or my mother. 'All right, Marty, I think we've done enough for one day.'

Marty smiled and stood up. She was sweating, a feeling she hated. It was partly due to the drugs and partly because the whole place was overheated. She wandered back to her room and sat down. Angus Pearson was fact-gathering. He wanted to know about events rather than feelings and thoughts. That would come, she knew that, but she'd be prepared, she'd be more than ready for him.

They were pleased with her, they said, when what they meant was that they were pleased with themselves, proud of their ability to cure with a prescription of drugs and meaningless psychobabble. Dig deep enough into the past and you'll find the answer. Doctor knows best.

Doctor knows best. Daddy knows best. It was all the same to Marty. They were all fools. Only Marty knew best.

The months passed and her sessions had been cut down to once a fortnight with Angus Pearson and one afternoon in group therapy. And what a drag that was, how eager were those pathetic perverts and weirdos to spill out their innermost thoughts, their hopes, their dreams and ambitions. Unless, of course, they were all playing the same game as herself. Maybe they were, but she had no interest in the other inmates on the locked ward although she pretended to like some of them. To have liked them all would not have been natural, to have disliked them all would have been abnormal. And Marty was striving for normality, as hard as it was from a chemical straitjacket. She had soon picked up the terminology.

She brushed her hair, watching her distorted reflection in the so-called mirror. It was made of something unbreakable and was stuck firmly to the wall. The windows were too high to reach and there was a mesh grille over the light bulb sunk into the ceiling. 'For the sake of self-harmers,' she muttered, unable to understand how anyone could keep cutting or injuring themselves.

It had been suggested that she was well on the way to beginning the slow progression of rehabilitation to the outside world. But to do so she would have to continue playing the game.

It was a few minutes before two o'clock. Marty walked down the corridor, escorted by a nurse, in order to be punctual for her session with Angus. She smiled at the woman she secretly called her jailer. The woman smiled back, glad that Marty wasn't one of the troublemakers.

'Sit down, Marty.' Angus indicated a chair in front of the desk. 'You look very nice today.'

She had put on some make-up. 'Thank you.' She sat down opposite the middle-aged man and smiled her gratitude for the fatuous flattery. No one could look nice when they carried an extra stone and a half in weight. The drugs were responsible for that. She had tried eating less but found this only exacerbated their effects on her nervous system. It was hard enough to think clearly as it was and sometimes she slurred like a drunk. It didn't matter. As soon as she was out she would stop taking them. And she had been taking them. She had soon learned all the tricks such as keeping the pills under your tongue then spitting them out later, but apparently they always found out so she swallowed them. It was a black mark against you, a further delay in the fight for freedom if you were labelled uncooperative.

'The staff tell me you've been taking an interest in the art classes. Do you enjoy them?'

'Yes. It's soothing. It makes me feel relaxed.' Lower your

eyes demurely, clasp your hands loosely in your lap. There's a good girl. Then look up and smile. Always smile. Her jaw ached from it.

'Good.'

She had hoped to impress him but seemed to have failed. The art teacher would have shown him her paintings, nothing was private here. Art therapy, it was called, and what you drew was supposed to be a reflection of your thoughts. The real sickos sloshed black and red all over the paper and themselves; Marty painted wild flowers, very badly but with delicate shades and a delicate hand. See? her work said. I'm perfectly sane.

'I'd like you to tell me, from the time you were small, what you consider to be the main events in your life.'

Marty stifled a sigh of boredom. Angus just wanted to hear the same old things. He was simply asking in a different way. She went through it all again.

What she didn't tell him was the truth, how she used to creep into her father's bed while her mother made the morning tea. How, even at an early age, she knew she had a certain power over him. The first time she had touched him he had slapped her in disgust. But she had still clung to him, she still sat on his knee or held his hand whenever she could. He would never have deserted her, run off with another woman.

'Did your father have sex with your mother?'

Of course. Sex. Childhood and sex. One or the other. She had known they would reach it at some point. 'Yes.' She'd heard those vile night noises, the grunting and groaning.

'Did your mother ever suspect what was going on?'

'I'm not sure. Maybe right at the end, maybe that's why she killed him.'

As Marty grew up she heard rumours concerning Edward Rowland, how his sexual couplings were not concentrated solely within his own house. There was a housewife and a shop assistant and a farm girl, so local gossip would have it. It wasn't true, of course, not when he could have had Marty.

'Not because he was seeing other women?'

'No. There were no other women.'

Angus was tired. He was sure he was wasting his time. 'What did she do with the body?'

'She buried him under the concrete in the slaughter-house.'

The place should be burned down, Angus thought. Marty claimed to have been abused there, she believed her father was killed and buried there, her mother had met her death on the concrete floor, Laurence Peters had been shot in its doorway and little Josh had been incarcerated within its walls. It was a list of horrors. How many had been perpetrated by Marty?

This was the one aspect of Marty he couldn't fathom. Unless it was wishful thinking, why did she insist her father had been murdered? Once he got to the bottom of that they might start making progress. But not today, they'd both had enough. 'See you next time. And keep up the good work in Art.'

Marty went back down the corridor, catching a glimpse of herself, head and shoulders, in a thick pane of glass, curtained from behind. She had the start of a double chin. How she hated herself for becoming like the others: over-weight, spilling her food when the drugs made her shake, learning the language of an institution. She must work even harder towards her release.

At the end of September Hannah and James were married at the register office on the Hoe. George Allison and Hannah's father were their witnesses. Pauline and Andrew accepted the invitation with alacrity, which surprised Hannah.

Joyce, determined not to cry, spoiled her make-up five minutes into the ceremony. One tear dripped on Josh who was sitting on her knee. It made him giggle. This time her daughter would be happy, James would make sure of that. Sonia saw her tears and squeezed her hand. 'She'll be fine,' she whispered, anxiously watching George who was clutching their own wriggling child.

Joyce nodded. Sonia, in her finery, looked stunning. Paul and Lorna Freeman and Gareth and Judy Chambers were the only other guests. They had left Gabrielle with a friend.

Outside they posed for photographs, each taking a turn with the camera then seconding a passer-by to take them all together. It was typical West Country weather. A sea fret obscured Plymouth Sound and moisture hung in the air. At least it was mild.

Hannah wore an oyster slub silk dress and matching coat. The simplicity of her outfit was subtle and flattering. She smiled for the camera shyly, like a first-time bride, happy again despite the knowledge that Marty would not remain at Oakhaven for ever. That problem would be tackled when it arose, if there was a problem. Perhaps they could cure her, perhaps she would not want to return to the area.

Gareth winked at Hannah as he took a final picture of her and James, then passed the camera back to Phillip.

'Hungry?' James asked, knowing Hannah had been too nervous to eat breakfast.

'Starving.' She took his hand as they walked down past the putting green, deserted now, and over to the Moat House Hotel where they were having lunch. A table for thirteen plus one high chair had been reserved by James. Josh was able to sit in a normal chair to eat. Unknown to Hannah he had also asked if they could provide champagne and a cake.

'I can't believe it's over already,' Hannah said. 'I was shaking like a leaf this morning. Thank you all for coming.'

'You know I'd never have missed out on a chance to drink champers,' Sonia said, raising her glass. She was surprised Gareth was there. He was a nice man, no doubt of that, and so was his wife, and Hannah was fond of him, but he was still a reminder of unhappier times.

'Oh, James!' Hannah exclaimed with surprise when they had eaten and a waiter produced the cake.

James took her hand and stood up. 'Come on, let's cut it. I know the boys will eat some.'

Phillip toasted the bride and groom and James said a few words in response and then it was time to disperse.

'I'm very happy for you,' Judy Chambers said, kissing Hannah on the cheek. Although they had not met before that morning there was little she had not heard about Hannah Peters, now Hannah Fulford. She said no more, neither did Gareth although they both knew that the future was uncertain as far as Marty Rowland was concerned. Whatever the psychiatrists might say, Gareth had told Judy that, as far as he was concerned, Miss Rowland had an obsession with Hannah. Judy prayed he was wrong.

A week later Hannah, James and Josh returned from a honeymoon in Guernsey where the weather had been kind and Hannah had stopped taking the pill. It had been a joint decision.

James went in to the factory and Hannah stayed at home with Josh. On Mondays and Thursdays he went to a playgroup where Hannah chatted with the other mothers. They saw Sonia and Anthony, either at Hannah's house or in Chagford. They were often accompanied by George. There were also visits to and from both sets of grand-parents and the occasional night out with Lorna and Paul. Hannah would only leave Josh with his grandparents, she still had not reached the stage of trusting him to an outsider.

'At last,' James said one evening. 'I've finally got rid of the flat. The contracts were exchanged this morning.' Unlike Laurence, he paid all the bills and provided for Hannah and Josh. 'Is it time we talked about moving?'

Hannah turned away. It was November, Josh had passed his second birthday. So very much had happened since his birth. Moving was the last thing on her mind. She had news of her own but another such occasion made her fearful of imparting it.

'Hannah?' James glanced around. Josh was in bed, he was starting a cold and had gone up at five thirty. Flushed and snuffling, he had reached for Bunny and closed his eyes. The fire blazed in the grate, the table lamps were lit and the dining-room table was laid for two. 'Hannah, what is it?' He reached for her. 'Tell me, am I right in thinking . . .?'

She nodded, tears running down her cheeks as she saw the joy in James's face. He held her tightly and stroked her hair. 'Oh, God, I'm going to be a father.'

Hannah pulled back a little. 'You won't think any the less of Josh because of it, will you?'

'How can you ask? You know I love that little boy as if he were my own. Can we tell people?'

'Of course.'

It was almost an hour later before they sat down to eat. James rang everyone they knew and Hannah let him. Last time she had the same news to impart there had seemed to be nothing to celebrate. 'It's due about the first week of June,' he told Sonia, who asked to speak to Hannah.

As she took the receiver she realized why James had wanted to make those calls. He had no one of his own to tell. His parents had been killed in a road accident when he was in his late teens. Her family was all the family he possessed. 'Congratulations,' Sonia said. 'And don't forget to invite me to the christening.'

'You want to be godmother or is it the champagne you're after?'

'Both. Take care of yourself, Hannah. I must go, George is coming for dinner.'

Hannah was sick for a few weeks and then she blossomed and tried to explain to Josh that he would have a brother or sister to play with in the summer. Josh was unconcerned.

Another Christmas came and went. They all spent it at George's place, at his insistence, his house being larger than Sonia's. Everyone brought a contribution but it was George who cooked the turkey and set the shop-bought

196

pudding alight then provided everyone with extravagant gifts. 'He's turned into a family man,' Sonia said, but with humour, secretly proud of him.

Two days after New Year's Eve, which James and Hannah had spent quietly at home, Gareth telephoned. He did not preface his conversation with the conventional seasonal greeting, it did not seem appropriate considering the news he was about to impart. Instead he asked after Josh.

'He's fine. And, Gareth, guess what? I'm pregnant.'

Oh, God, he thought, don't let the same thing happen twice. 'And the best of luck to both of you. All those sleepless nights, don't tell me about it. Look, Hannah, I thought I'd let you know that Marty's been taken off the locked ward.'

Hannah's stomach churned. 'Is she allowed out?'

'Only with an escort. But it means they think she's getting better. It's only a matter of time now. I'm sorry, but I had to warn you.'

'Thank you, Gareth.' She put down the phone and took a deep breath. The next baby wasn't due for another five months. Would Marty have been released by then? Would she try to steal this one? No one could say. Josh was tugging at her skirt. She picked him up and held him, kissing him so hard he squirmed and laughed. 'Not this time,' she told him. 'This time I'll be waiting for her.'

Chapter Fourteen

Marty smoothed the ugly dress over her hips. None of her own clothes fitted her now but she refused to spend decent money on larger sizes. Once she was out she would stop the pills and go on a diet. Eighteen months she had been locked up, and now she was on an open ward where she had had to learn new rules. She no longer had to endure the ritual of keys, the clanking and slamming of doors as the nurses changed shifts or went off for their breaks.

I could leave, I could simply walk out, she told herself, knowing she wouldn't. She stared out at the grounds from the dormitory window. They were as institutionalized as the people housed within the building. The grass was cropped short, the trees stood in rows and the empty flower beds had been carefully dug the previous November. The bare Devon earth, rusty red, was heaped in the perfectly edged circles cut out of the lawn, the lumps broken down by the January frosts. Later, dwarf marigolds and salvias would be planted in concentric rings, their clashing colours harsh on the eye, as they had been last year. What a lack of imagination it showed. But imagination was discouraged in mental institutions.

There was a different type of inmate to contend with now, neurotics and the occasional alcoholic, which was a drag, but she made conversation, joined in their endless card games and offered to help with the tea trolley at a quarter to four in the afternoons. Good old Marty, full of community spirit, pleasant and cheerful towards her fellow patients, almost ready for the outside world. She had

had all those months in which to think. Laurence was dead. She'd not had a chance to mourn him, not with all the drugs dulling her senses. Nothing else mattered now except revenge. Hannah was free, Hannah had Josh and probably James. Marty had nothing, not even memories because that afternoon Angus Pearson had managed to rob her of those.

'Marty, how do you suppose you came into your inheritance so easily?' he had asked her an hour or so earlier.

'Because there was no one else. I told you, my father was dead.'

'But in that case it would need to be proved, there would have to be a death certificate, investigations, both the police and your lawyer would have needed to verify this before making you the sole beneficiary. How do you suppose they did this if he was buried in the slaughterhouse and no one knew he had been murdered?'

Marty had laughed. 'It's obvious. He was gone more than seven years, therefore he was presumed to be dead.'

'Possibly, but inquiries would still have taken place. However this is beside the point. You're ready to hear this now, you've made tremendous progress. When your mother died the police were called in because it was a sudden death. Naturally they had to trace the nearest relatives. I have to tell you, they found your father first.'

'They dug up the concrete?'

'Marty, that just isn't so and you know it. You went almost immediately to the farm, you'd have noticed if they'd done so. They asked in the village. It was that simple. Your father ran off with the barmaid. A bit of a cliché maybe, but that's what happened. Your mother divorced him a year later and he remarried. They're still together, living on a farm in Somerset.'

'I see.' Marty had stifled the scream, fought off the panic. It wasn't true, it couldn't be true. Her father would never have left her. But the rumours came flooding back, the talk of other women in the village. Was that why her mother

199

was so cold, why she avoided the village and her neighbours? Had she known what went on behind her back and
been so humiliated that she couldn't face people? 'I didn't
know he drank,' she had added calmly, for something to
say, knowing that to show too much emotion would have
delayed her release. 'And my mother never told me about
the divorce. There weren't any papers in the house.'

'It was a long time ago, she probably destroyed them. So
you can put all this behind you, Marty. Your father wasn't
murdered, he isn't even dead. What I'd like to discuss now
are your feelings about him. For instance, would you want
to try to make contact with him?'

'I don't know. I need time to think about this.'

'Marty, you have to understand that you were a very
disturbed young woman, that no matter what you say, you
were never abused. Both the child psychiatrist you saw
and your father have confirmed this. Your school was so
worried about you, as was your mother, that they suggested psychiatric treatment. Fortunately you have a good
brain and your illness didn't interfere with your work.
Later you managed to hold down a career. Have you
thought about going back to it?'

Never, she had thought, but that was not what Angus
had needed to hear. 'Maybe, in time. There'll be too much
to do at the farm for a while.'

Marty's version of events had puzzled Angus until he
had read the notes from the child psychiatrist. It was quite
clear that Edward Rowland had found another woman.
Marty had told her headmistress that Gloria Rowland had
killed her husband and that someone should tell the police.
Even though the headmistress had been aware of the situation – she had seen Edward in action for herself and the
girl from the pub had simply gone home one evening and
never returned to work – she had felt obliged to do so in
case they were all wrong. But it turned out the whole
village knew. However Marty had been in denial. The man
she had loved inappropriately could not have left her,
therefore he had to be dead. And who better to blame than

the mother, who may well have been unapproachable if she knew of her husband's extramarital affairs. Any woman would be hurt and angry. And maybe she had realized what her daughter was trying to do. 'Marty, are you all right?' Angus had watched her, waiting for some sign of emotion. To learn, after fourteen years, that the father you thought was dead was in fact alive would be a shock for anyone. To someone in Marty's position, who had adored her father for all the wrong reasons, it could be far more traumatic.

'You knew all the time, didn't you? Why didn't you tell me any of this before? I've been here for over a year and you've never said a thing.' She felt she had been tricked. Her breathing was ragged but she had controlled it just as she had done the tears which threatened to fall. 'I must've been mad to have believed what I did. At least I know the truth now.'

'I didn't tell you because you weren't ready. Because you'd never have accepted it. Don't you realize how much progress you've made, that you're now able to face the truth? Marty, you're almost there, you know. To be able to admit you were not well proves it.' He had smiled. 'Anyway, your social worker's coming tomorrow to take you out.'

When the session was over Marty went back to the dormitory: she had not been ready to face the other patients. She was frightened. She had not been ill, she was not mad, so why had she said so? She did not need a psychiatrist. And how had Angus Pearson been able to do that to her, make her see what she did not want to see, what she had really known all along? I must be careful, she thought, I must be extremely careful. He might make me say other things. It's the drugs. The drugs were tampering with her mind. What was in them to alter her so much? She only knew what they told her. Maybe they lied, maybe they would give her something that would make her say she killed her mother. And then what? 'Then I'd never get out of here,' she whispered.

Because she had killed her, for the house and for the money. For Laurence. Well, she still had two of those things.

She walked over to her bed and lay down, picturing the long, hot walk that afternoon early in August. She had returned from a trip and had four days off. Laurence was no nearer moving in and she wondered if he was having second thoughts about divorcing Hannah. Maybe he had changed his mind about her pregnancy. She could not risk that. If she could provide all that Hannah had provided, money and a lovely home, he would come to her. Once he was under her influence she would lure him away completely. Sex was a powerful weapon. Marty knew that much.

The crops had fully ripened and were dazzling to the eye. The hedgerows smelled dry and the road was dusty. But she couldn't risk the car being seen, nor could she take the bus to the village. Even if she wasn't recognized, the presence of a stranger would be noticed. So she walked.

Marty knew her mother's habits, had known they wouldn't have altered over the years. The new potatoes would be coming to an end, the old ones nearly ready for digging, not that the season mattered. At four o'clock Gloria Rowland would mount the ladder in the slaughterhouse and choose her vegetables for her evening meal. There would be carrots and swede and potatoes and maybe parsnips if they weren't too woody. The cabbage was cut daily.

It couldn't have been easier. Gloria Rowland was in the slaughterhouse, on the upper level, her back to the ladder, unaware that her daughter was watching her. Silently, Marty had climbed the wooden rungs and, without uttering a word, pushed with all her strength.

Incomprehension flickered in Gloria's eyes in the fleeting seconds before she hit the floor she had cemented herself, the floor Edward was supposed to have concreted instead of running off with a tart. That was her last thought before she died.

Marty climbed down. There was blood on the floor. She stepped around it and went outside, leaving the door open, just as she had found it. She had had the sense not to touch anything except her mother. How fragile she had felt beneath her cotton dress.

She stayed in the house, sitting in a kitchen chair for the length of the night, regaining her strength, awaiting daylight when she would begin the walk back again. At six thirty she had gone outside. Gloria Rowland was pale and still; her blood had dried brown around her head. It might be days or weeks until she was found. Nobody came to the farm apart from the postman and the van that delivered groceries. But Marty could wait. She was used to waiting.

She lay now on the rough cotton bedspread, aware that she was sweating. What if her parents hadn't divorced? Her father would have inherited the farm and the money and would have gone to live there with his woman. Marty would have had nothing.

Clutching the bedclothes, she fought down the rage that even the medication could not control. Enjoy your son while you can, Hannah, she thought. And when I've finished with you I'll decide what to do about my father.

'James, it's started.' Hannah was clutching the phone, bent double.

Josh watched her wide-eyed. 'Tummy ache,' he said with a nod of wisdom.

Hannah touched his head as she put down the phone. 'Look, darling, Daddy's coming home to take me to the hospital. The baby's coming. Remember we said you'd be staying with Grandma and Grandad? They'll bring you to see me, how about that? Now, let's go and get our cases.'

James looked terrified when he arrived. Hannah smiled and assured him everything was all right but she felt a pang when they dropped Josh off with her parents. 'He'll

203

be fine,' Joyce said. She was looking forward to having him to herself for a few days. 'Let me know the minute there's any news,' she told James as he bundled Hannah back into the car. His worst fear was that the baby would come before they reached the hospital.

It was a perfect spring day. A light breeze blew Hannah's hair back from her face as they drove. During the months of her pregnancy Hannah had healed. She knew how much she owed to James, how he had made living possible again. His love encompassed both her and Josh. They had watched him grow, were enchanted as he learned to talk, whole sentences now. A proper, sturdy little boy who knew nothing about the week of his life his mother had missed. And James, ever careful of her feelings, had asked, now that he was talking and calling him Daddy, if they might change his name to Fulford.

'I'd like that, James. He never knew his real father, and it'll be less confusing for him, especially once he starts school.' They had already agreed that Josh should know the circumstances of his birth and Laurence's heroic death as soon as he was old enough to understand all the implications. 'But do you mind if I discuss it with Pauline and Andrew? I'd hate them to think we'd just written Laurence off as if he'd never existed.'

Hannah had done so. 'You see, I wasn't sure if you'd mind, if you'd prefer the line to go on,' she had said, knowing that to some people the continuance of the family name meant a great deal.

It was Andrew who answered. 'No. It'll make life easier for him, especially when he has a brother or sister. It doesn't matter to us, Hannah. Once, I think it would have done, but we can't rewrite the past. James has been to you and Josh all the things that Laurence should have been. Let Josh take his name. We really don't mind.'

That had been some time ago. Another pain ripped through her. Hannah tried not to groan and wondered if James was already regretting offering to be at the birth.

It was over far sooner than Hannah had anticipated.

'Hello, Lucy,' she said when the nurse placed the baby in her arms.

'Lucy,' Josh repeated a few minutes later, delighted with this new word. Joyce was holding him, the telephone against his ear. James had rung to say that Hannah had had a baby girl and everything was all right.

'And you?'

'I wouldn't like to go through that again,' James said, laughing. 'Hard work, if you ask me. Anyway, we'll see you later. Hannah can't wait to show Josh his sister.'

James went back to the four-bedded ward where Hannah was leaning over on one elbow admiring her daughter in the plastic crib. 'She's like you,' she said, thinking back to how like his father Josh had been at birth.

'You look worried.' James touched the baby's face, hoping that bad memories weren't surfacing.

'Not worried, just thinking about how Pauline and Andrew will react.'

'They sounded pleased when I rang them.'

'I know. But Josh is their flesh and blood, Lucy isn't. I'm always so afraid of hurting them.'

'I don't think it matters now. They're used to the situation. And I know how grateful they are that you're still so close to them. Some people in their position lose touch with their grandchildren altogether.'

'I expect you're right.' Hannah smiled as Lucy began to cry. 'There'll be a lot more of that to come,' she said, picking her up carefully.

Three days later Hannah went home and found that Gareth Chambers had sent some flowers. He could not know that his thoughtful gesture was like a warning, that Hannah felt a resurgence of panic. She now had two babies to worry about and Marty was out there somewhere, released to a half-way house.

Chapter Fifteen

Despite her protests Marty had known that one of the conditions of her release was an adjustment period at the half-way house. It seemed unnecessary when she had a house of her own and plenty of money upon which to exist but she agreed to go there simply because she had to.

Angus Pearson had told her there was no longer any reason to keep her at Oakhaven, it was time to rejoin the real world.

And now it was over, she was free. Almost free. No more accompanied shopping trips with the well-meant suggestions for cheap, nutritious meals she would never dream of cooking. Prices had gone up, the psychiatric social worker told her, as if she was stupid, as if that wasn't the norm. So what? She could afford them.

Angus had talked of the farmhouse and her future plans. He had also mentioned money so perhaps he had hoped for a nice big donation towards research or the unit to which he was attached in return for her cure. He could hope on.

Glenside, the place was called. Ridiculous when the building was smack in the town centre and they were hundreds of miles from Scotland. From the outside the house looked characterless although her room turned out to be nicer than she had expected. Eight weeks, they had told her, two months and then she could return to Lower Denntiscombe Farm.

The half-way house was tolerable and at least she could

go out on her own. Marty found she was a little nervous on the first few occasions, hesitant when buying necessities. She had not realized that what applied to others also applied to herself. She had become institutionalized.

There were four residents plus Dave, a community psychiatric nurse who lived with them, alternating with Brian every few days. The men seemed quite at home sharing with two overweight females, one of whom was so zonked out on Largactil it hardly seemed worthwhile waking her up in the mornings. The two male residents were both thin; one had a stringy beard and smelled of sweat and tried to get Marty to go out with him. 'You're not my type, sweetheart,' she told him, wondering if he ever took a bath. There would never be another man now that Laurence was dead.

She counted off the days. Dave reported back that she was taking her medication unsupervised. She knew this because she had an outpatient appointment with Angus Pearson once a fortnight. Soon it would only be once a month.

'We'll miss you,' Dave said when she stepped out into the street on her final day. He tried to hug her but she pulled away, wanting no one to touch the mound of flesh she had become. Her small case contained the clothes she had worn as an in-patient and whilst at the hostel. Even after eight weeks and plenty of washing the smell of the institution lingered. She dumped the case and its contents in someone's wheelie-bin and walked, unencumbered, towards the city centre.

No comment was made when she drew a large sum of money from the bank but someone must have noticed the account had been untouched for some time. How good it felt to hold the notes, to stuff them into her wallet until it bulged. Standing orders would have been paid, of course, sums for gas and electricity she had not used, water rates and council tax. She must be well ahead on payments.

Despite her air of confidence there were forgotten things she had to get used to again. So many of her needs had been attended to by other people for a long time. Loaded down with fruit and vegetables, meat and fish, she decided to buy two dresses. Only two because she would not need them for long. The clothes she had left at the farmhouse would fit her again soon. How she hated her body, how Laurence would have hated it. The minute she reached home her diet would begin. It would start with the disposal of the pills which had caused her gain in weight.

She had no car this time, it was still at the farm and had probably rusted. The journey involved two buses and a walk of two miles. It was hot, unbearably so, and the bags were heavy. Her clothes stuck to her and her thighs rubbed together uncomfortably. Dust rose where her feet went. The grasses grew high in the hedgerows, ripe with seeds which scattered when she brushed against them and stuck between her toes in their open sandals. The crops were tall, almost four feet high. Marty stopped for a rest. She could smell the ripening wheat. A skylark sang but she could not see it. Crickets started up their chirruping, silent once more when she had passed by.

Puffing, unfit and sweating, she finally reached the farm. 'Oh, no.' How stupid she had been. She had imagined it would look just the same as when she had left it. The slaughterhouse doors hung open crookedly, weeds pushed up between the cobbles and one side of the hen-house had rotted away. Gone, too, were the hens. No one had told her where, but her social worker had been given a key. Marty made sure she had got it back. She would have to start all over again but the work would help with her weight loss.

Inside, a layer of dust added to the hushed atmosphere of a house which had stood empty a long time. Dead insects littered the floor. The fridge and freezer doors stood open. Someone had thoughtfully removed the food and defrosted both appliances. The electricity supply was switched off. The social worker again? she wondered, for there was no one else to care. Well, it must have been: she had told them that she had no friends or relations to keep an eye on the place. She hadn't known about her father then.

Summer was at its height. The fields in the distance were turning gold. A buzzard hovered over a copse on the hill. 'I'm home. And I'm never leaving again,' she said, dizzy with the exhilaration of freedom.

She opened the kitchen window to let in some air then turned to the bottle of wine on the table. She had bought it along with her groceries. Would there be a reaction? She had taken her morning medication, but that was seven hours ago and she'd taken none since. I'll take a chance, she decided. She had been abstemious ever since her arrest. The men in the hostel had offered her beer but she had always refused it. She had been terrified that the combination of drugs and alcohol would loosen her tongue and she might start talking about her mother.

'There's nothing wrong with me, and there never has been,' she said as she crushed the contents of the tablet bottles and washed them down the sink. She felt better immediately. 'Except I'm too fat. Salad tonight, with fish. And when I'm back to my normal size I'll get the boy.' The quarry, she decided, they'll never find him in there. They'll never believe I'd do it again. And this time I'll make sure I'm not caught. She laughed, surprised at the sound. It echoed around the kitchen. 'And then I'll seek out my father. And what a reconciliation that will be.'

She sat and made plans. By now Laurence' s son probably attended the playgroup in the village nearest to where Hannah lived. Hannah had mentioned that he would do so when he was older, there was nothing wrong with Marty's memory. That's where she would watch first. 'No!' The exclamation took her by surprise, so loud in the quietness of the house after the constant noise of Oakhaven and Glenside. She sat upright. What if Hannah had moved, had gone to live far away where Marty would never find her? She shook her head. No, Hannah loved that house too much. She'd still be there. She had to be.

A month passed. Marty kept her appointment with Angus Pearson. 'You look remarkably well,' he told her.

'Thank you.' She had lost almost a stone and felt better for it. There were another ten pounds to go.

He talked of general matters. Marty guessed he was testing her. There was no mention of the past, only the future and how much work she had done at the farmhouse. She left with a sigh of relief and drove home.

The weeds had been killed, there were hens in the run again. In case anyone bothered to check, Marty collected repeat prescriptions from her GP and had them filled at the same chemist's each week. The staff there had come to know her. Once she got home the pills went the same way as the others. It wasn't as if she needed them. She didn't care about the expense, she must be seen to be doing the right thing.

One Saturday afternoon she dialled Hannah's number. Her voice when she answered made Marty feel sick. She sounded the same and she sounded happy. In the background were other sounds, Laurence's son, and a man's voice. And something else. Something she did not want to think about. She hung up without saying anything.

A family, she thought, the bitch has a family and I have nothing. She picked up a mug and hurled it across the room. It smashed into shards on the flagstone floor.

Hannah put down the phone and turned to James, white-faced. 'It was her, it had to be.'

'Don't, Hannah. It was probably a wrong number.' But James was inwardly panicking. Gareth had rung him at work and told him that Marty was back at the farmhouse. 'I thought I'd leave it to you to decide whether or not to tell Hannah,' he'd said. 'She might be harmless now, for all I know – some people can be cured – but I thought I ought to warn you anyway.'

'Thanks, Gareth,' James had said, unsure himself

whether or not to tell Hannah. In the end he had done so.

'They wouldn't have let her out if they weren't certain everything was all right,' he'd said, holding her to calm her fears, but wondering how anyone could ever be certain. 'Anyway, just in case, don't take any chances with the children.'

And from that moment Hannah had changed. Josh was never allowed to play outside unless one of them was with him. Lucy's pram was never left unattended. Four weeks had passed since Marty's release from the half-way house and nothing had happened, not until that silent telephone call. 'What can we do, James?'

'Nothing. Oh, Hannah, I can't bear to see you like this. Look, let's move. Let's get as far away from here as we can. Josh hasn't started school or anything, it won't make any difference to the children. I'll put someone in to run the factory. You and the babies are all that matter.' He looked across at Lucy, now four months old. The thought of the same thing happening to her sickened him. 'We've got enough money to rent somewhere until this place is sold. We can go anywhere you want, Hannah.'

Hannah reached for Josh and pulled him on to her knee. 'No. I'm not running away from her. I'm not going to live with the fear that wherever we are she'll try to find us. If necessary, I'll face her head on.' And if necessary, I'll kill her, Hannah added silently. But let her come soon, as I know she'll come, let this new period of waiting be over. Deep down she had always known it would come to this, that Marty was never going to let go.

More phone calls followed, the caller never speaking, just making a presence felt at the end of the line. Hannah told Gareth but they were never able to trace the number. Whoever was ringing hung up too soon.

At the end of October Hannah was hanging washing on the line when the phone went again. She went inside holding Josh by the hand. Lucy was asleep upstairs in her cot.

211

'Hello, how are you?'

Hannah's elbow jerked. She stepped back in shock and trod on Josh's foot. He began to cry. 'What do you want?'

'Laurence. But I can't have him now, can I? It's your fault, you bitch. You'll pay for this.'

'Wait.' But Marty had hung up.

'It was a direct threat,' Gareth told her later. 'We'll tap the line.'

'What good do will that do?' Hannah asked. 'And if she's on the phone it means she can't be hanging around the house.'

Gareth shook his head. He was drinking tea in Hannah's kitchen; James was on his way home. 'You say you recognized her voice but we need proof. She didn't give her name, did she?'

'Oh, so I'm the lunatic now, am I? I'm the one who's paranoid,' she shouted. 'I'm sorry. It's just that I can't go through all that again. I can't live in fear for my children, never taking my eyes off them. Isn't there anything you can do, Gareth?'

'We've spoken to Angus Pearson. As far as he's concerned she turns up regularly for her appointments and shows no signs of relapsing. Her GP confirms she collects her prescriptions and we know she has them filled.'

'But?'

Gareth sighed. 'But she's a clever, manipulative woman. She might not be taking the medication.'

'You know, don't you? You know that she's not going to leave it there.'

'Yes. But until she acts, there's nothing we can do. We need proof, Hannah, that's the bloody trouble.'

'So I risk the lives of my children until you get it.'

He didn't answer. There was nothing he could say. 'Have you thought about James's suggestion, that you move?'

'She'll find us. She doesn't have to worry about a job and she's got the money.'

212

Hannah was right. All they could do was to sit it out until Marty Rowland made a wrong move. But how much would that cost Hannah and her family? It was a price no one should have to pay.

When James arrived he found Hannah and Gareth and the children in the kitchen. They were all subdued. 'Look, playgroup's broken up for half-term, why don't we have a holiday, get right away for a week, longer if you like.'

'No, James, that won't solve anything. We've got to stick this out.'

Two days later Hannah saw Marty. She was strapping Lucy into the car-seat, Josh was beside her trying to fasten his own seat-belt. She happened to look up and across the river. Standing beneath the leafless trees was a figure. Hannah would have known it anywhere. Her legs buckled. She gripped the passenger door, her knuckles white. She was being watched. The phone calls were no longer enough for Marty. How soon before she would act? Be normal, she told herself, get behind the wheel and drive into the city as you intended. But, instead, she drove to the factory to find James.

Nothing happened for two more weeks. Playschool had resumed. Hannah had not wanted Josh to return but James made her see sense. 'We'll go there together and explain the situation. The gates are locked anyway, no one can get in until it's time for the children to leave.' He explained how they weren't the only ones, how security in all schools had been tightened after too many tragic events. As if Hannah didn't know.

'But this is Josh we're talking about. Josh and Lucy.' She was close to tears.

'I know that, Hannah, but we can't let this poison their whole lives.'

The building that housed the playgroup stood on the corner of two of the village streets. It had been converted from an old cottage and had a fenced-in garden at the back. The fence was high. The children, being small, were never left unattended. At the end of each session Hannah

213

went inside with the other mothers, taking the pram, never relinquishing her grip for a second, her eyes scanning the noisy excited group of children for Josh. Josh now attended twice a week.

On Friday afternoon as he ran towards her Hannah bent to hug him, one hand still on the pushchair. He always smelled of chalk and playdough and whatever else it was that all schools smelled of. In his hand was a scribbled drawing. He peered in at Lucy, standing on tiptoes. 'She's asleep,' he said, poking her, as if this was an affront when he had a picture to show her. 'It's for Daddy, anyway,' he said.

Hannah straightened up and turned round. Josh held on to the pushchair automatically. Hannah had told him always to do so. Outside, beneath the bright autumn sky, she was paralysed. She closed her eyes as if she could eradicate what she saw. Bile filled her throat. Walking quickly away on the other side of the road was Marty. Marty knew where Josh could be found. Marty had come back for her son.

'Mummy, come on.' Josh was tugging her hand. Slowly, as if she was walking through treacle, Hannah got the children back to the car and strapped them in. Then she drove home.

'She was there, outside playgroup,' Hannah told Gareth as soon as he arrived in response to her call. They were in the kitchen again, where they had all spent so many hours when Josh had been missing. Hannah was making tea for them both and buttering bread for Josh. Lucy began to stir, nearly ready for another feed, but she wouldn't cry yet.

'There's nothing I can do, Hannah. You know that, don't you? Walking down the village street isn't a crime. She hasn't actually done anything.'

Hannah spun round, the buttery knife in her hand. 'And what if she does, Gareth? What happens then? What if she succeeds next time? And if she doesn't, if she's caught in time, she'll have another short spell in a mental hospital before she's let out again.' Her arms dropped to her sides.

'I'm sorry. I shouldn't be taking it out on you. God, I always seem to be apologizing to you.' And I always seem to be on the verge of crying, she realized. If I break down now I'll be no use to my children.

Gareth looked at her and saw the change, the reversion to the woman he had first known. Thinner again, more drawn and with a permanent air of anxiety. How could he help? There was nothing the police could do, no protection they could offer in the face of no evidence. He sipped his tea and thought about it whilst making childish conversation with Josh. 'Look, I've got a suggestion,' he finally said. 'But whatever happens, you didn't hear it from me.'

Hannah sat down and put a plate and a beaker of juice on the table. Josh had developed the habit of folding the bread before biting into it. Mashed banana ran down his chin. She clasped her hands loosely and rested them on the table. 'All right, I'm listening. What is it?'

'You'll have to speak to James, he might not agree. And it might not work anyway. Hannah, if this were to come out, the case would be thrown out of court. Entrapment is no basis upon which to charge anyone. But there'll be no risk and there's always the chance that nothing will happen.'

'Go on. I'll try anything, Gareth. Anything at all.'

He nodded towards Josh who was watching them from beneath his lashes as he chewed at the crust, listening to every word.

'We'd better wait until he's had his tea then you can tell me,' Hannah said.

Had Hannah seen her? She wasn't sure. Marty walked away quickly, without looking back. So, she had been right, that noise she had heard on the telephone was a baby. The bitch had had another child. James's, I suppose, she thought. She couldn't wait until Laurence was cold before spawning another brat.

Marty had seen Josh, too, but he was much bigger now,

a little boy, no longer a baby. It would be much harder to take him now, he'd put up a fight. But the baby. Why not take the baby? She smiled. It was perfect. Let her keep Laurence's brat, she was welcome to him. Marty would take the baby and drown it in the flooded quarry. Did Hannah leave it outside in the garden? No, she couldn't chance that move a second time. There must be a way she could do it without getting caught.

She went to the village every day, always buying something in the shop to make her appearances less suspicious. She soon learned that Hannah only brought Josh to playgroup twice a week. Watching carefully from behind the window of the tea-shop she saw that the gates were locked until the mothers and fathers arrived. There was no way she could get at Josh, not there. It had to be the baby.

Hannah, she noticed, had taken to leaving the car at home. She now approached the playgroup from the footpath, always with the pushchair, its hood up to protect the child. Sometimes Hannah's lips moved. 'Talk to it while you can,' Marty whispered. 'It won't be with you for much longer.'

The next time Hannah came for Josh she left the pushchair by the school gates. Marty smiled. She thinks I've gone away, she's getting too confident. Eating a scone and sipping tea, she decided what she would do. That she would be recognized in the village did not concern her. It would all be over so quickly no one would notice.

The days grew shorter. High winds brought down the last of the leaves. Marty still watched but she made sure Hannah never saw her. She's over-confident, now, she realized. That's the beauty of patience. I'm used to waiting. Hannah thinks I've given up.

On a Thursday when Josh wasn't there Marty tried a practice run. It could be done. She would be shielded by the parents as they made their way out. She knew exactly where to park and the car engine would be running. By the time Hannah noticed the pram was empty, she'd be gone.

Even if she shouted, with all those other mothers and the children getting in the way there would be confusion and it would be too late.

She knew she must act soon, before the school broke up, before winter proper when the road to the gravel pit became inaccessible. Besides, she had already managed to trace her father and it was his turn next. His number was in the book. E. W. Rowlands, the address that of a Somerset farm. She had dialled those digits twice, leaving it until the evening in case the woman answered, then hung up. There was no question about it, it was his voice all right. How could she ever forget it? But how to deal with him was another matter. She'd think of something, something appropriate. Pretend friendship? Lure him back to the farmhouse alone and kill him in the slaughterhouse like the others? No, the tart of a wife would know where he'd gone. There'd be a way. In time she'd think of something. And Marty had plenty of time.

Hannah had seen her in the tea-shop, just as she had on other occasions, but that was because she was always looking for her. There was no mistaking the figure she had come to loathe. She sensed it would happen soon, that Marty's patience was running out. She put the brake on the pram and walked towards the front entrance of the building through which, in a matter of minutes, she and Josh would emerge. Hannah stood sideways to the door, one eye on the road as always.

Her stomach lurched. She was right. The time had come. Marty stepped out of the tea-shop and crossed the road. Not sprinting, there was no need when so many parents were milling around with their children, busy chatting and buttoning up coats. Hannah watched and waited.

Marty's car was close to the pushchair, closer than she had hoped for because it wasn't always easy to park right outside. She reached beneath the hood just as Hannah turned to face her. Hannah was smiling.

'Get away from my pram,' Hannah shouted, hoarse-throated, causing heads to turn, mouths to drop open, just as she had intended.

'You bitch,' Marty screamed, rage welling up. 'You fucking bitch.' She grabbed the pram and threw it into the road.

Someone screamed, one of the mothers. The rest were silent, petrified by shock.

An approaching car swerved to avoid the pram as it flew through the air. It hit the windscreen. There was a loud crack. The elderly driver stamped on the brakes, an expression of shock on his face. He wasn't going fast but he lost control, clutching his chest as pain struck. The car skidded, two wheels mounted the pavement, the bumper caught Marty's legs. She was flung in the air and landed beneath the wheels just as the driver corrected his line to try to avoid her.

A bird sang in a tree, otherwise there was no sound. A second later chaos broke out. A teacher ran inside to phone for an ambulance, everyone was talking, appalled by what they had witnessed, children were crying in incomprehension. Someone, a man, knelt beside Marty, another, a woman, was rifling through the driver's jacket for glyceryl trinitrate pills for his angina. Only Hannah stood still and silent, gripping Josh's hand so hard that it hurt.

The pushchair lay on its side, two wheels buckled, one still spinning. It was broken, irreparable. It didn't matter. It was empty. Lucy was at home with James just as she had been every time Hannah had brought Josh to the village since her conversation with Gareth.

'Mummy.' Josh started to cry. He didn't know why, only that something was terribly wrong and that his hand was hurting.

Hannah picked him up. Marty's body was limp, unmoving. Someone had covered her torso with a jacket, someone else was using a mobile phone, calling the police as an ambulance was already on its way. The driver had got out of the car and staggered towards the pavement. He now sat on the kerb, his face grey, his head in his hands, heedless of his smart business suit and the lessening pain in his chest, knowing only that he had killed a woman.

Hannah found she was on her knees, cradling Josh. She was crying. Josh stroked her face. Marty was dead. It was over. Like Gareth, Hannah had known there would be no peace, not until the woman had destroyed her. What she had hoped for was to prove that Marty wasn't cured, that she was capable of doing the same thing again. A reprieve was the most she had expected, another year or so while Marty underwent further treatment. Not this, not the end of the nightmare.

How can I feel this way? she thought. How can I feel nothing but joy that someone is dead?

She looked up as the first police car arrived. Gareth got out of the second and took her arm, leading her back to the unmarked car. 'We'll need a statement,' was all he said as he drove her home. 'You'll need to explain that you started walking to the village to collect Josh because the walk did you good and he wasn't getting enough exercise. You'll need to explain that you took the empty pushchair in case he tired on the way home. Okay?'

Hannah nodded. Gareth had thought it all out.

James was standing in the window, nursing Lucy who was fretful. He saw Gareth get out of the car. Then Hannah and Josh. The pushchair was missing. James went to the hall and flung open the door. Hannah, hardly able to stand, still responded to her daughter's crying. 'Give her to me,' she said, her voice no more than a croak. Lucy stopped whimpering. Hannah and Josh started crying again.

'It's over,' Gareth said. 'It's all over, James. I think we could all do with a drink.'

A week or so later James brought home a copy of the *Evening Herald*. Hannah sat down beside him at the kitchen table and together they read the article printed on the fourth page.

'The inquest into the death of Marty Rowland, 31, who

was killed when a car mounted the pavement took place yesterday. The coroner recorded a verdict of accidental death, and exonerated the driver, saying that he had no chance of avoiding hitting the deceased after she threw an empty pushchair directly at his windscreen causing it to shatter.

'Miss Rowland had been undergoing psychiatric treatment because of a similar incident involving Josh Fulford, James and Hannah Fulford's older child, in which Laurence Peters, Hannah's first husband and Josh's natural father, was shot dead.

'A post-mortem revealed she had not been taking her medication which might account for her second attempt to snatch a baby.'

The press had pestered them but they had expected that. Hannah and James refused to comment. They'd been through all that before. But Josh was quoted. 'Lucy's my sister,' he'd said before Hannah could stop him. 'Someone tried to take her away. That's very naughty.' Afterwards they had laughed.

'It's over, Hannah. It's really over.' James looked at his wife. They were still unable to believe it. 'She can never hurt us again.'

'I love you, James,' she said, kissing him full on the lips, dispelling his fears. Maybe she hadn't at first, although she'd always liked and respected him. Maybe she had married him in order to protect Josh from Marty. Whatever her motives, they no longer mattered. What she had said was true. She loved James Fulford, her husband, Lucy's father and Josh's too. Now they could all start living again.

✗